THE WAYWARD

TABITHA CAPLINGER

BLUE INK
PRESS

ISBN 978-1-948449-17-5

Library of Congress Control Number: 2022950037

Cover by Megan McCullough

https://meganmccullough.com/

Published in the United States by Blue Ink Press, LLC

THE WAYWARD

THE WAYWARD

To the ones who rage against false comfort,
who fight for their dreams and the dreams of others,
who won't let the darkness steal what makes us truly alive;
Don't grow weary in well doing.
Stay rooted in the One who is true freedom.

In the fifth month of the nineteenth year of the second millennia A.D, the Necanians came.
They are the Saviors to the world, the Bringers of peace and prosperity.
All who obey them are blessed.

Inscription on the Armistice Monument in Hope City.
Dedicated on Peace Day in the year 2029.

CHAPTER I
WILDER

Winter came early to Beartooth. Frigid wind whistled outside the greenhouse windows as Wilder and her best friend, Korah, spent the afternoon helping Solomon tend to his indoor garden. The old man had tried to protest the intrusion on his favorite place in the whole settlement—a structure fashioned out of salvaged windows and glass doors. Wilder knew he preferred the quiet and being alone with his plants. He told her once it was where he felt most connected with God. A recent tumble had twisted his knee, making his gait a bit wobblier and his walk a little slower, so his objections were ignored.

"That boy...what's his name...is going to be the death of me," Solomon huffed, retrieving his fallen cane for the twentieth time in the last hour. Between the greenhouse humidity and his own frustration, sweat glistened on his black skin. He patted his forehead dry with a handkerchief.

"Griffin. That's his name and you know it." Wilder watered the pots of herbs on the top shelf.

"And he's twelve and you like him. You're just mad because

he's the reason you have to use that cane until your knee heals, which was all an accident," Korah added while wiping her potting soil-covered hands on her apron before blowing a strand of brunette hair out of her eyes.

"Accidents happen when people are being careless," the old man griped again.

"Yes, and bad attitudes about them don't make knees heal any faster." Wilder finished her watering and set the pitcher down on the shelf. She pulled down the sleeves of her tan sweater before grabbing her coat off the hook by the door.

"I don't like it when you get preachy." Solomon snorted through a half smile.

"Well, I learned from the best." She took the small seedling from his hands. "Come on, it's getting close to supper time. We'll walk you home."

"I don't need you to—" he began.

"Don't tell us what to do, old man. We can take you," Korah said, cutting him off. Her lips were pursed, and she rapidly tapped her foot on the ground as she held his wool jacket out to him.

Solomon held up his hands in surrender. "You two know you're my favorites, right?" he said, a grin stretching from ear to ear.

"Of course we are," Wilder said.

The whole greenhouse was a compilation of distressed doors and windows gathered from deserted townships when Beartooth had first been built. Everything in their settlement, aside from cabin logs cut straight from the forest, were remnants salvaged from former lives. Like the greenhouse, the crude elements had all been fashioned together into something new and beautiful in their imperfections—a masterpiece of scraps left behind when the Necanians rebuilt the rest of the world in their image.

After he'd donned his coat, Wilder took Solomon's arm and helped him to the paint-chipped door. The three stepped outside the greenhouse.

"Can we help you?" Solomon's tone cooled like the outside air as he squinted toward the snow-dusted path that led from the forest to the edge of their settlement.

Walking toward the greenhouse was a man. He seemed tall, compared to Wilder anyway. Though most people were tall compared to her. He removed his knit hat revealing a mess of light brown hair which was left in even more disarray after he ran his hand through it before scratching the traces of a beard which covered his chiseled jawline. He smiled, his lips crooked and his tanned cheeks a little pink from the frosty wind. He looked to be only a little older than Wilder.

"Hello," the man greeted. The deep tones of his voice filled the still forest with rough echoes.

"Hello," Solomon responded. His body tensed and his brow furrowed a touch.

Wilder matched the old man's wariness. They didn't get many visitors, especially this time of year. Wilder knew enough from his attire—an olive-drab jacket, faded jeans, and scuffed brown boots with a dirty rucksack tossed over one shoulder—that he wasn't from the Necanian's domed city. She had never been south but had seen old images and had heard stories of the people's sleek black and white fashions which seemed to accent their new pristine lives with the Necanians. This man looked nothing like that, though. While those in the city rarely dared travel this far from their home, that didn't necessarily make this man a friend. Some of the other northern camps housed a more dangerous sort.

"The name's Declan." The man reached out a cracked hand.

Solomon shook it then asked, "What brings you all the way

out here, Declan?"

The man's smile shrank, and his head dipped down just a little before he replied, "You probably don't get a lot of tourists, but I promise I'm not looking to bring any trouble. Just hoping for a place to stay for a night or two, until the coming snow passes."

Solomon rubbed the back of his neck. "We could probably accommodate that...as long as there's no trouble."

"You have my word." Declan nodded solemnly.

"I'm Korah," the girl interjected, smiling wide and waving, "and this is Wilder." Korah, ever more trusting and hospitable to strangers, pointed her thumb at her friend.

"Nice to meet you, Korah." Declan's crooked smile returned. "And nice to meet you...Wilder."

The way Declan said her name caused something in Wilder to jerk, as if she'd been asleep. It was settling and disturbing all at once—a ripple in the water. Etiquette told her to shake his hand or offer some other courteous response. Another voice swore this man *would* be trouble, it just wasn't sure what kind. Jumbled between the two was this peculiar fear that if she touched him, she might catch fire right in that spot. Wilder had never encountered that kind of feeling before. She didn't know what to do with it, so she didn't speak. She only nodded curtly then helped Solomon keep his footing as they walked toward his home.

"You can stay with me," Solomon offered Declan as they reached the group of cabins. He pointed his cane to the second tiny house on the left. "I think that would be best." Solomon was kind, but there was caution in his tone. If anyone was to risk their safety, it would be him. He would keep this stranger close.

"Of course," Declan said.

"I'll bring you both dinner in a bit," Wilder said. While it wasn't unusual for her to cook for Solomon, she reprimanded herself for the offer upon seeing Korah bite away a sly grin.

The old man raised his brow. "I won't say no to a free meal." He smiled at her and ushered Declan inside his door.

* * *

A big snow did come, blanketing everything in a layer of gleaming white while they all slept. Wilder stood on her weathered front porch the next morning, watching the soft falling flakes, and wrapped up in the colorful blanket Melvina, her friend and the camp's healer, had crocheted for her. Shrieks of laughter interrupted the peaceful scene as the children ran out of their cabins to play. Fresh snow always called out to them, never getting boring no matter how often the winter brought it. Wilder laughed as they rolled on the ground making angelic imprints and tossed snowballs. She spotted Griffin's curls peeking from under his knit cap. He grabbed a handful of white and molded it into shape then turned and hurled it across the slushy street. The other boys all ducked out of the way and Griffin's eyes widened as he watched his snowball hit the back of a stranger...Declan.

"Sorry, mister." The boy's voice cracked as he spoke.

Declan didn't turn around or even seem to acknowledge the boy's apology. He reached his hand over his shoulder and tried to dust the snowy residue off his back. His silence worried Wilder. She started to call out to help mediate the situation.

Before she could speak Declan turned to the waiting Griffin and said, "Not a bad throw, but if you pack it a little tighter and more evenly, you'd have better accuracy and speed. Let me show you." The man reached down and formed his own snowball then threw it at the other boys, hitting one square on the chest. "See?"

The boy's faces stilled with shock for a split second before melting into huge grins.

"He's on my team!" Griffin called.

Within moments, the center street of their encampment became the great snowball war of 2074. The children yelled and ran and squealed with utter glee. The stranger who joined them seemed to no longer be a stranger at all. That fire rose inside Wilder again, flushing her cheeks, as she watched Declan play with the children. She had known this man for just a few hours. She barely spoke more than a handful of words to him the previous night when she brought dinner to Solomon's cabin where he had stayed.

Yet, electricity tingled beneath her skin when she thought about him, watched him. She wanted to slap herself for feeling it. She wasn't that girl. She didn't become some gooey mess around men. She didn't giggle and flirt. She did not believe in love at first sight—not that she was saying this was love—and she would not start now. No, whatever this was it was a fluke. The snow would pass, Declan would go on his way, and she wouldn't give him another thought. He wasn't her type anyway. She preferred someone more sensitive, artistic, and intellectual. *Perhaps he is all those things wrapped inside rugged masculinity.*

"Shut up," Wilder muttered to herself, rolling her eyes at the cringe-worthy thought. She shook her attention back into the real world where snowballs still whizzed to-and-fro.

Declan stood in the middle of the ruckus staring at her. When her eyes met his, he smiled and waved. Wilder lifted the fingers that held her blanket around her in a weak wave of her own. A snowball hit the side of Declan's face, and a laugh burst forth before she could stifle it. The man's smile only grew grander, more handsome. She bit her bottom lip and retreated inside her one-room cabin, scolding her swooning as she went.

CHAPTER 2
DECLAN

Six Months Later

Since losing his parents and escaping Hope City when he was thirteen, Declan had never lingered in one place for too long. Since his original getaway from the Necanian dome, he had traversed a few thousand miles of what had once been America, coming across varying settlements along the way. Most were nothing more than places to get a good meal and a safe night's sleep. He'd stay a couple days here, maybe a week there, then he would be on his way to nowhere in particular. He hadn't expected Beartooth to be any different, but it had been six months now, and he still wasn't ready to leave, though he didn't really know why.

Strike that, he knew exactly the reason—Wilder. She revealed herself in small, sparing doses when it seemed she had no other option but to engage in conversation with him. However, Declan savored every single interaction and couldn't bring himself to say goodbye to her or her home. But he'd also miss the solitude that this small camp so easily afforded him. In his free time, he would hike to a clearing near the river for some target shooting to clear his mind.

Unfortunately, a couple of the other young women in the settlement noticed his hobby and had asked for a shooting lesson. He had wanted to say no but couldn't think of an excuse fast enough. The consequence was an afternoon of flirtation, interrupting his tranquility. It wasn't all bad. He would be lying to say their less-than-subtle advances didn't feed his ego just a bit. Today he was helping two such young women by having them practice aiming for a bullseye target he had fashioned using a bit of charcoal on a dying whitebark pine tree.

"Hi, Wilder," one of the young women called out as he was digging in his rucksack for more bullets. He glanced up upon hearing her name.

"Hi there, Lydia...and Mary. It looks like you all are having fun." Wilder stopped on the worn dirt path with a basket of blackberries in her hand. Her pink lips curved into a smirk.

"We are." Mary touched Declan's arm and giggled.

"I bet." Wilder rolled her blue eyes, and he swore her fair cheeks reddened. If Declan didn't know any better, he would think she was jealous. He *hoped* she was jealous.

"Want to join us?" Declan asked before she could retreat toward camp.

"I'm not interested in an excuse for you to put your arms around me and lean over my shoulder to flirt," Wilder said. The other girls stiffened at her remark, but he was barely able to suppress his own chuckle at her candor.

"No problem. I'm fine with having to come to your rescue later when you can't defend yourself," Declan said, slowly turned back toward the targets, waiting for her rebuttal.

"Who says I can't defend myself?" Wilder asked. "And what exactly am I defending myself from?"

"You never know what could happen." Declan shrugged then reloaded his pistol with the bullets he'd retrieved. "Wolves are around...there could be a rogue bear in the woods...marauders..."

Wilder guffawed. "A rogue bear? Marauders? Really?"

"I like to be prepared for anything." Declan glanced at Wilder over his shoulder then focused on the target. He fired three quick rounds, all hitting within an inch or so of the bullseye. He was showing off. He didn't like that about himself, but it was what she did to him. He felt the need to impress her, and he found it was harder to suppress the urge to do so as the weeks at Beartooth passed by.

"Well, we wouldn't want you taken down by a band of marauders on *my* account," Wilder said, a hand on her chest. She moved to stand next to him. "Are you equipped for a sword fight with pirates too?" She laughed again, the melody igniting a warmth in his chest.

"Actually, yes," Declan replied.

Wilder brought a hand to her mouth, stifling her giggle. "Then I guess we can just count on you to save us."

"You don't strike me as the type of girl who *wants* to be saved." Declan had her there, he saw it in the way her lips pursed, her eyes squinted slightly, and her freckled nose scrunched.

"Fine." Wilder set down her basket. "Show me how you use that thing, then step back and let me try on my own. No funny business. I'm not into playing out some romance novel scene."

He held his hands up in mock surrender. "Whatever you say, ma'am."

Wilder rolled her eyes again. "Cute," she jibed, tucking her cinnamon waves behind her ears.

"I know I am." Declan winked at her, ignoring her raised eyebrow but not the very real blush. He barely noticed Mary huff and Lydia cross her arms over her chest, both annoyed when he stepped away from them and closer to Wilder, her presence taking all his attention.

He was a man of his word though and showed her how to hold the gun, how to turn the safety off, and aim and shoot, all while she watched attentively. Wilder took the gun from him and made him step back. She lifted the pistol and eyed the target. Time ticked by while she stared at the thing but didn't flinch. She lowered the gun, took a breath, then raised it again. Declan was beginning to wonder if she would ever actually pull the trigger, but finally she fired, and it hit just to the left of the bullseye.

"Not half bad," Wilder said with a pleased smile.

"That was a good shot," Declan admitted, "but the bear might have had enough time to filet and grill you before you got it off."

"Hey, if I'm accurate, I only need to shoot once," she retorted.

"True, but—"

Wilder cut off his reply by stepping forward to shoot again. This time she didn't hesitate at all before firing three shots, all finding their mark smack in the middle of the concentric circles. "I guess I'm a natural," Wilder said, putting the safety on before she handed him back his gun.

Declan closed his fish mouth. "No one is *that* natural."

"They are when their daddy taught them to shoot when they were eight," Wilder responded, picking her basket of blackberries back up. "I don't like guns, but I can use one. So don't worry. I'll keep you safe from the marauders, and you can handle the pirates."

"I get sea sick," Declan said, soliciting another bewitching laugh before she walked away.

When she peeked back over her shoulder at him, it was settled. Wilder, without even trying, had rooted herself in his heart. And that rooted him there, in Beartooth.

CHAPTER 3
WILDER

Four Months Later

Wilder pulled the heavy quilt over her shoulders and groaned into her pillow. She blinked itchy dry eyes and licked cracked lips. She fumbled for the glass of water on her bedside table only to discover it was empty. She grumbled again. Her tongue still tasted of the sour concoction Melvina had given her the night before. The ache of her muscles had seemed to ease though, so perhaps Melvina's remedy was working. It was a thought which made having to drink the bitter fluid a little more tolerable.

"Look who's awake," a deep voice came from a corner chair.

Wilder turned to see Declan stand. She opened her mouth to question him, but it was like cotton and her throat scratched so words were slow to emerge.

"I took the night shift," Declan explained. "Melvina didn't want you left alone after taking that stuff." He pointed to a mason jar which sat on the little kitchen table that was still half full of a yellowish liquid. "I'll make you some tea."

Wilder watched him fill the kettle and set it on the wood stove as she slowly pulled herself to sitting. She pushed damp hair off her forehead and wiped the corners of her mouth.

Declan wet a washcloth and came to sit on the edge of her bed. He reached to wipe her face but Wilder held up her hand. He smiled awkwardly and gave her the rag.

"Thank you," she managed to croak out. She wiped her face and neck. She was certain she needed a full bath, but this did offer a little refreshing in the moment.

"Do you want anything to eat?" Declan offered. "Mel brought soup. Korah left some bread. Or I could get whatever you—"

"Just the tea for now."

He nodded and returned to brewing her cup.

It was odd. Declan had been in Beartooth for ten months now and had only been in her cabin once. That was just last month when they'd had a dinner to celebrate his joining the council. Before that, he would occasionally stop to bring her firewood, leaving it on her porch and offering some flirty comment and a wink. She would roll her eyes and stifle more genuine smiles. Sometimes they would converse about something more substantial, like the weather or the harvest. Declan had come to care about Beartooth, Wilder had no doubt about that, but she resisted the idea he actually cared about her in any real way.

Solomon insisted there was more to Declan than outward charm. He'd told Wilder of their late-night talks and convinced her, and the other council members, that Declan would be a benefit to the camp's leadership. He'd told them that he thought Declan's knowledge and experience of the world outside Beartooth would be helpful, that this new member of the community had earned his respect and deserved theirs. Solomon had come to trust Declan, so much so, in fact, that he'd once told Wilder, in confidence, that he could foresee Declan taking his seat as head of the council within a couple years when he was ready to pass the baton. She had laughed. Solomon had laughed back at her, telling her she'd see it too, if she let herself.

Why wouldn't she let herself? Being sick stole the energy of denial, making her honest enough with herself to admit that she was afraid. If she didn't look beneath his surface smirks and handsome features, she wouldn't have to open herself up to a possibility that came with the risk of heartbreak. Others in their community always thought Wilder brave, but she never really thought it about herself.

"Here." Declan brought her favorite mug, filled with steaming black tea. "I think this is how you like it."

Wilder took a sip. The hot liquid soothed her throat. It had just the right amount of honey to sweeten it the way she liked. How had he known?

"Are you feeling any better?"

"Yes," Wilder said. "I think that I am."

"Good, I..."—Declan looked down at his hands—"*we* were all worried about you."

Wilder took another sip of tea to cover the blush that brought heat to her cheeks at his slip up. He had been worried about her and she liked the way that felt. It was different from when he would joke or flirt and it all just flitted on the surface. This was stirring something deeper—something real.

This whole moment was something real. It wasn't just a teasing glance that gave her fiery shivers on her skin, it was his genuine care that warmed her soul. Wilder entertained the notion that Declan's suave advances had been about something more than simple attraction. It was seeming more and more possible that she had misjudged him in this regard.

"I'm sorry to have worried anyone." Wilder smiled and reached clammy fingers to touch his hand briefly.

The smile Declan returned made Wilder's breath catch. His green eyes danced, twinkling in the stream of light from the morning sun.

Wilder took her hand back and sipped her tea again.

Declan swallowed and ran a hand behind his neck. "I...uh... looked over your bookshelf while you were asleep..."

"You can borrow something if you want," Wilder said.

"Actually, I was wondering if I could read something to you?"

"Oh." Wilder's mouth was dry again. Her stomach filled with butterflies. She nodded. "Yes, I would like that."

"Any particular book?" He pulled a chair beside the bed.

"*Pride and Prejudice*," Wilder replied. "Have you read it before?"

"No." Declan perused the shelves for the tome. "We didn't have books in the city...well, we had one... here it is." He pulled the Austen novel from its shelf and ran his hand over the navy-blue cover.

Declan sat down in the chair, opened the book, and began to read.

Wilder nestled against the pillow to settle in for the story. She closed her eyes, just listening to his voice for a moment. He stopped to snicker at a line, and she opened her eyes to watch him, finding she preferred seeing his expressions while he read.

Wilder had been afraid to open her heart. She hadn't

thought herself brave. Sitting here though, sick and disheveled in her bed, with Declan beside her, having taken care to make her tea and read to her, she still didn't feel brave. But she was beginning to feel safe.

CHAPTER 4
WILDER

Five Months Later

Children danced about as everyone clapped their hands in time. Wilder laughed, breathless with joy, as she sat under twinkling lanterns and autumn stars. Declan sat beside her with his hand wrapped around hers. The sparkling lights matched the gleam in his eye as he smiled wide. A fire inside she had once fought now added a glow to her life. She could tell you the moment it had started —her resistance weakening as he'd read of Mr. Darcy. A thousand tiny moments had come after, building a love she couldn't live without. It took four hundred and fifty-seven days from their first meeting to this, their wedding night. Over that time, snowball fights, shooting ranges, and awkward conversations had shifted into long walks and deep talks of histories and futures. In the shelter of evergreen forests, strangers had become soulmates.

"I have a surprise for you, Mrs. James." Declan squeezed Wilder's hand and pulled her to her feet.

She tugged at the lace of her skirt to keep it from dragging on the ground and followed him past the mismatched wooden tables and chairs, which had been pulled from everyone's homes for the occasion. She stepped beyond the smiling faces of their friends—their family—to the little clearing on the other side of the candlelit reception.

"What are we doing, Mr. James?" she whispered in Declan's ear.

"This," he whispered back and his breath made her skin tingle all the way down to her toes.

He placed one of her hands on his shoulder and held her other up as he put his right hand against her waist. She heard the pop of the record player then the piano notes. A gravelly voice wafted above them. They began to sway to the tune.

"Sound familiar?" Declan asked.

"Vaguely," Wilder teased, but she knew exactly what he meant. The first time he'd kissed her, they had been on a walk together. He had stopped and asked her for a dance. She'd laughed about dancing with no music. He'd told her he had never really danced before so he was sure things would get funnier. But then he'd pulled her into his arms and rested his cheek near hers, humming. The hum had turned into sweet lyrics of an old love song. She hadn't laughed again. She had leaned into him and listened to his timid song, knowing it was melting the last bit of her reluctance in her feelings for him.

"I thought *that* was the happiest day of my life," Declan said now, pausing his feet and moving a hand to her cheek.

Wilder leaned into his palm. She closed her eyes and tried to etch this moment into her memory. In the length of a song, she wanted to sear into her mind the warm glow of lantern light, their love, her family who was there with them, and the pure joy that seemed to radiate from the two of them.

As the melody of their song faded, the clink of metal against glass created a new tune that grew louder as chants of "kiss, kiss, kiss" were added to the refrain.

"We have to give the people what they want," Declan said.

She returned his grin with one of her own. "Wouldn't want to disappoint."

Declan pulled her closer. His lips covered hers, and she tasted the honeyed cake and buttercream remnants, which only made the moment sweeter. The reception cheered and the musicians struck up a new tune while everyone clapped in rhythm as they surrounded the couple in a new dance.

Eventually, Declan led her off to the side. He watched the crowd with wide eyes and a full, bright smile. He rarely danced, but he observed it with obvious pleasure.

"You know, I was eighteen before I heard music, real music," Declan said. He chuckled but punctuated it with a sad sigh.

The Necanians, the builders and rulers of the domed cities, didn't have music. They had outlawed it. Though Wilder had never understood why.

"Why would you want to remove this?" She hadn't meant to ask the question out loud. Any talk of the Necanians always soured Declan's mood.

"I don't know," Declan said. "But they did. They stole the stories of songs and traded them for obedient silence." He mumbled the last part like he was repeating something he had heard elsewhere from someone more poetic, perhaps. His face dimmed a touch more. A tear flashed in the corner of his eye. "The Bringers of Peace," he scoffed at the Necanian's epithet. "They are really just the thieves of life, slowly stealing the soul of humanity."

Wilder was certain he had heard those words before from someone else. The way he said them was like they came from another voice, one familiar but distant. "Declan?" She linked her fingers with his.

Declan looked at their intertwined hands then to her face. He wiped the tear from his cheek before kissing hers. "Not here," he whispered. "Not in the north, not with the people in the mountains." He turned his attention back to the dancing. "They can't steal this." His smile returned and he began to clap along to the music.

Wilder clapped too as she watched her community alive with celebration. Korah and Sam danced with as much glee as they had on their wedding day just a couple months ago. Melvina held hands with a group of children twirling in a circle. Solomon played his drum while Griffin sat beside him on the guitar. Every face, every soul in this place made Wilder grateful. She was glad to never know Necanian rule. She was glad to have been born in Beartooth. Their village's isolation in the mountains meant that they could get away with their own way of life that was separate from the Necanians. She would be glad to spend every day for the rest of her life in this spot, with this man by her side.

She grabbed Declan's arm and began to pull him onto the makeshift dance floor. "Come on!"

He resisted. "Oh no! My dancing quota is over for the evening."

"You would deny your wife this small request on our wedding night?" Wilder feigned disappointment.

"No one wants to see me make a fool of myself to music," he said, although she noticed he was inching forward.

"Not true." Wilder tugged him harder. "I certainly do."

CHAPTER 5
WILDER

Five Years Later

Founders Day celebrations were slated for a week from Thursday and Wilder had been put in charge of leading the festivities for the second year in a row. She should have spent the morning engaged in more productive planning but had somehow lost herself in introspection over the birth of Beartooth.

She realized how little she truly knew of the world outside her home camp—almost nothing except what Declan had shared in stories of his past or what she had learned in history lessons as a child. She could not see the domed cities of the Necanians from her forest compound. Sitting on the covered porch of her weathered cabin, she viewed the totality of her life experience—trees shedding the death of winter as spring burst forth in emerald buds, birds swooping across the bright, azure sky, and friends moving about their day with simple purpose.

This was what she knew of life. She had no personal frame of reference for exactly how much had changed fifty years ago when the Necanians came to Earth. Decades before she was born, they introduced themselves to the world—all brightness and grace in lean, muscular humanoid bodies—and the world had been smitten with them.

Most of the world anyway. Wilder had only ever seen pictures of the aliens from old news and magazine clippings. In the images, she found reasons one might be enamored with the ethereal beings; their white skin glistened with translucent, silver scales, accented by the sheen of their long white hair and luminescent eyes. She understood the ease with which one might relent to such a creature, especially one powerful and spinning promises of peace and prosperity. But in Beartooth, elders spun stories laced with distrust and concern. Whatever the rest of the world saw or did, Wilder's people did not revere the Necanians and passively refused to serve them. Declan hated them. The Bringers were the very reason his parents were gone, though he didn't like to talk about it.

The aliens were also the reason her parents and grandparents had fled north into the cooler mountain climates to build this village. They were no longer alive, all having died peacefully and naturally as they all eventually would, but their stories and warnings had remained in her memory. In isolation from the rest of the world, they established a community which gave homage to a vintage era. They ate what they could grow or hunt. They survived without modern comforts in order to be as self-reliant as possible. They lived like ghosts of an earlier time, a time when the world wasn't lost. They resided in a smaller world. One Wilder treasured.

In the five years Wilder and Declan had been married, Founders Day had come to be, at least for her, a time of musings of the nature of the world, Beartooth, and its beginnings. She had rarely pondered such things before, but Declan had opened her eyes to the gift her home truly was. However, she'd lost herself in those ruminations for too long this morning. Founders Day wouldn't plan itself.

Wilder read over her to-do list in an effort to bring her thoughts back to the matter at hand. Korah had taken charge of food, insisting they keep to the traditional venison roast and refusing to hear any talk to the contrary. Wilder would follow up with her this afternoon. Korah's husband, Sam, was tasked with setting up the tables and chairs in the clearing at the southern end of the settlement. She would check with him the day before the feast. Melvina had asked to organize the art and music, gathering creative representations of their community creed. They were having tea in the morning and Wilder could discuss her progress then. Solomon would once again regale them with the story of the founders—*pilgrims leaving everything behind because they would not abide.* He, she knew, needed no check-ins or follow-ups.

He told the tale the same every year. Wilder could quote it verbatim:

In the beginning, we were considered nothing more than nonconformists to be shrugged off as unenlightened. Then we became rebels. Not the kind who struck fear, but the ones who created a certain disdain in the hearts of seemingly better men. We were pushed back, our ranks shrinking until our exile outside the shining city. We have lived forgotten by the rest of the world except in cautionary tales spoken to unruly children. We are harmless in their eyes, too few to disturb anything real in their society. We're merely the outliers, the people in the mountains, 'the wayward souls who are lost to a better life.' But we are not the lost ones, friends.

Wilder chuckled at the verbiage while checking an item off her list. Solomon had a flair for the dramatic in both his Sunday sermons and his bonfire stories. He told this story—of fathers and mothers coming together to create something

23

secure for their children and their future—as though it were a sermon with a message of hope. Wilder appreciated the old man's passion. Even if she never quite understood its cause. For her, hope had always been certain and unthreatened.

"Have you been out here all morning?" Declan climbed the three porch steps in two strides. "Because I swear you were sitting in the exact same position when I left after breakfast." His brow arched over green eyes that brightened with playfulness.

Wilder set her journal and pen on the small side table then stretched her back. "I lost track of time contemplating history, life, love, and the future." She reached out her hands to Declan and he pulled her to her feet.

"Life, love, and the future, huh?" He smirked. "Am I part of this contemplation?"

"Well, Mr. James," Wilder said, smoothing the collar of his flannel shirt. "I do remember some promises—vows if you will —regarding sickness and health and until death parts us, so I would say you do play some role, yes." She giggled and stood on tiptoes to kiss his cheek.

Declan returned the kiss to her lips then wrapped her in his arms.

She loved the smell of him—sandalwood and sweat mingling with the pine that always wafted through the woodsy air. She breathed it in deep, like it was an elixir renewing her heart with each inhale.

"How are you feeling today?" he asked.

"Not pregnant, if that's what you're wondering."

He sighed.

She understood. It was the same question with the same answer they asked every month. Enough days were marked off the calendar to give them pause but not so many to lower her spirits. There was a time for everything, and their time would come.

Declan kissed the top of her head. She felt the apology in it but had told him enough times that there was no need for him to say sorry. Finally, he had conceded instead to silence in moments like these. He always fought a tinge of pessimism—a remnant of the harder life he lived before finding Beartooth, she supposed.

"Did you and Sam get the glass patched in Solomon's greenhouse?" Wilder asked. She let him go and started to walk inside.

"For now," he said, following her. "On the supply run tomorrow, we'll need to find a new window or glass pane to do the job right."

"Good." Wilder set a copper kettle on the wood stove. "The sooner it can be fixed, the better." She pulled two cups from the wooden shelf and set them on the table next to a half loaf of bread, then started slicing a ripe tomato.

"I'll be sure of it." Declan stood over the sink, washing his hands in the leftover dish water. He dried them on the cotton towel. She noticed when she glanced over at him that his shoulders had drooped and that his jaw was clenched.

"Is everything okay?" she asked.

"Yeah." He offered his usual charming grin, which melted some of her concerns.

They didn't disappear completely, though. She could guess what worried him. She had sat next to him in the elder meetings where he'd spoken of the Necanian scouts roaming farther north, and the best- and worst-case scenarios this could imply. Declan, a man of action, never liked sitting and waiting, especially for a bad outcome he could do something about. But what was to be done over mere reports from other camps? Her people looked to

Declan as a leader, especially during their supply runs, as he had the most experience in the lands outside their village, having been a nomad for so long before he'd settled in Beartooth. But her people also had the wisdom of time and experience to know that the Necanians had never before seen them as a threat and had never once bothered them since their exile from the domed cities.

Wilder swallowed down her rising fears, saturating them with that hope her people coveted, before returning to slicing the juicy tomato. For fifty years, they had remained secure and untouched in Beartooth. Even if Declan's rumors were true, what harm would the Necanians do to them? The people of Beartooth were not a threat or an enemy. What was the word Solomon used? Outliers. They were merely harmless outliers.

CHAPTER 6
WILDER

"You don't have to do this," Wilder said, sitting on the edge of their bed, watching Declan button his shirt.

A new day's sun peeked through the deep green trees and sparkled through Wilder's cabin window. The dancing light contrasted her melancholy mood. Ever since the previous day's lunch, she'd fought to keep anxious thoughts in check. Declan had been uneasy for the rest of the day, despite his efforts to hide it, and his uneasiness was contagious. Fear was normally so fleeting for her. It alarmed her—how her gut wrenched with a sense of dread she was suddenly unable to tamp down.

"We need the supplies," he reminded her.

"Do we really? You've been worried that more and more Citadel guards have been scouting farther north. You've said they might be up to something, and we don't need a window or fabric and paper that badly." Wilder bit her bottom lip and turned her gaze from his green eyes to her own fair fingers fiddling with the tattered hem of her cream tunic.

"Wild." The mattress dipped under Declan's weight, and

his hand rested on her knee. "It's not just paper and fabric, though we both know Neema might drive us all to an early grave if she doesn't get a new dress for her birthday." His low chuckle seemed forced when he brushed a strand of her hair behind her ear. "There are things we need for the feast, and you could use a new journal," he added as his calloused fingers gently turned her chin toward him. "I'll be safe. I promise." A soft kiss landed on the corner of her mouth. "Besides, this isn't my first rodeo. We'll be in and out as fast as we can."

"You'd better," she said, then tugged at the collar of his shirt, pulling him into another kiss. "I'm kind of used to having you around now," she muttered against his mouth, reluctant to let him go, but with a last inhale of his coffee-tainted breath, she pulled away.

"Right back at ya." He winked and kissed her cheek once more before standing up. "I love you."

"I love you more."

"I love you most." Declan grabbed his backpack and left.

* * *

The sun dipped low in the evening sky, the charcoal hues of a stormy night looming above the last remnants of daylight. A light spring rain tapped against the tin roof. Wilder looked back and forth between the window and the ticking clock, waiting for Declan to be home and safe. She had read, and paced, and found chores to do to keep herself distracted from the nervous knots twisting her stomach. She'd told herself he was safe like always, and that she was being ridiculous. She just wanted it to be over and for this anxiety to be a blip she would barely remember. It would be over soon. Declan would come through the door with a wink and a crooked smile, and she would rest.

Headlights flashed outside the dingy window and tires spit mud onto the porch. Wilder ran to the front door and jerked it open.

"Help! Someone get Melvina!" Griffin's yell pierced Wilder's ears. She turned from her porch to see him hop out of the back of the muddy jeep.

"What's going on? What happened?" Wilder nearly tumbled down her porch steps.

"We were ambushed by Citadel guards at the trading post," Griffin answered, his voice trembling like the hand he ran through his curly hair. "Sam was hurt."

Wilder wrapped an arm around him. Griffin was barely seventeen. This had been his first time riding with the group toward the city. "I'm sure he'll be okay, Melvina's a miracle worker." She tried to reassure the young man, but one unspoken question was breaking down her own sense of calm. *Where was Declan?*

"Wild?" Solomon asked for her attention as he stepped into her view.

She looked at the old man's creased face. Shadows and sorrow further darkened his black skin. Something was wrong. Solomon always smiled. Even when his lips weren't curled upward, his brown eyes always danced. There was no music behind them just now though. She looked past him toward the scene unfolding at the jeep, trying to understand what would cause such emptiness in her friend's eyes.

Melvina had recruited a couple of the others to help carry Sam to her cabin. Korah walked beside her husband, holding his bloody hand, and whispering into his ear. A small cluster of people who had come out from their homes at the noise began to gather. Wilder noticed that hidden among the adults, the ever too nosey Neema and Finley had crept outside, both still in their pajamas. Without another word, Griffin, who'd noticed them too, slipped away from Wilder to help lead the two children back to their mothers. The chaos of the team's return settled into an eerie silence, with only the splashing rain and occasional sounds of distant thunder to break the quiet. A weight pressed on Wilder's chest making it hard to breath. No one who remained at the jeep looked at her besides Solomon. Her mind dizzied. *Had she missed Declan? Had he gone with Sam? Why didn't he stop to see her, give her a quick hello kiss to let her know he was okay? He was okay, wasn't he? He had to be okay.* She turned her head, frantically surveying the settlement.

"Wilder." Solomon grabbed her by the shoulders, halting the external gestures of her panic, but her insides continued to shudder with worry.

"No." Her response was a whisper. "No," she muttered over and over, putting the pieces together before bursting into a sob of realization.

"I'm sorry," Solomon said. He wrapped his hands around her arms, attempting to embrace her.

"No!" She shoved him back. "No!" The cry made her throat hurt.

The old man reached for her again. He pulled her close, but she fought against him. She tried to writhe away from his comfort like Declan's life depended on her refusal to accept this. She pounded her fists against his chest and shoulders. All the while, Solomon gently tugged her closer until she had no more room to fight him.

Wilder's legs went numb, and she collapsed into Solomon's arms. Instead of holding her up, he knelt with her, cradling her as she wept. The sky let loose with a downpour which rivaled her tears and soaked through her clothes, but she couldn't move, and Solomon didn't leave her.

CHAPTER 7
WILDER

Four and a half months later

Declan had died on a Tuesday.

That still didn't sit right with Wilder. Dying, like being born, seemed more like Sunday business. It should come when you aren't distracted by the trappings of the mundane. Something so large shouldn't happen on any old day of the week, like laundry. But death comes when it wants, and whenever it comes, it makes your everyday different. Not one day in the last one hundred and forty-two felt the same as before that awful night. They all hurt. They all held an emptiness she couldn't recover from.

It's difficult to grieve someone you never got to bury. The people of her village, her friends, had helped her place a memorial stone, of course, but no body had been brought back to fill the ground beneath it. Wilder used to visit the stone daily—now weekly—each time aching with the hope that

Declan might still be alive—merely taken and held for some crime he couldn't have committed. Perhaps this sliver of hope was what now crushed her? A lie to sustain her each night she spent alone.

Alone. It's not something Wilder thought she'd ever be again and yet, here she was, working to solve the riddle of how to return to life without Declan. The first day she stepped into this new reality, the world had moved around her in a quick beat, one that didn't match her own. Her breath had heaved. Her heart had pounded inside her ears, drowning out the whispers of condolences and the chirping of the birds. She used to love to listen to the birds, but now they were hard to hear. Her existence still marched slower, out of rhythm with everyone else's. Her insides stung while her outside was painted with the face of someone trying to move forward, all the while she was struggling to balance between the two. She couldn't just stop though. So, Wilder tied an invisible black band around her heart and kept walking the tightrope of grief.

"Knock, knock." A melodic voice and a soft tapping on the porch beam woke Wilder from her memories. "I brought you your favorite rye bread," Korah said as she took the seat next to her, setting the breadbasket on the table. "The one made from your great-grandmother's recipe," she added.

"You don't have to feed me." Wilder uncurled her legs and set her bare feet on the cool wood planks.

"Don't I though?" Korah asked. "A girl needs more than tea to survive."

Who says I want to survive? Wilder thought the words, but didn't dare speak them. Even if she expected she could deliver them with enough sarcasm to not be taken seriously, Korah was her best friend and would see through the fake humor into the pain which never relented. "Thank you." Wilder decided on a normal, thoughtful smile then reached for a slice of the still warm bread.

"You're welcome," Korah responded, grinning with her entire golden-brown face. She tucked a black curl behind her ear. "Neema and Finley are dying to have another reading lesson, by the way."

"What time did you tell them to come over?" Wilder asked with a half-full mouth of the delicious baked goods.

"At eleven." Korah fixed the same piece of hair again even though it had not moved from its place.

"You want to tell me something," Wilder guessed and took a sip of her chilled tea.

Korah nodded. "Yeah, I do."

"It's not like you to hold back. Should I be worried?" Wilder asked, moving a little forward in her wicker seat and leaning toward her friend.

"It's nothing bad. It's good, actually...really good." Korah fidgeted with a patch on her denim pants.

"Then why are you not telling me the good thing? I like good things." She touched Korah's hands.

"Well, it's a good thing, but I'm afraid it will make you sad." Korah always worried about making Wilder sad.

Wilder wondered if deep down it was because Declan had never come home while Sam had survived with just a scar to remind them of his once grave injuries and their good fortune. But she never resented their fortuity. If a trade could have been made, Declan would have never let Sam die in his place, and she would never wish her grief on her best friend.

Wilder gave her friend's fingers a light squeeze. "Just tell me."

A hesitant smile curved Korah's mouth gradually upward. "I'm pregnant...about twelve weeks."

"That's definitely a good thing!" Wilder leaned further

forward to hug Korah. She did feel sadness poking around the edges of her joy but shoved it away with a deep breath. "It's a very good thing."

Korah pulled back and wiped her wet eyes. "You really think so?" she asked. "I know you and...you were trying before...and I don't want you to hurt more because this just throws it in your face and..."

"Korah, you don't have to be so worried about me all of the time." Wilder touched the necklace she still wore. It was a gold circle with stamped wildflowers—a gift from Declan after her first miscarriage. "You are allowed to be excited about this, even around me. You're my best friend, I want you to be happy." She clutched the pendant then released it with a deep sigh.

"I am," Korah said, clearing her own tears the same way.

Wilder gave her friend another hug. She could mourn for the things she would never have later.

CHAPTER 8
WILDER

"Please, just one more story, Auntie Wild," Finley said while batting his long eyelashes over blue, puppy eyes.

"Yeah, just one more...it can be a short one." Neema's smile broke through the fake pout she used whenever she wanted to get her way.

"You both know your cuteness no longer works on me." Wilder closed the story book on her lap.

"Can't blame us for trying." Neema shrugged her shoulders and giggled.

"No, I can't. But you're supposed to be at Melvina's in thirty minutes for a science lesson, and I suspect you are both hungry, so you should run and grab lunch beforehand." Wilder patted the top of Neema's black braids and repeated the gesture on Finley's sandy curls. "Go on, now. Maybe I'll treat you to a bedtime story tonight...*if* you're good."

"We will be!" the two gleefully promised. They jumped up and hugged Wilder before skipping out the door, nearly knocking Solomon down the steps.

"Watch it, now!" the old man gently scolded as the children laughed across the path toward Melvina's. "Those two are going to be the death of me," Solomon said, dusting the garden dirt off his pant legs.

"They keep you young," Wilder countered.

She returned her books to the corner shelf where she kept her collection of treasured tomes. She glanced over classics from Austen, Lewis, Tolkien. Her fingers brushed the spines of *The Wizard of Oz* and *A Wrinkle in Time* that had both been her mother's. They were remnants of a world which now only existed in little camp libraries like hers. She paused at the copy of *Night* by Elie Wiesel. Declan had smuggled it from its hiding place in his childhood home. It was the only book he'd read until meeting her. She remembered so many evenings spent reading aloud to each other from these yellowed pages and discussing their favorites books while debating the first story they'd read to their children one day.

"I suppose you're here to check on me because Korah told *you* she told *me* her news." Wilder turned her attention away from her books and back to Solomon as she grabbed the kettle off the wood stove. "Want some tea?"

"Yes, to both." Solomon took a seat at the beat-up old table. "Are you okay?" he asked.

She poured hot water over loose leaves into porcelain cups. "I wish everyone would stop asking me that."

"We will...eventually." Solomon smiled as he took the cup she offered him. "You know it's because we care about you."

Wilder sat down in the chair across from him and dripped honey into her teacup. "I know, but all the asking doesn't help."

"Does it hurt?" he asked.

The truth paused on the tip of her tongue. If it was anyone other than Solomon, she wouldn't say it. She would drag it back down and replace it with something more polite or acceptable. He had seen her uncontrolled pain though, had helped hold her together at her most vulnerable, and it made her feel braver, safer with him. "Sometimes it does," she replied.

Solomon glanced at her over his teacup then set the delicate thing on the table and leaned back a little in his chair. He breathed in and out several times, like he was trying to slow down the thoughts bouncing around behind his chestnut eyes.

"I suppose it would," he finally said. He pulled himself forward again, his wrinkled fingers playing around the edge of his green cup. "Grief is a hard thing. We all want it to be gone in a flash, with a thought. But it's like a persistent weed, strangling out all the prettier flowers. No matter how many times you try to pull it up, it just grows back."

"It spreads, too." Wilder took another slow sip. "Everything is tainted by it; these cups, this table, the room, the camp, the river, the trees, the sky, the stars...it all reminds me of him. Everything reminds me of him. I can't escape it—I can't escape him."

Solomon reached out, resting his black calloused hand on her pale one. "He's gone, Wild. He wouldn't want you to keep on like this."

"You think I don't know that? The problem is people die, love doesn't." A hot tear streaked down Wilder's cheek. She wiped it away before it could drip from her chin.

"No, you're right. If it's real love, it doesn't ever die."

"Then what is a person supposed to do?" Wilder asked.

Solomon drank the rest of his tea in one swallow. "I guess they work to get really good at not letting the weeds destroy the whole garden."

Wilder offered a quivering smile. "You're quite profound after spending a morning in the greenhouse."

"I'm profound all the time. With age comes wisdom, my dear." Solomon chuckled as he stood. He walked behind her and kissed the top of her head. "I left a basket of fresh vegetables on your steps. Get them before something else does."

"You didn't have to do that. I could have come and gotten them myself."

"I don't *have* to do a lot of things, but that isn't going to stop me from doing them," Solomon said as he headed for the door.

"I'm glad I have you, old man."

Solomon glanced over his shoulder with a bright smile lighting his whole face. "Of course you are." He put his cap back on his head and left.

Wilder watched him walk back toward his own cabin through her screen door, chuckling when Neema and Finley ran into him again on their way to Melvina's.

She shivered. The air outside cooled with every day that fall closed in, but the sunshine still felt warm where it filtered through the trees, whose leaves were just beginning to surrender their green for bolder colors. Reds, oranges, and yellows were scattered among the emerald branches, and soon they would take over for a brief, glorious period before falling.

It was a busy time in the settlement. Winters were cold and long in the mountains. Once the first snow came, there would be no going back to the city for supplies. After Declan, they'd all decided to be more cautious in their excursions, anyway.

They would take fewer trips out. They would learn to do without, not wanting to rely so heavily on the favor of strangers or the indifference of the Necanians. They still didn't understand why Declan's crew had been ambushed that day. As far as they knew, they had broken no laws. Their best guess was that someone had mistaken them for criminals, or falsely reported them as such to the guards. The elders spent weeks after the incident trying to figure it out and strategizing how to move forward. Wilder had been promoted to Declan's seat as chair of the council—probably as some way to honor him— but she was barely able to focus on anything said back then. She couldn't remember any actual words that were spoken. She remembered fear charging in and them squelching it. If these people, Wilder's people, believed anything, it was that fear was the enemy. And they would not kneel to it.

They made new rules for going to the city. They camouflaged themselves to blend in, took less time, and spoke to fewer people. They gathered only the essentials they couldn't provide for themselves. Teams had gone back on a supply run only once since April. During that trip, the team was left unbothered, but even that hadn't sat right with Wilder.

Why? Why had Declan's team been ambushed and this one left alone?

Knowing wouldn't bring Declan back, but she told herself it might've made things easier, made her feel better. She suspected it wouldn't, not really. But it's human to want to know why—to want the details and the answers— to believe every bit of knowledge might shrink the pain until it finally disappears completely. Pain doesn't work that way, though. Wilder knew it. Grief could not be cured. It was an illness she must simply learn to live with.

Wilder stepped out onto her small porch that wrapped around to the side of the rustic, weather-beaten cabin she called home. In the furthest corner, overlooking the banks of a small stream, sat her wicker chairs. Declan had found them for her. They were a little beat up, the paint peeling. Melvina had sown new covers for the pads out of some faded material she'd scrapped together. Declan had set the chairs on their back porch, leaving them as a surprise on their fourth anniversary. It was his last gift to her. Wilder would sit there to read and watch the birds while she sipped tea out of her favorite chipped porcelain cup. Declan used to join her and read or whittle.

Now she sat there and thought about Declan and his absence. She shouldn't torture herself, but she couldn't close the doors in her brain that allowed memories of him to walk in. Wilder fidgeted with the tattered strands of her knitted blanket and mentally began a slideshow taking her from his first day in to Beartooth to his last, reminding her of all she'd lost and would never have again. She didn't cry this time. She was out of tears for the day. Instead, she closed her eyes and willed the picture of Declan's smile to be seared into her mind —equally afraid of remembering and forgetting.

CHAPTER 9

CASIMIR

The sun reflected off the mirrored walls of the city's buildings in glistening streams—an offering of warmth and light to its masters.

That is how Casimir saw things. The world and everything in it existed solely for his pleasure. That was the power he held. Anything that irritated him could be dismissed with the wave of his long, pallid fingers. He enjoyed dismissing things and people. He relished in the weakness of humanity and how it bolstered his strength.

He liked to stand in this spot, the spire of his steel tower, and watch the humans through the glass of his grand window. He considered them nothing more than ants, scurrying about as though they had purpose. They walked through their days, working, eating, and sleeping, and thinking they were happy because they were comfortable. He believed if you gave humans the illusion of safety, they would grip it with grateful hands and continue in their ignorant bliss...*most humans*.

The large door opened with a slow creak before a servant's voice spoke, "High One."

"What?!" Casimir's growl echoed off the marble walls and floor.

"My apologies for the interruption, High One, but General Wolstan has returned from the northern regions," the servant answered.

"I can make my own introductions, Felix," a larger man said as he strutted into the room.

His long white hair was braided on one side, revealing the traditional three silver rings etched into his face near his temple which signified his class and family—one circle shy of Casimir's. "Hello, brother."

"Wolstan," Casimir said, acknowledging his sibling with the slightest tilt of his head before sitting at his desk. "I hope I am not displeased by your report."

"I live to please you, brother." Wolstan placed his fist on his chest and smirked. "The raid on the Lakota encampment was successful."

"So, I can assume it was destroyed?" Casimir asked.

"It was," Wolstan replied. "The majority of the rebels were brought back to the Citadel and are being taken to the ward as we speak. A few resisters were made an example of and…" Wolstan looked at the ground.

"And?" Casimir noted his brother's sudden sheepish glance. It was unlike Wolstan, the warrior, to show any form of weakness or hesitation.

Wolstan cleared his throat and returned his gaze to his brother. "Some of the Wayward managed to flee. We sent scouts after them but lost their trail about three miles outside of the village."

Casimir raised a fist and moved to slam it onto his desk, but stopped short of the collision. He stood, straightened his buttoned black jacket, and approached his brother with three long strides. "How many?" he asked.

"About a dozen," Wolstan replied. "Give or take."

"Give or take..." Casimir intended his echo to be calm but menacing. "Do I need to be worried?"

"No. They were weak, mostly women and children. No one of worth."

Casimir placed a hand on his brother's shoulder, digging his long white nails into the fabric of Wolstan's pressed, charcoal coat. "They may be no one of consequence, but they most certainly have worth." His fingers gripped tighter, and his growing claws pushed deeper with each word he spoke. "Perhaps if you miss the next Sacrament, you will remember that and not be so careless the next time?"

"Of course, brother." Wolstan's jaw tightened. "I apologize for my lack of reverence."

"All is forgiven." Casimir released his hold. Drops of blood seeped through the fabric where his talons had been. "This time."

Wolstan bowed his head then turned on his heel to exit.

Casimir walked back to the window, stared out into the setting sun, and licked the remnants of blood from the tip of his finger.

CHAPTER 10
WILDER

The bonfire flickered and crackled. Sparks danced in front of Wilder and up into the crisp air before disappearing against the night sky. The children laughed at Korah's attempt at a scary story. To be fair, Neema was not easily impressed when it came to scary stories. Even for an eight-year-old, she was a skeptic of all things spooky, and interrupted to question every detail to prove whatever tale you spun could not possibly be real.

It was exasperating, and the main reason Wilder, the camp's resident story master, never bothered with telling ghost stories or the like when Neema was around.

"Help me," Korah whispered as Wilder took a seat on the log bench next to her.

"Nope. You knew this would happen. I will not rescue you." Wilder snickered then warmed her hands near the flames.

Griffin picked up his guitar. "I'll save you, Ms. Korah." He ran a hand through his long curls, pushing them out of his face and into a messy heap on one side of his head, then began to strum his fingers along the six strings.

An upbeat tune floated into the air, mingling with the hiss and snap of the fire, and eliciting a squeal from Finley. He held out his little hand to his friend. "Dance with me, Neema!"

The two children joined the other young ones as they all jumped, spun, skipped, and turned all around. Some of the adults entered in while others clapped their hands to the rhythm and hummed along to the melody. It was yet another vibrant, joyous moment of life in action. Prior to her wedding, Wilder would have taken it for granted—this kind of expression—but Declan's words echoed around the moment...every moment.

He had grown up in one of the domed cities with the Necanians. There were so few in their community who had ever even really seen one of Bringers, and those who had were all older now, being but children when they first arrived. They hadn't talked about them much, but their disdain and distrust of the creatures was always just a little stronger than everyone else's.

Everyone except Declan.

He had detested the ethereal beings and everything they stood for. Once or twice, he had too much to drink and fell into bed, into darker memories. That's when he would talk about them.

Wilder had rarely asked and almost never remarked. She simply listened to him speak of what his life was like before. He spoke about being controlled, of being afraid. He'd never wanted to be those things again. He'd longed for a freedom that hadn't yet seeped deep enough. Wilder had ached for him, knowing he'd still been haunted by the past. She would curl up beside him in their bed and wrap her arms around him, lay her head against his back, and will all of her hope and love into him as he talked until he eventually fell asleep. Oh, how she longed to fall asleep with him just one more time. To have just one more bonfire dance with him.

In the longing lingered a gratitude. Declan had made her appreciate her people's freedom and spirit. He had made her thankful for the life she lived, one where they had art and where music was passed down like sacred legacy.

Even now, Griffin transitioned to play a Bob Dylan song. He'd probably heard it on one of Melvina's old records. Wilder had heard it before too. She actually knew it quite well. She couldn't read music, but she had memorized every note of this ballad. Once, those chords felt like magic tickling her skin, but now they stung. A refrain that, before, had made her feel like she was floating, now made her feel chained with heaviness.

Wilder choked on smoky air and a sob. It surprised her. So did the warm tears that dripped down her chilly cheeks.

"Are you okay?" Korah touched her arm, concerned.

It had been their song from thier first kiss as they'd stood beside the river with the spring blossoms dotting the landscape in brilliant color to their wedding dance under the twinkling glow of the autumn evening.

Griffin stopped playing abruptly. "I'm sorry, Wild. I totally forgot this was the song..."

Wilder swallowed down the rest of her tears and shook her head. "Don't be sorry." She reached over and patted Griffin's knee. "The happy memories keep me going and that song is a happy memory."

She wished that wasn't true.

On her worst days, she wished she could peel every trace of Declan from her brain. Traces of love fed the endless torture of grief.

"I'm fine," she said. "I promise."

It was another lie. A small one to keep the others from talking to her about things she didn't want to share out loud.

"Keep playing. Don't stop the fun on my account." Wilder stood up and moved away from the light of the fire to stretch her legs and catch her breath.

Korah came up behind her. "Want me to walk you home?"

"No, it's still early. I just need a minute." Wilder wiped her face with cold fingers that poked through her knitted gloves.

"It's okay, ya know? Feeling sad or angry or whatever you want to feel? You don't have to hide it on our account." Korah wrapped an arm around Wilder's waist and leaned her head on her shoulder. "We still miss him too."

"I know." Wilder rested her own head against Korah's.

Declan was their friend, their leader. He had kept everyone safe, taken care of them. Everyone liked him but they had only known this one side of him, the side that was kind but seemed hard, rough when he talked, tougher than everyone else. Wilder knew a softness most had never seen. He had been focused and serious, but he'd also had this way of breaking tension with some quick-witted joke. He knew how to make everyone laugh and how to make her smile.

When was the last time she really smiled?

They missed him, but they didn't miss him the same way, not with the same depth. They couldn't because they hadn't known him like she had. She didn't want to discount their grief, but they weren't truly ready to fully take on hers. Perhaps she wasn't keeping it from them for her account, but theirs. She was protecting them from falling into a well too deep for them to climb out of. She sacrificed herself to it to protect them.

Declan would not have wanted her to do that, but it's what he would have done.

In the break from the music, the sudden sound of branches breaking in the tree line drew everyone's attention.

"Who's there?" Sam stood up from where Korah had joined him and called out into the shadow-filled woods.

"Griffin, you all take the children back inside. Now!" Melvina ordered the teenager.

Griffin nodded and ushered Finley, Neema, and the others back toward the rows of cabins.

Another branch cracked and the leaves rustled.

"We don't mean anyone any harm, but we will defend ourselves. You best speak up, whoever you are," Solomon said from where he stood next to Melvina.

Wilder walked forward until she was standing next to him. She squinted into the darkness until the outline of dark figures began to emerge from the forest.

A dry voice called. "Help us...please."

It came from a woman. She was holding someone else up, who, as soon as they came into view, collapsed to the ground taking the woman with them. Others followed behind, almost all stepping out from the darkness of the trees only to fall to the ground.

"Get some water. And more light!" Melvina yelled, rushing toward the visitors.

"Yes, ma'am." Wilder and Korah ran to obey.

* * *

About a dozen strangers came through the tree line. Most were women and children. A couple were elderly men. Some were injured. All of them looked like they had gone days without much water and little or no food.

Melvina brought them all back to the chapel. It was the only building in camp large enough, and she said it was the best place for them until she could organize their needs and place them in temporary housing among the settlement.

"Who are you? Where are you all from?" Melvina's ivory skin wrinkled across her forehead as she pushed her long gray braids over her shoulders and passed out bread and water.

A woman, the woman who had first called for their help, took a cup from Melvina. She was probably in her fifties, with long raven hair and brown skin. "My name is Sarai. Our camp was in the Black Hills..."

"Was?" Melvina had finished passing out the supplies and came to sit down next to Sarai. "What happened?"

Sarai took a sip of the water. She peered around the room, tears pooling in her eyes as they met the frightened faces of her people. "The Necanians came."

Solomon stepped forward. "What do you mean? Why would they come this far north? What did they do?"

"We think they've been sending scouting parties to collect information on our camps," Sarai answered.

"Yes, we know." Melvina stood back up and continued her caretaking as she spoke. "But they've never so much as made contact. They just skulk around the mountains, spying."

"Actually, they have...made contact." Sarai's voice was cold and quiet. "At least one other camp just south of ours was hit about a month earlier. They haven't been just keeping watch on us, on our numbers. They have been plotting attacks."

"But why? We haven't done anything to threaten them," Wilder said. The muscles in her chest constricted around her lungs.

Sarai replied, "We aren't a threat. It's something else."

Melvina set her water pitcher down and wiped her hands on the burgundy-patterned fabric of her shaggy, layered skirt. "What exactly did the Necanians do to your settlement?"

"They came in long after dark. We didn't see them until it was too late. They pulled people from their beds, dragging them into the night. A few of the men tried to fight and they"

49

—Sarai seemed to choke on her words—"they beheaded three of them. The rest they stunned with some sort of weapon then tied them up like dogs, taking them as prisoners. We were the only ones to escape. They came after us, but they don't know the mountains well enough and can't handle the cold, so we got away."

Solomon rubbed the back of his neck. "How many of you were there in your community?"

"A little over one hundred." Sarai's eyes drooped with regret while her jaw remained clenched.

Wilder's own settlement wasn't that large, maybe a third that size. She couldn't imagine losing any one of her people in such a grotesque manner. The thought of such an intrusion to their peace and security terrified her. Would that intrusion come to them?

"How did you know to come here?" Solomon crossed his arms in front of his chest.

"Declan told us if we ever needed anything that he would help. We came looking for him. This is his home, isn't it?" Sarai began to look around the room again as if she only just then realized Declan's absence from this conversation.

Wilder's legs wobbled as she took slow steps toward the stranger. The shaking traveled into her belly and through her chest and up out of her throat until it dispersed in the quiver of her voice. "How did you know Declan?" she asked.

Sarai's eyes widened. "You must be Wilder."

"How did you know Declan?" Wilder repeated the question with a more dangerous tone.

"Did?" Sarai asked the question quietly. She closed her eyes and released a heavy sigh as realization for Declan's absence settled. When she looked back to Wilder, tears hovered in her eyes. "He'd been known to come through our camp on occasion," Sarai said. "Every few months he would stop in for a couple of days, then he would pack up and be on his way. A few years ago, the visits stopped. I assume that's when he found this place—and you. Then, last winter, he shows up carrying a duffel of shortwave radios he'd salvaged. He wanted the camps to be able to communicate. He was getting suspicious of the Necanians." The woman paused like she was waiting for some acknowledgment of her presentation being fact, but Wilder had none to offer.

Declan had shared his vague suspicions but had never mentioned anything to her about connecting with other camps. If anything, he'd worked to calm Wilder's own nerves.

"So, he did go through with implementing his plan?" Solomon's question was quiet, not directed at anyone in particular; more like a thought he didn't realize he'd said out loud.

"We did tell him to do what he felt was best," Melvina said. "If he did reach out to the other camps, he must have felt like the situation deemed it necessary. He would never endanger our home otherwise."

"What are you talking about?" Wilder asked. "You both knew about this?" Anger, frustration, doubt, fear, betrayal, grief all swirled around Wilder's head, and she had a hard time keeping her balance. She placed a hand on the back of a nearby chair to steady her body, but it did little to steady her heart.

"Wild," Solomon said as he rested a hand on hers. "We weren't sure. Of course, you knew from being present at the elder meetings that Declan had expressed concerns. More scouts were being seen farther outside the city walls, and he said he just had this feeling they were plotting something."

"He didn't have proof," Melvina interrupted. "Just his gut, but—"

"But you both knew," Wilder interrupted. "You knew that he wanted to contact other camps, that he was more worried than he admitted about something. You *knew* and you let him go to the city, you didn't tell me."

"He'd mentioned to us privately that he wanted to contact the other camps, to warn them, but we didn't know he had." Solomon's voice sounded sad. Wilder thought she could hear the old man's own regrets whispering between his words. "We trusted Declan. He was our leader on these things because he had experience in the outside world, and we told him to do what he needed to do to protect us."

"It was about more than protection," Sarai cut in.

"What do you mean?" Solomon asked.

"Well, Declan's messages started as warnings and check-ins, wanting us to keep watch and stay alert. He asked that if anyone noticed anything odd or if they had issues with scouts or Citadel guards near their communities, especially if they harassed us in any way, to let the other camps know."

"But it didn't stop there?" Melvina asked.

Wilder didn't want to hear anymore. How could she not know what her own husband had been doing? How could she not see how worried he really was? Why had he kept it from her?

"No," Sarai answered. "The first of spring, Declan called a meeting. He asked that leaders from each settlement meet. He wanted to discuss a plan."

"Wait, in late March he left for a few days, said it was a hunt and he wanted to be alone. He wanted a retreat." Wilder hadn't wanted him to go, like she never wanted him to be away from her, but she'd understood that a man like Declan needed space at times.

He'd spent so much of his adult life as a solitary nomad that the confines of a singular village would press on him. He'd needed to breathe and stretch and wander just a little. It hadn't been the first time he went away to be alone.

But this time he'd lied to her.

Not just this time...in the winter, too.

"He wasn't hunting? He was meeting with you?" Wilder asked Sarai.

"Not only me," the outsider said. "There were leaders from six camps in all. Declan shared his concerns about the sudden Necanian interest in the northern region. He wanted to formulate a plan to keep the Bringers at a distance. He wanted us to be ready to defend ourselves, if necessary. All of the camps felt it was too much, though. They were content just being able to communicate if there was an emergency but saw no need to plan for one. They thought Declan was being overly concerned, with no real evidence to back it up. They feared they would appear aggressive to the Necanians if they did anything further."

"Declan never mentioned any of this..." Solomon muttered to himself.

"I suppose he was waiting to see what the other camps would do before presenting anything. He didn't want to cause a panic. He didn't want you all"—Sarai turned directly to Wilder—"he didn't want you to worry."

"That sounds like Declan," Melvina whispered.

It did. Perhaps Declan had meant to tell her, and then the others by the next elder meeting. It would have been held the first of May, and she was sure he would have said something then, even if not everything. But he never saw the first of May.

"I need some air." Wilder excused herself, escaping to the cool night.

She stared up at the stars, the foggy puffs of her quick, heavy breaths blurring their brightness. She sniffled and wiped her nose on her sleeve. The evening's revelations opened the door for her faithful companions; fear, sadness, and anger twisted and writhed inside of her. She knew Declan; he would want to be the one to solely carry the full weight of his suspicions and worries, to allow his people as much peace as he could afford.

Peace now evaded her. They had been partners in this life, that's what he'd always told her, and yet he hadn't lived it, not completely. She'd even shared her own concerns the day he... he left her, and it turns out that he'd known she was right and had offered nothing but false assurances. Why? Why not let her in? Why not allow her support in bearing this burden? She would have gladly bore it beside him. She could have helped him.

Sarai's voice interrupted Wilder's misery. "He didn't like keeping you in the dark."

"Did he tell you that?" The words sounded bitter even to Wilder.

"No. He didn't have to. I could see it in his eyes when he talked about you." Sarai's shoulder brushed Wilder's as the woman stepped beside her.

Wilder didn't know her, didn't like being vulnerable in front of a stranger, yet she couldn't even find the strength to dry her wet face.

"When he first came back into our camp after his long absence, he told me about you," she said. "The way he spoke of you...it brightened him. But that last time...." She shook her head. "He loved you, Wilder." Sarai's hand lightly squeezed Wilder's as she continued, "You were the world to him and keeping this from you was the heaviest of his burdens."

Wilder squinted back up at the stars, inhaling through her runny nose before responding, "I know Declan loved me—"

Sarai squeezed Wilder's hand again, this time tighter than before. "Then don't let this one transgression taint his memory. You knew he wasn't perfect, and this would have been one argument, one fight you would have forgiven him for easily, if given the chance to have it."

"You're probably right," Wilder said, "but given that chance, he might still be alive, and forgiving that might prove more difficult."

"Forgiving him for dying?" Sarai asked but didn't wait for an answer. "You will never be able to forgive that, my dear, because it doesn't require forgiveness. Only acceptance. After all, right now you aren't angry with him for dying, you're angry with yourself because you think, had you known his thoughts, you might have stopped it from happening. That serves no purpose because we can't change what has already been done."

"We can wish we could." Wilder's shoulders drooped, her limbs hanging heavy.

Sarai pulled her into a hug, whispering into her ear, "Yes, we all have wishes that bring us more pain than hope. We can know that and still not stop ourselves from wishing."

Quelled emotions flooded the deep well of Wilder's grief. She wept on this stranger's shoulders, opening herself.

CHAPTER II
WILDER

T he next morning, Wilder sat in her wicker chair sipping her tea as the sun crested over the horizon, ushering in a new day.

Sleep had been impossible to find after the night's admissions.

A rooster crowed somewhere in the settlement. Soon everyone would begin to emerge from their warm cabins. Normally this would mean joyful chatter and the sounds of happy children embarking on their playful adventures. But something had settled over everything after last night's arrival of the Lakota survivors. Even without the whole community knowing the details, Wilder was sure they knew enough to be concerned, to be cautious.

The time of refugees breaking through the tree line in search of asylum had ended in the decade after the Necanians came, and camps like Beartooth were formed by members of the rebellion. Of course, there was the occasional traveler... but nothing like this, not anymore.

* * *

It was still early in the day when the council gathered.

Wilder, Solomon, Sam, Korah, and Melvina sat around the wooden table in Melvina's cabin. Sarai and one other of her camp's leaders joined them. They sipped cups of tea and nibbled at the scones Korah had baked. Dark under-eye circles and dreary movements made them all look as tired as Wilder felt.

Sam ran a blistered, brown hand over his short black hair then scratched the back of his neck. "What are we going to do?" he asked.

He was a man of few words, but always kind.

Since Declan's death, Sam had always been sure that Wilder had wood for her stove. He never asked her if she was in need or told her he was doing it, but the pile of logs on her porch was always restocked.

She wouldn't have even known Sam was the one doing it had she not caught him in the act one morning. She'd asked if he wanted breakfast. He'd politely declined in three short words then went on about his day.

"Do we need to do anything?" Korah asked. "We don't know that the Necanians are coming here, too. Is panicking the right move?" Korah's normal smile curved downward into a slight frown. Her hands rested on the table. She fidgeted with her plate and fork.

Sam placed his hand on hers. "No one is panicking," he said gently.

"Sam's right. This isn't about fear," Melvina said. "But we do need a plan. If they've been attacking other camps, they will come here eventually. We need to be prepared."

"Prepared? How? We can't fight them," Korah argued. "We

don't have the manpower or the weapons. Even if we could stop an attack, they would just come again and again."

"Some from other camps are leaving, moving farther north or deeper into the mountains," Sarai offered without looking up from her tea.

Wilder's heartbeat thumped loud inside her chest, breaking the heavy silence even if just in her own ears. Sarai's suggestion made sense, yet it was not one that had occurred to Wilder. Wide eyes and open mouths around the table proved it had not occurred to the others yet either.

This was their home.

This was the only home she had ever known. This was where she, Sam, and Korah were raised. Solomon and Melvina helped build it with their parents. Their blood and sweat were embedded in this place. This was the corner of the world they had all carved out for themselves, the place they'd lived, and the place they hoped they would die and be buried.

Solomon moved in his seat, making it creak. "If we leave, if we run, we will always be running," he said. "If not us, then our children and their children."

Their children.

As heavy as this all weighed on Wilder, what did it feel like for her friend? How must the fear and worry be multiplied with a child to think about? She and Korah grew up together. They'd dreamed of falling in love and getting married and having children. Hoped they could raise their children here, catching frogs by the river, learning constellations on clear nights, picking peaches in the grove. They wanted to show them everything that meant something to them. Could they do all those things somewhere else?

The generation before them had left everything they'd ever known. They gave up the comforts of their lives, refusing to succumb to what they saw as subjugation by the Necanians.

They created a new life, and now their subjugators had come again and wanted to steal and destroy what was theirs alone.

Declan had been right. The Bringers of Peace brought no peace, just death and pain.

"Solomon is right," Wilder said. "If we run, we will always be running. We shouldn't have to run. We shouldn't have to leave our home. We did nothing wrong." Wilder's heart beat faster with each word. She was shaking, angry, and scared... but also ignited with a ferocity to protect her people, to secure their future.

"Then what do we do when they come?" Sarai asked.

Wilder looked at their guest. "You'll help us?"

"Declan was right about the camps working together. We are with you. It's time we all stood together."

Around the table, dim faces were lighting again. This small gesture of solidarity offered a glimmer of hope against their enemy. Perhaps more camps would now feel the same way as the Lakota.

"Solomon," Wilder said, "you and Sarai can find Declan's radio and begin to reach out to other camps. Perhaps more will feel the same way."

Solomon nodded.

"I can put together a patrol. We can set a schedule, have eyes watching at all hours. When they come, we can have a warning," Sam suggested.

"Melvina and I can create an emergency plan for the children. Where they should go, what they should do to stay safe if an attack comes," Korah added.

"Yes—do it, both of you" Wilder agreed, shifting uncomfortably. This was the first time since being given Declan's seat she'd had to speak with authority. It sounded strange in her own ears. She wasn't sure she could lead. But if this was who they needed, it was who she would become.

CHAPTER 12
CASIMIR

C asimir stood at the head of a long black table in the middle of a white room with high ceilings. The members of the Necanian High Council were all in place, awaiting their leader's words.

Casimir smelled their fear and submission. He breathed it in pleased.

"We have done much during our time here, on this world," Casimir began, addressing the room. "We were wise in our approach to these mortal beings. We took our time gaining their trust—their favor. We walked among them and said little. Occasionally we would pull a child from a fire or stop a car from crashing. We made their evening news, and they saw us as heroes."

"They still do," Wilhelmine, Wolstan's wife, said.

Casimir loathed her and the interruption, but he refrained from lashing out, instead merely offering a curt nod in her direction before continuing. "Soon we were invited to the grand houses of the world's leaders. We were asked to speak at their Peace Summits. Our counsel was revered. They called us the Bringers of Peace and offered us their world, one decision at a time, until it all belonged to us. We have done well with it. We have kept the humans asleep to their slavery. We silenced the faith-filled and the artists, deeming them instigators of division. We made them wary of differing opinions with fear they did not know they held. Now they are worker bees, keeping the lights on for their master."

Wilhelmine spoke up again. "Except the Wayward ones."

"Yes, except them." Casimir sneered at the thought of rebels lingering, of the outliers he intended to bring to a swift end. "That is why we are here today. I have devised a plan for the people in the mountains."

"Why?" Hesperia, his youngest sister, asked. "They do no harm. They keep to themselves."

Casimir allowed her presence solely to ensure his blood-line's influence. She wouldn't dare stand against him, but her soft nature irritated him.

He paused, inhaled a calming breath, then smoothed the silver buttons of his charcoal jacket. "They are a remnant of everything we are not and of all that made this world weak. As if that weren't enough reason to hold disdain for them, certain camps have also begun to plot against us. We have even captured one of the agitators as proof of their malice toward us."

"Their very existence is a danger to us," Wolstan said to their sister.

Hesperia looked down in silent compliance.

"Very true, brother," Casimir said. "But I have decided that we need their existence. The Wayward may provide a solution to another problem."

"What is that?" Abas, one of the oldest among the council, asked.

"In the beginning, sacrifices for the Sacrament were plentiful. Using the vilest of the humans—their murderers and their criminals—even bolstered our favor with them as those miscreants disappeared before their eyes and under their noses. But now there are fewer among them to cull."

"Our laws have worked too well?" Wilhelmine wondered.

"They have worked perfectly," Casimir answered. "But if we continue to take from the general population, we will not be able to keep the nature of the Sacrament hidden from them and..."

"You fear they will revolt," Wilhelmine said.

"I fear nothing of the humans, but we are still outnumbered here. We still rely too much on their labor." The words of admission turned sour in Casimir's mouth. He hated the humans and the need for them. "More of our kind will come, and when they do, we can show the humans their chains in full. Until then, we must tread carefully. The rebels can become the perfect provision to meet all our needs, now and in the future."

"How?" Abas asked. "Their numbers are few, they cannot possibly be enough to sustain the entire Necanian population, at least not for very long?"

"No, they are not enough," Casimir replied, "but they could be."

"What are you suggesting?" Hesperia whispered.

Casimir pulled out the tall black chair he had been standing behind and sat down. He clasped his hands together and rested them on the table. All eyes were on him, eyes of fear and eyes of jealousy. He met each pair in succession, holding a stare until they averted their gaze from his own. He breathed deeply, savoring the power he held over them.

"We need a proper supply of souls for the Sacrament," Casimir explained. "While the Wayward's numbers are few, they *are* humans. And humans reproduce—like vile insects always creating more of themselves. We will capture the rebels and use them for this purpose."

"Human reproduction is untimely and messy," Wilhelmine said, her lips twisted in disgust.

Casimir again restrained his anger with a deep sigh and the bow of his head. "We have taken the necessary steps to streamline the process."

CHAPTER 13
HESPERIA

The clacking of shoes on marble floor echoed a cadence which served to sharpen the otherwise silent walk.

Hesperia kept a slight distance as she followed the rest of the High Council down a long corridor. They all seemed eager to follow her brother, Casimir, into the bowels of their shining fortress to learn his full plans.

Hesperia was terrified.

She was unlike the others. She didn't have the same taste for blood and death. Often, she wished she were something entirely different from what she was. She longed to shed her scaly skin and escape the trappings of her species.

It had not always been this way. As a child, she was happy to be Necanian. She would spend hours reading over the history of her kind, plumbing the depths of every tradition and law. She once thought her white hair and glimmering skin beautiful. She'd been proud of the etchings on her temples that told the world which regal bloodline she was born of. The round, multiple rings of her family, markings that matched her two brothers and made her feel invincible.

She would be lying to say she didn't know when things changed for her. It was when they arrived here, on Earth. To her people, she was an ignorant youth, a curious and wild adolescent. But to the humans, her 127 years were multiple lifetimes.

She'd let her inquisitive nature draw her too close to the humans. Too close to him—*Theo*.

He was no one of significance—a servant in their house. She'd supposed he was handsome by human standards, but the outer shell of his appearance meant little to her.

He was music.

He was laughter.

He was stories.

He was this world she had never known, one that was warm and full of life and imagination. He hid books in his room and would read them to her in varying voices and tones. He would sing her sweet songs. He would touch her hand, or her hair, and she would feel things she never felt before. Love.

Was it?

She couldn't know because love wasn't something Necanians possessed. That feeling was something she hadn't laid hands or heart on. Perhaps she'd loved him—if she could, in fact, love.

He was a transgression.

That is what Casimir called him—a distraction from their cause. He made her soft. But she'd felt stronger when she was with him, and she couldn't stop herself from seeking him out even after Wolstan had warned her.

She wished she'd heeded.

Instead, she'd seen him drained of everything that made him lovely.

They'd forced her to watch as Theo's soul burned its way out of his beautiful sapphire eyes, feeding Casimir, who had more than his fill before leaving the servant cold and still on the Sacrament floor.

"Here we are," Casimir said from the front of the line, pulling Hesperia back to the present.

They were stopped in front of a large red door. Casimir turned the knob and it clicked. The door squeaked as he pushed it open, like it was heavy.

"Inside you will see our future," he said, and lights came on in the room behind him.

The members of the council stepped inside, including Hesperia, though her forward progress was reluctant at best. What she saw made her body and breath stop for a moment.

Hanging from the white ceiling were large bags. Each was attached to tubes and wires, filled with fluid. Through the transparent plastic were the outlines of human bodies.

"This—*this* is how we will use the rebels." Casimir sounded delighted at the scene. "The men and women who are viable are kept here and their seed and egg harvested as often as is possible. Insemination along with fertility testing and egg harvesting happen in this room," he said, gesturing to an odd white chair with silver stirrups. "In the adjoining room are artificial wombs which will grow the offspring until reaching maturity for consumption."

Wilhelmine stood staring at one of the suspended bodies. "But a human soul is not favorable or filling for several years. How does this help us now?"

"We will need to continue our rationing for a time as our first crop grows. We can gather much of what we need from these donor vessels, even freeze some to stagger crops so there is always a harvest to yield. In this way, we can have multiple crops growing simultaneously. We then only need to keep enough mature adults on hand at any given time to keep production running. In fact, once all the eggs have been harvested from a female, she is no longer useful and can be used in the next Sacrament."

Nausea rippled through Hesperia. Consumption. Production. Crop. It was all so clinical, so methodical. Her stomach turned that she was even a party to this at all.

"So," Abas said, "we ration the adults we have now... until proper sacrifices are produced?"

"Yes," Casimir replied. "But there are still hundreds of rebels in the northern regions. We already have plans to expand. We will begin by culling all that we can and bringing them here to be added to their brethren while larger facilities are prepared."

Wolstan spoke up from beside Casimir. "These were taken from just two camps. I already made orders to send dispatches to two others after I take a regiment to a settlement in a fortnight."

Casimir's mouth drew upward in a sly smile.

Hesperia wanted to scream, wanted to argue. But she couldn't. Her voice was dead inside her throat, unable to push out. Even if it could, they wouldn't listen to her. She had no voice in her brothers' minds even when she did speak.

She was still a child to them, and a stupid one at that. Theo's death had really been *her* punishment. If she were to speak against Casimir now, death would still be the consequence.

But this time, she feared it would be her own.

CHAPTER 14
WILDER

The air had turned crisper in the mountains. Wilder usually loved when you could feel and see the seasons changing in an homage to the great cycle of life. But as autumn took full hold, she felt too distracted to enjoy the shifting sights and smells of nature.

A year ago, she would have been up early. Heavy cardigan wrapped around her shoulders, sipping tea outside, and watching the dawning sunlight glisten through the vibrant colors of turned leaves. Today she remained curled under layers of blankets, working up the courage to get out of bed.

Two weeks ago, they'd made plans to defend their home and protect themselves from a possible Necanian attack. With it came a long to-do list and a request for Wilder's voice in all of it. They all came to her with their questions and suggestions. She felt so very inadequate to make the final decisions, yet her people seemed to have a confidence in her that she struggled to find in herself.

She hoped she wasn't leading them astray, that this course they were on would keep them safe. She fumbled through it all afraid, very afraid of being wrong. But fear was a luxury she shouldn't keep close for too long.

Wilder tossed aside her blankets and stretched herself up and out of bed. She stoked the dying embers of the fire in her wood stove and tossed in a fresh log to help fight away the chill. The cooler air and frigid water forced her to make quick work of washing her face and getting dressed. Then she sat in front of the fire to brush her hair. She was fashioning it into a loose braid when a knock sounded against her door.

"Who is it?" Wilder asked.

"It's Mel. I brought you some breakfast," Melvina replied as she turned the knob to let herself inside. She peeked in through the cracked doorway.

"You can come in," Wilder said. "But you didn't need to bring me breakfast."

"I know." The older woman set a basket down on the little dining table then removed her wool shawl from around her shoulders. "You've been dealing with a lot lately, trying to make sure we are all taken care of, and I just thought it'd be nice for someone to take care of you...at least a little."

Melvina opened the basket and pulled out some freshly baked bread and fried bacon. She'd also brought butter and jam. "And before you go into a whole spiel about how you can take care of yourself and everyone worries about you too much and all that jazz, don't. This isn't out of worry, just love. Now, sit."

"Yes, ma'am," Wilder obeyed with a smile. Inside, though, she bristled up like she always did when someone did something nice for her.

She didn't used to be that way, not until Declan's death made her a widow. Things felt different after that. She felt pitied, and she hated that feeling. She didn't want pity. She knew that wasn't the reality behind all the kindness offered her, but it was hard to feel otherwise. She didn't want to feel uncomfortable by their caring actions though. She wanted —*needed*—to feel the love they offered. She needed to pull some strength from it.

"I'll put some water on for tea," Melvina said. "You help yourself."

"Thank you," Wilder replied.

Melvina nodded and went to work filling the tea kettle and setting it on the wood stove before sprinkling dried tea into the bottom of two cups.

Wilder watched her while buttering a slice of the warm bread.

Melvina was some sort of anomaly, Wilder thought. She walked to the beat of her own drum. She didn't care what anyone thought of her—with her mismatched layers of patched clothing, her long, braided gray hair, and the henna flowers she kept drawn on her ivory hands and arms. She was joyful and boisterous and opinionated. They all loved her. She nurtured them. She was a mother, doctor, and counselor. She told stories of the world before the Necanians had come, stories her mother had told her. She talked of art and music as she concocted her natural remedies from the herbs and roots that she kept on her shelves. She was a healer with a knife on her belt.

Melvina had told Wilder once that, while everyone thought the knife was just for hunting, it wasn't. She said it was so that she never felt weak and defenseless again.

To Wilder, Beartooth had always been safe and, at first, she wasn't sure what the old woman meant. She came to surmise that Melvina had once suffered something horrible. She had been attacked or seen an attack that tried to steal her security.

Wilder wanted to ask. She'd tried once, but Melvina had made it pretty clear she wouldn't give any more power to the pain of the past. She'd said she was free of it but had also learned from it and wouldn't let it happen again. That was all that needed to be spoken of the matter. Melvina had touched the blade cinched to her belt, like she was making sure it was still there. Wilder never brought it up again, though she still often wondered.

"Honey in your tea?" Melvina asked her now.

"A little."

Melvina finished making their cups of tea and joined Wilder at the table.

Wilder took a bite of the warm bread, sweet with jam and dripping a bit on her lips as the butter melted. This was one of her favorite breakfasts. She enjoyed every bite, even licking the sticky sweetness that was left on her lips. Melvina didn't speak another word the whole time she ate, packing everything back in her basket when Wilder was finished.

"I'm sure everyone will be wanting to talk to you soon," Melvina said.

"Me too," Wilder said and sighed. "Thank you again for the breakfast and the company...and the quiet."

"Silence is underrated at times, but it can be good for the soul. Sometimes we just need another person to be in the room with us and it's enough." Melvina smiled and patted Wilder's shoulder on her way to the door.

Wilder stood up. "Mel."

Melvina paused in her exit and looked back. "Yes?"

"Why is everyone looking to me, trusting me? I'm not a leader."

"In my experience, most people who think of themselves as great leaders usually aren't. Whatever you think of yourself doesn't matter so much as what you think of those looking to you to lead them. They trust you because they know you care about *them*," Melvina answered.

"But what if I make a mistake?"

"Not to put more pressure on you, dear, but that should be a *when* instead of an *if*. You will make a mistake. And when you do, you'll figure out how to make it right. We'll all be here to help you." Melvina smiled again. She tugged her shawl tighter around her shoulders. "Besides, we do nothing in and of ourselves. There is a greater Power who does the real leading."

She winked, then walked out the door, shutting it behind her.

Wilder stared at the empty space in front of her. Wilder had misplaced her faith, or perhaps she simply set it down and walked away from it. She hadn't stop believing, had she? She still sat in on Solomon's weekly services in the dilapidated chapel at the north side of the settlement. Was that belief or routine? Or was it a show so the others wouldn't know her anger and frustration with a God who was supposed to love them and help them and save them? Who was supposed to save *him*.

Wilder James was angry at her God, which felt more painful than just not believing in Him anymore. So she'd tricked herself into thinking it was the latter. She'd forced herself to grow numb to His touch and deaf to His voice. She hid from Him and told herself He was the one hiding.

Now she felt suddenly very exposed. A tear tickled her jaw line, followed by another and another.

"No," she whispered, "not now, not when I need to keep the wall up. Now is not the time to be broken."

"Broken is not a bad place to be." Solomon's voice startled Wilder. He stood there, just inside her cabin door, watching her with a look.

"How can you say that?" Wilder asked him. "With everything we are facing, I can't fall apart."

Solomon stepped closer and took her hand in his. She felt

the callouses on his fingers and palms against her soft skin. Her lip trembled when he looked into her eyes.

"You think you can hold yourself together? You think broken is a bad thing to be? He just wants to put you back together, to fill in the cracks so you are stronger. He can work with broken because it's honest. The hiding and pretending, that's what'll make you weaker."

"How can I trust Him again after what happened?" Wilder breathed heavier. Her heart beat faster, and her palms were sweating. She was about to capsize back into grief, on the verge of drowning.

"Oh, darlin', that is the million-dollar-question. There isn't a pretty answer to it. But did you trust Him before because everything was always good and perfect and comfortable? Or did you trust Him because you knew that no matter what— good or bad—He loved you and was with you? Do you trust Him because things feel good or because He *is* good, even when you don't feel it?" Solomon's hand tightened around hers. The more she felt his grip, the more she lost her own.

Wilder brought her free hand to her face, masking her eyes and the deep sorrow she knew was surfacing in them.

Solomon hugged her to his chest. "I know this isn't easy. I'm truly sorry for that. I wish I had magic words that would make it all make sense, but sometimes it just doesn't, and we can ask why and never get to know. That's faith, not knowing, not understanding, but still trusting."

"How do you do it?" Wilder muttered her question into Solomon's shoulder.

"I just do. I'm sure plenty of people would think I'm crazy. Not believing seems easier, but there is pain in both. The difference is with one, there is also grace, and sufficient isn't a strong enough word for what it does in us."

"I feel so lost without Declan."

Solomon's embrace grew tighter around her. "I know. But he was never your compass. It's time to find North again."

"What if I can't?"

"You ask a lot of questions but aren't asking all the right ones," Solomon replied. He pushed her back until she was looking at him in the eyes again. "What if you can? What if you did? What does that look like? What does that feel like?" He smiled wider with each question.

Wilder leaned into his words, feeling them seep deep into her. Strength pushed with them somehow. The shaking inside her stopped, and her feet felt firmly planted. She took a deep, clean breath.

"There it is." A chuckle punctuated Solomon's words.

"What?" Wilder arched her brow at him.

"The hope. It just glimmered right there in your eyes. I saw it." The old man laughed and kissed her cheek.

Wilder laughed while wiping her soggy face on her sleeve.

"I haven't heard that laugh in quite some time." Solomon's whole face brightened.

"It's good." Wilder's agreement held a silent question of residual uncertainty.

"Real good."

CHAPTER 15
WILDER

Wilder breathed in deep and rubbed the final traces of tears from her face. "I suppose you didn't come here just to stave off my spiritual crisis?" she asked Solomon.

"No, that was just a pleasant coincidence," the old man said and winked. "Sarai wants to speak to you, and Sam wants to show you the watch towers he's completed. They asked me to come get you."

"Okay then, let's get to it."

Wilder didn't really want to walk out into the world. She preferred a retreat back to the security of her blankets. She'd barely been awake for an hour, but the morning's emotional journey had exhausted her.

Solomon had helped her uncover a glimmer of hope, but it was such a small hope in comparison to the depths and darkness of her sadness. She wondered if it would be enough. She couldn't be sure of anything other than her need to find healing, for their sake and her own.

Stepping off her porch and out into the bright sun which

filtered through amber leaves was a good start. Nature was always a source of peace for Wilder—a reminder that death is part of life. It's not a part that anyone wants. No one longs to see the brilliant beauty of life fade and fall to the winter of death. But death was not the end. She could not let Declan's death be her end. It had buried her under a cold deep snow, but it was time to find herself again. To emerge into a new life without him.

Without him.

She choked on that last thought. Moving on felt like giving up, and she didn't understand why. There hadn't been a body, but he was indeed gone. Wilder didn't have the time or energy for fairytale dreams of men coming back from the dead. She had work to do, work that needed her alive.

"Good morning." Sarai's voice lilted into Wilder's thoughts as she looked up and saw the woman waiting for them on the bench outside Solomon's cabin.

"Morning," Wilder said. "Solomon said you wanted to talk to me?"

"Yes." Sarai stood. "I've been trying to reach out to the other camps on the radios but haven't gotten any sort of response. I don't know if they have been attacked, as my camp was, or if they simply didn't turn the radios on."

"Is there another way to get a message to any of these camps?" Wilder asked.

"I don't think so," Solomon said. "Not without someone going in person."

"I can go," Sarai said.

"Is that safe?" Wilder asked.

"I know the area between here and Wolf Point pretty well. They are farther north, so I assume the Necanians wouldn't have breached that far."

"The settlement at Wolf Point is a pretty rough one if the stories are true," Solomon interjected with concern.

"I've heard the same stories, but Wolf Point is our best shot in a short amount of time to get help," Sarai replied. "And I can hit another camp or two on the way if I take the right path."

"When do you want to go?" Wilder wasn't sure she liked the idea of sending someone out alone, but she knew they would need more allies if their suspicions about the Bringers were correct.

"The sooner the better," Sarai answered. "If I wait too long, I'll be caught by the coming winter. I can have supplies together and be on my way in just a couple of days."

"You shouldn't go alone," Solomon said.

"Are you offering to go with me?" Sarai asked the old man.

"My knees would never make it," Solomon answered with a laugh. "But I'm sure there is someone from here who can keep you company."

"I can move faster on my own," Sarai said. "I know the dangers and am fully capable of watching my own back. I wouldn't do this if I wasn't sure."

Wilder hesitated to respond. Sarai seemed like a fully capable woman. She had gotten the Lakota survivors here with almost no supplies. But could she really ask her to do this? There was no choice. "All right. But please be careful."

"My people lived among these mountains for centuries, long before the Necanians. Surviving them has been handed down from generation to generation. I will be fine." Sarai wrapped her hand around Wilder's. "I want to do this."

Wilder nodded.

"I'll help you get supplies together, then," Solomon said. "Wilder, Sam is in the South end, just past the groves."

"Okay." Wilder let go of Sarai's hand so she and Solomon could do what they needed to. She began the walk toward the groves. The time alone would be welcome as she trekked down the narrow path through the trees.

Korah skipped up to her. "Can I keep you company?"

Wilder sighed. "Sure." *So much for alone time.*

"You okay?" Korah asked. "I know you hate it when I ask you that, but I can't help it. You won't tell me anything otherwise."

Korah was right. Wilder wasn't much of an open book lately. Even when asked, her answers were calculated. She always pretended parts. Perhaps it was time to stop that. "I've been better."

"Do you want to talk about it?"

"Not right now, but maybe later," Wilder replied, linking her arm with Korah's as they walked side by side. "I would like to talk about you though, how are you feeling?"

"Well, I think the morning sickness is finally over, thank goodness. I need to enjoy food again."

Wilder giggled at her friend's reply. "That's good."

"I think I felt the baby kick."

"You think?"

"Well, it's weird and, I haven't exactly ever had a tiny human growing inside me before, so I'm not sure." Korah rubbed her hand across her still-subtle baby bump.

"I think you felt it. I think that little munchkin couldn't wait to introduce itself to its Mama." Wilder pulled her friend closer until they could lean their heads together.

"I can't wait to meet him." Korah smiled down at the bump.

"Him?"

"Just a feeling," Korah said.

"You've always had a good intuition," Wilder said. Korah's smile dimmed. "What's wrong?"

"I'm just worried. I know it doesn't do any good, but I can't help it. If the Necanians come..."

Wilder stopped walking. She took her friend by the shoulders and said, "If they come, we will be ready. We have a plan. We will follow it, and it will work. We have to believe that."

Korah nodded slowly, and the two started walking again.

"Mel and I worked out the path for the children and sick to take. We will go north farther into the mountains. Mel says there's a cave up there we can take shelter in," Korah said. "We've already put together a supply cache outside of the settlement to gather from if we need to make an escape."

"See," Wilder said, "you've got a good plan. I know it doesn't silence all the fear, but it'll help fight it."

"I don't want to have to run. I don't want to leave the comfort of our home here." Korah stared at the path in front of them. Her eyebrows pinched together.

"I know. I don't want that either. But comfort isn't always reliable or possible. Leaving comfort behind doesn't mean leaving joy behind though. We can still have that."

Even as she said it, she realized that the idea of joy felt very foreign to her. It hadn't always been so. Walking down this forest path with her best friend reminded her of that. She knew it once, and she could know it again.

* * *

"What do you think?" Sam asked, looking up at the platform he and some of the others had built in the trees. "We can see pretty far out from that height. We're finishing the ladder now. Another crew is building one farther east, and we will also build one to the southwest. If the Bringers come, they will most likely come from the south."

"Looks good. If you see something, how will they get word to the camp?" Wilder asked.

"They have torches," Sam replied. "Someone at camp will be watching for the signal. We did a test run last night and could see the fire fine. Even if the Bringers make it within 100 yards of this spot, we will have twenty to thirty minutes before they breach the camp to move everyone out."

"What if they try to surround the settlement?" Korah asked.

Sam reached out to touch his wife's arm. "I doubt they would because they won't expect us to have an escape route or any kind of defense plan," he answered. "But if they did, they would have to come close enough to spot us before spreading out and flanking the camp because of the river crossing and that western ridge. They don't know these woods like we do, they will play it safe and try to catch us off guard."

"You've put a lot of thought into all this," Wilder said. "I trust you."

Sam's lips drew into a half grin, and he nodded. "There's a lot at stake. I want us to be as ready as we can be. It's what Declan would have done."

"It is," Wilder said. "Well, don't let me keep you from your work. Gonna walk back with me?" she asked Korah.

"Yes, but can we stop and pick some apples on the way? I think my husband deserves a pie for all this." Korah kissed Sam's cheek, and he smiled wider before kissing her forehead.

"I'll be home for dinner," Sam said. He went back to his work and Korah and Wilder started toward the apple trees back in the groves.

CHAPTER 16

HESPERIA

Hesperia didn't know why she was doing it, heading into the sub-levels of the Citadel.

Instead, she should have stayed in the safety and comfort of her suite. She could escape the disappointed and malicious looks of her brothers in that comfort, but she couldn't escape the images ravaging her mind. Ever since the High Council meeting—seeing that room and hearing Casimir's plot—a haunting feeling twisted her stomach.

She was Necanian. She was supposed to be cold, methodical... unattached to these creatures they ruled over. She had no soul.

But...

But she had been touched by one, Theo, in a way that left her changed. In her weakest moments, she wished to go back to the prison of her indifference. Instead, she would hear the music play in her memories, and that indifference now looked like cruelty. It brought with it the pain of compassion for these humans. But it was slipping further away from her with each passing day.

That was why she was here, on the dark stairwell that brought her deeper under the bright Citadel. Into the bowels of the old city. Dim lanterns cast shadows along the dingy concrete walls—cracked and covered in faded graffiti. It had been a subway station or shelter of some sort, she thought. Its past wasn't as important as its present...as a dungeon.

Casimir had built cages into the walls to hold his enemies. In the last half century, world leaders, men of faith, artists, and even Necanian usurpers called this dreary place their final home. Their stays were always short-lived. Casimir didn't believe in mercy, and torture only brought him brief pleasure before his anger made him murderous. So, when Hesperia realized a human captive had been chained here for months, she needed to see it for herself. Either this man held some value— information perhaps— worth the High Ruler's tolerance, or Casimir hated him too much to allow him a quick death.

The two guards wouldn't stop the sister to High Ruler Casimir, and they wouldn't question her either. Her brother saw her as a disappointment but not a threat. He had no reason to keep Hesperia from any part of the Citadel. He also had no reason to believe she would even come to the dungeons, much less forbid her from them.

Truth be told, no one spent much time thinking about her at all. Wolstan came by her room once or twice to check in on her, more out of his sense of obligation to family rather than any genuine concern, but he'd left for the mountains. No—no one worried about Hesperia or what she did or where she went. She was a ghost in this place.

A sound, a groan, emanated from the far end of the chamber.

Hesperia walked along the line of empty cells until

reaching the last one. It was darker here, but her eyes adjusted quickly. The irises instinctively transformed, lengthening to that of a cat. Darkness was familiar to the Necanians. They pretended to long for the warmth of light, but it was merely part of their facade as the Bringers of Peace. The dark was where they really felt most at home.

Another groan, more of a growl, echoed to her ears.

Hesperia stopped and peered through the iron bars. A figure was shackled to the wall, a male human. His body hung weak and limp. He looked dirty and thin. Dried blood crusted along the side of his face from his temple down to his ragged beard. The metallic scent of it pricked inside her nose, accenting the otherwise musty air. Hesperia wrapped her smooth fingers around the prison bars. Her silver bracelets jangled against their rusty metal.

"Who's there?" The man's head jerked up and his jaw clenched. He pulled his shoulders straighter and pushed himself taller with shaking legs.

Hesperia didn't say a word. She didn't make a sound. What could she say?

The man sniffed the air and growled again. He was losing himself the way humans did when they were fed on in small doses, their souls depleted little by little. The human would only be able to make out the slightest glint of her white skin in the minuscule light that reached this far corner.

Hesperia stood still, curiosity freezing her in place. His clothes weren't the neat black and white uniforms of the people in the city. A lion tattoo marked his forearm. His messy hair spiked and jutted in haphazard patterns. He breathed in haggard, heavy pants. His heartbeat thumped faster by the second. He looked angry and his body tired and pained. His eyes revealed a deeper ache. Hesperia observed the traces of tears that cut through the blood and grime on his cheeks.

She opened her mouth to finally speak, but he began to mumble.

He stuttered the same unintelligible word over and over as his heart rate calmed. The ferocity that surfaced was being pushed back by this whispered mantra.

Hesperia watched a fresh tear follow the stained path along his face and drip from his lip. She leaned in close, straining to hear what he was saying to himself.

"Wild," he muttered through a broken breath.

Hesperia couldn't bear it any longer and retreated down the hall.

Perhaps she'd hoped seeing this prisoner would remind her of her Necanian ideology, restore her belief in her brother and his mission here. But this human, whoever he was, wasn't her enemy and she couldn't imagine that he deserved this cage.

CHAPTER 17
WILDER

Wilder nibbled at the slice of warm apple pie Korah had brought her. It tasted more tart than she normally liked, but the buttery warmth was comforting. She needed a little comfort. So many thoughts about her morning conversations ran through her head. She'd curl up in bed later and write them all down in an effort to make sense of them...if that were possible. She saw the truth in Solomon's words but that didn't mean living it out would be easy.

Assuming she wanted to.

Wilder had gotten comfortable with her anger—familiar with the fight—and that offered some strange security for her. Letting go, giving in, moving on—those things seemed scary. Wilder had lived nearly twenty-five years of her life without Declan. And yet the whole person she had been before him lay ripped asunder.

Life without him felt like life without herself. She couldn't just move on without first sewing herself back up. But a scar would always remain.

She expected everything to be like it was before Declan, but that wasn't possible. Was that the real problem? They had become one flesh, and nothing would undo that math. What if so much of her anger and frustration wasn't just from losing him, but from realizing *she* would never be the same?

She longed to go backward, but life moved forward. God had given her a gift, one that changed her, and He'd taken it back, leaving a hole. She wanted to fill the hole with the old Wilder, the young one who never knew anything different, but it could only be filled by the person she was becoming now, through this.

Solomon was right. This wasn't about being unbroken... but being put back together. It reminded her of those clay pots she'd read about in one of Melvina's books. Over time, they crack and chip. They aren't thrown away, but instead, the cracks are filled with gold. They aren't hidden, like something to be ashamed of, but rather cherished. Her cracks wouldn't defeat her. Her broken heart could be repaired. Wilder would never be the same, but there could be beauty in her healed brokenness.

Wilder got up, took her dishes to the little kitchen counter, and set them in her sink. She pulled the tea kettle off the wood stove and poured some of the hot water into the tepid suds. She hummed a happy song while she cleaned the plates. For a few glorious minutes, the only thing on her mind was that tune.

With the rest of the hot water, she made herself a cup of tea and wrapped up in her favorite blanket. She stepped out onto her porch to sit in her corner chair. Through the treetops, a million brilliant stars shone down on her. She felt so very small just then, and yet so very much at peace.

Movement suddenly bustled through the camp. It was too late and too cold for it to be children playing. Wilder stood up to see some of the men running from the South woods. She looked into the trees and spotted the small orange glow of the signal torches.

"Wilder," Sam called out, running from his cabin across the street to the bottom of her steps. "The night watch saw something. Davis says it was a company of Necanians."

Wilder's chest constricted with a gasp. Her palms began to sweat. She wasn't ready for this. But ready or not, it was happening, and they needed to follow their plans. "Have Korah and Mel start moving the children and the weak out of the settlement," she commanded. "Have everyone else grab weapons, and be ready to hold them off long enough for the others to get a safe distance away."

"And you?" Sam asked her.

"I'll help here." Wilder went inside to grab one of Declan's guns, a rifle. She paused when she touched it, a second of memory mixed with anxiety. She swallowed it all down and forced herself back into play—ready to fend off these marauders. When she got back outside, she saw parents quickly hugging their children, wives saying goodbye to husbands, a daughter kissing her elderly father's cheek as some joined Melvina and Korah with their emergency knapsacks in hand. Korah looked in her direction with teary eyes. Wilder smiled weakly at her friend then nodded for her to go.

"We'll find you or come for you soon," Wilder yelled as a final reassurance then headed toward Sam and the small militia he had formed who were prepping to take their places in defense of their home.

"Stay steady, don't give away your positions if you can help it." He gave final orders, and they all nodded their understanding before separating.

Wilder and Sam took their position in the rickety steeple of the old chapel. From that vantage point she could see the whole settlement. She listened for the quiet rustle of feet on fallen leaves. Mostly it was from those of her people headed to safety, but at the far end of the camp, it was more subtle. She squinted at the tree line, silently waiting for their enemy to emerge. Her gun aimed toward the empty streets.

"Where are they?" Sam whispered.

A dog barked toward their right. Wilder heard some command in a language she didn't recognize from the same direction. A door was kicked in and something broke. A gun fired.

"Hold steady!" Sam yelled out.

Glass shattered followed by another sound—a weapon of some sort maybe? Then there was a scream.

All of Wilder's muscles tensed, and the hair on her arms rose. She looked back and forth waiting to see them, to see anything. A bit of white flashed against the greens and browns of the trees and cabins.

Out into the middle of the settlement's main path stepped a large figure dressed in gray. Moonlight made him, his white hair and skin, seem to shine, except for the darkness of his red eyes. He was tall and muscular. Behind him came two more of his kind. One was dragging the bleeding body of a comrade and the other was holding Ellen, Griffin's mother, with a blade against her throat.

"Come out, come out," one in the center yelled. Their leader, maybe.

Sam clicked the safety off his gun.

"No," Wilder said.

"I can make the shot, take him out," Sam said.

"I know you can, but they'll kill Ellen and who knows who else before we can take them all out. For all we know, there are a dozen others just waiting for us to reveal ourselves so they can pick us off."

"Then what do we do?"

Wilder wasn't sure. She wasn't scared of a fight. At least she didn't think she was, but afraid or not, this just didn't seem wise.

The Necanian leader glanced around him, seeming to verify where his own soldiers were. They had no way of knowing how many Necanians there were and they couldn't afford to let even one get through to those on their way to safety.

"I am already losing my patience," the Necanian said. "We came here in peace, but you killed one of my men in cold blood. That crime is punishable by death."

The one holding Ellen pushed the knife closer to her neck. Ellen began to tremble. Wilder had become the leader, officially or not; she carried the weight of her people. She needed to do something now. He said he came in peace. Wilder didn't believe that for a second, but perhaps she could use it to buy them some time.

CHAPTER 18
WILDER

Wilder set her gun against the planks of the wooden wall. "You stay here, and if things go sideways, start shooting," she told Sam.

"What are you going to do?" he asked.

She looked at Sam. "What I have to do."

Then Wilder stood up and called to the Necanian. "I'm coming down... peacefully."

The Bringer nodded. He gestured for the others to lower their weapons. They all did as far as Wilder could see, except the one with the blade to Ellen's neck, though he appeared to loosen his grip a bit.

Wilder walked out the front doors of the old church and down the street toward the Necanian. She didn't raise her hands in any kind of surrender but moved slowly, maintaining eye contact in an effort to solicit calm and trust.

"Are you responsible for these people?" the Necanian asked her.

"Yes," she answered. "My name is Wilder James. I lead

them." The words sounded weird to her still. It had become truth over the last weeks, but she never said it out loud, nor had she wanted to. Now was not the time for humility or insecurity. She was looking into the face of their enemy, and she must appear strong and confident.

The red of the Necanian's irises changed to gray then blue —probably the moonlight playing tricks on her. His mouth curved just a bit. "I am Wolstan, brother to the High Ruler Casimir, general of his armies." He placed a fist against his chest in some sort of salute.

"What are you doing here?" Wilder asked, taking no time for pleasantries.

Wolstan laughed. "I like you. Most humans snivel or stutter."

"Answer the question," Wilder said. "We have broken no laws, done no harm to you."

"Yet you are armed and attacked one of my soldiers with no cause," Wolstan retorted.

"Was there truly no cause?" Wilder asked. "Your soldier entered her home without invitation; she merely defended herself from an intruder. We are all defending ourselves from intruders. That is against no law."

She watched his jaw tighten. "Perhaps you are correct, and this has all been a misunderstanding."

Though he appeared to be conceding, Wilder suspected it was nothing of the sort. He was hiding something, perhaps hiding his true intentions because he had been caught off guard by her camp's preparedness. This was not a friendly visit under the cover of night. This Necanian meant to ravage Beartooth like they had done to the Lakota.

"Feel free to clear things up," Wilder said.

Wolstan looked around the camp then back at Wilder. "We

heard there was trouble in the northern settlements. A rogue group pillaging villages. We came to find and dispatch them so they could cause you no more harm."

Bringer of Peace—the name was as much a farce as his explanation. The Necanians were up to something. Even if Wilder could stop this incursion from proceeding, peace would only be temporary. She needed to think quickly. She needed to not just get them to leave, but to determine their complete plans. "We heard of an attack on another community," Wilder said.

"You are in communication with the other camps?" Wolstan asked. His head tilted just a centimeter to one side, and his eyes squinted as though he was at least a little surprised by her revelation.

He was digging, trying to find out something. It was a slip up that gave Wilder what she needed. "You assumed we were not?"

"We know very little about the northern settlements," Wolstan replied. "That has clearly been a mistake."

Wilder raised an eyebrow at his insinuation.

"We have underestimated you all," Wolstan added, failing to cover his displeasure.

"It appears you have," Wilder said.

Her mind churned out calculations on how this could all go. With just a word, her people could charge and surprise them, but these Necanian soldiers were trained. It would end bloody and not necessarily in her favor.

She guessed Wolstan was thinking the same thing. It seemed they were at an impasse. Further diplomacy was probably her best option, but what could she offer that would be enough?

Wilder smiled sweetly to ease the tension growing between them. "I can assure you that if the rogue group you spoke of were to come near our camp, we will know and will gladly get word to you so you can deal with them as you see fit."

Wolstan nodded. "We want only for you to be safe. We have stayed at a distance from the Wayward for far too long. Casimir seeks to change that."

The Wayward. The name elicited an uncomfortable sigh. "That is good to hear," Wilder replied, hoping she hid the chill, the suspicion in her voice, well enough. "We want only to remain at peace."

"My lord desires to unify. He no longer wishes to have the division between the people in the mountains and the loyalists in our cities. It has already caused enough pain and heart-break." Wolstan's expression shifted slightly. She could see it, him taunting her.

"What do you mean?" Wilder cautiously conceded to his provocation.

"Perhaps you had not heard? About six months ago, one of the Wayward was getting supplies at a trading post just outside the city walls and was killed. It was tragic that the animosity felt for your kind led to such an incident." Wolstan watched her closer with every word he spoke.

Wilder bit the inside of her cheek to keep from breaking down. She couldn't let her enemy know her deep pain. He couldn't have known that the one he spoke of was her beloved. He would certainly take it as an opportunity to attack Beartooth.

Wilder sucked in a deep breath, exhaling it back out slowly giving her time to compose herself. "We heard. We hope those responsible were brought to justice."

"I am sure they were, but is justice enough?" Wolstan asked. "We ought to work together to ensure this never happens again. Perhaps if we knew more about your people, about the other settlements...?"

Wilder saw her opening. "Perhaps we could work together to create a deeper treaty of peace? I could offer such information."

"You would do that?" Wolstan stepped a bit closer to her, leaning in like he hadn't expected that response and was waiting for another surprise.

"Of course," Wilder replied. "If peace is the goal, then we share the same desire. I would be happy to assist."

"Excellent," Wolstan whispered.

"On two conditions," Wilder added.

"They are?"

"First, you let Ellen go, unharmed and without repercussion. She was only defending herself." Wilder waited for the Necanian to nod. He glanced toward his underling who immediately released Ellen. Wilder gestured for Ellen to get away, and the woman mouthed her thanks, then obeyed.

She turned her gaze back to Wolstan and said, "Second, I will go with you back to the city and give you whatever information you seek there in exchange for your guarantee of peace and safety for my people here. No Necanians will return north as long as I am in your care. Or other, more aggressive camps, may grow suspicious and thwart our peace."

Wolstan seemed to stare right through her as he weighed her words. "It is not necessary for you to leave your home," he offered.

Wilder knew what he was doing. He could lull her into a false sense of security, get information to help him raid other camps. But when he had all he needed, he would attack her people. Allowing him to stay at Beartooth though would only help him gain the upper hand. She would rather sacrifice herself. It would give her people time to retreat deeper into the mountains and Sarai the chance to warn the other camps. It might not save everyone, but she could save some.

"No, you take me back to the city, to your High Ruler, and we speak there," Wilder said.

"As you wish," Wolstan agreed. "My men will regroup a half mile south. You may gather your belongings and meet us there by sunrise."

"Agreed," Wilder said. Wolstan spoke something she didn't understand, then turned and walked out of the camp, followed by his soldiers.

The brush and nearby trees rustled as hidden soldiers headed in his direction as well.

When they were gone, Sam jogged up beside her. "What are you doing?"

"I'm buying you all time," she said.

"They'll kill you, possibly the moment you meet them," he said.

"No, they want to know about the other camps," Wilder said. "They misjudged us, and he's worried about that. Whatever their plans are, they will prove more difficult to implement than they have presumed. He needs to know what I know about the other camps. I'll make it to the city at least. That will give you all time to get to safety, to warn the others."

"There has to be another way," Sam said. "We can ambush them where they wait, take them all out."

"They will just send more," Wilder said. She touched his arm. "Get Solomon and Sarai and have them come to my cabin. Keep a watch here at the camp, and send someone to keep an eye on the Necanians so they don't backtrack."

"Okay," Sam replied and ran off to do as she said.

Wilder marched to her cabin and began to pack her things. How should she prepare for the journey ahead? A few items in an old backpack didn't seem sufficient for what she was facing, but she gathered them anyway. She folded her clothes just so and placed them carefully in the bag. Next came the book she had just started rereading, Declan's book, and her journal, followed by the tin of her favorite tea and the only photo she had of her and Declan.

She held it in her shaky hand, her fingers tracing its edges and then his face. Photos were a luxury. Solomon told of a time when people snapped images so readily, they often took moments for granted. They documented every second of their lives more than they actually lived them.

It was not so for her.

Memories were the only record she had of most of her life, priceless images held in the vault of her heart, save this one printed picture from Melvina's old polaroid camera. It was just a small square. The image was a bit fuzzy, but it was something she treasured now that Declan only existed in her memory. It was a piece of him she could still touch.

Solomon burst into her cabin and interrupted the silence of Wilder's thoughts. "I'm not going to let you do this."

"You will," Wilder responded. "It's our best chance at safety."

"You are sacrificing yourself," Sarai said, stepping into the cabin and closing the door behind her. Wilder saw she had a sadness clouding her eyes.

"I know I am. But if I can keep you all safe, even for just a little bit longer, it's worth it." Wilder sat down on her bed. "Besides, we can't be sure they'll kill me. Maybe I can change their minds about us."

Solomon sat next to her. "They have only ever had one goal and that is domination. They are interested in nothing less."

"True," Wilder said, "but there is more to it. I could see it in the Necanian's eyes, they have a bigger plan. Whatever reason they went after Sarai's camp, whatever reason they came here tonight, it wasn't just to get rid of us. It's why they didn't kill everyone at Lakota—why they took prisoners. We need to know why. Maybe by going there, I can find out and figure out a way to get word back to everyone."

"How?" Sarai asked.

"I don't know." Wilder sighed. "But I feel like this is the right move, like I have to go with them. I'm supposed to go with them." She turned to Solomon and took his hands in hers. "I have faith," she whispered. She watched tears trickle down his cheeks and his chin quiver.

"Then, I'll have faith too," he said, and hugged her.

Wilder held on to him a little longer than normal. She wanted this feeling of family, of security, to be burned into her so that when she was alone, she would have it to remind her of the reason she had gone this way.

With one last squeeze she pulled away and turned to Sarai. "Go to the other camps like you planned, tell them what's happening. Make sure they're ready."

"I will," Sarai promised.

"Sam," Wilder said and turned to the corner of the room where he stood waiting after joining them, "keep them safe. Only bring the others back to camp when you know it's secure, but be ready to move again in an instant."

"Yes, ma'am," he said and smiled. "Korah is going to be mad at you."

"Tell her I'm sorry," Wilder said as she stood up.

"It'd be better if you told her yourself, when you get back." Sam stepped toward her and gave her a quick hug himself.

"Yeah, it would." Wilder swallowed down more sad, anxious tears. She was so very tired of crying.

She grabbed her pack, then looked at each one once more. Wilder James had never been outside the boundaries of the Beartooth encampment. She'd never even wondered what lay outside her small utopia. This was her home. This place and these people were all she ever needed to be happy in this life. Others dreamed of adventure, but she dreamed only of growing old right here. She never thought she would say goodbye to that dream.

Now, she was.

CHAPTER 19
WOLSTAN

A falling leaf blew against Wolstan's face. He swiped it away and growled.

He hated this place. He despised the dirt on his boots and the smell of the damp earth and pine trees. His mood worsened with the thwarting of his plans.

When he returned home, his scouts would be severely reprimanded for their poor reconnaissance. They were not diligent enough in their work. They had found locations and estimated numbers, but they hadn't looked hard enough at these messy mongrel tribes to notice their resourcefulness.

They'd underestimated the Wayward, and Casimir would not be amused.

No, his brother would rage at this news. Wolstan needed to strategize his return. He needed to make it look like a victory so as not to suffer his brother's wrath. Casimir would not be as forgiving of Wolstan's failures as he had been with their sister, Hesperia's. There would be no forgiveness for him, Wolstan knew, so he'd have to plot his course carefully.

The dark night was giving way to the subtle light of the

rising sun. Wolstan watched down the forest path for the human woman, Wilder. Almost on cue, she came into view. Her manner gave no hint of anxiety or fear—of what might be to come. If Wolstan were not wiser, he would think her ignorant and laugh at her naïveté. He suspected that this very unassuming female knew exactly what she was walking into. She had a plan of her own.

It would fail, of course, because these weak humans were no match for the Necanians. They had full control of those living inside their city walls, and those outside were still too few to do any real damage. If this woman thought she could do anything of consequence for her people all on her own, then she was mistaken. She was no match for his brawn and certainly no match for Casimir's cunning.

She stopped just a foot away and looked up at him. "Shall we be on our way?"

"Of course," Wolstan replied.

CHAPTER 20
WILDER

The world outside of Beartooth was an apparition of a past age.

The Necanian vehicle hovered over the earth, but close enough for Wilder to see the remnants of old highways and rusty signs that were one bolt short of falling to the ground. They passed over several of the old towns and cities that had been abandoned when the Necanians built their large domes. Sanctuaries for Mankind, they'd called them.

People had left their homes to move into the promises they offered. All that was left of those homes now were collapsing buildings and empty houses, faded and dilapidated over time. Trees, flowers, and weeds took up residence where humans had once lived. Wilder watched ghost town after ghost town flash by her window. They were beautiful and sad—civilization being given back over to raw nature.

Watching kept Wilder's mind busy as they traveled to Hope City. Even with the speed of the Bringers' transportation, it took hours. The sun had come up, and now it was getting ready to sink back toward sleep again when Wilder and the Necanians were within view of the shining Citadel.

It looked like something out of one of her books.

The silver buildings gleamed as they stretched upward toward the clouds, nearly touching the protective, clear dome that arched over them. Light was everywhere, but it all still felt dead, cold. There were no trees or flowers. She had seen pictures of large cities from decades past and knew bits of nature had been sprinkled across their concrete landscapes. Not here. Not now. The only thing organic she could find was water spraying like geysers from metal fountains.

As they flew over the outer walls and breached the dome's entrance, the details got clearer. There were people, other humans, filling the walkways. They seemed less natural too. All dressed in mixes of gray, white, and black that looked more like uniforms with no adornments or individuality. They paused their steps and saluted the Necanians who passed by. Their gazes would turn to Wilder with no curiosity, just blank indifference. Their numb countenances left Wilder feeling uneasy.

Yet, she couldn't turn away from them. She wasn't sure what she expected from those who lived within the walls of the Necanian Citadels, but it wasn't this. These people chose to stay here and yet they still looked like prisoners.

The closer they flew to the center of Hope City, the more Wilder's insecurities heightened. She was out of sorts here. This place loomed so large around her that she wondered if it was false hope to think her people could do much in the way of stopping whatever schemes the Necanians had for the northern settlements. But she was here now, coming to a halt in front of the tallest skyscraper, and she would have to do her best to save as many of her people as she could.

"We will get you settled and then introduce you to the High Ruler at our evening meal," Wolstan said, stepping out of the now stopped vehicle and offering her his hand.

Wilder hesitated but took it, keeping up appearances along with the general. She took in the gleaming silver building and the shimmering faces of the servants who came to greet them at the doorway. They were all Necanian, to Wilder's surprise, down to the very last attendant.

"One of the servants will show you to a room where you can clean yourself and dress for dinner," Wolstan said as he walked beside her into the grand entry. "They will explain things to you."

Wilder opened her mouth to say something, but she couldn't think quick enough before Wolstan marched off in a different direction and left her staring at the white marble floor and walls around her.

A Necanian smaller than Wolstan approached. She was dressed in simpler attire and bore no markings on her face. But she was just as aloof as the general. "This way," she said.

Wilder nodded and followed the alien to a corridor on the right of the entry. They went up several flights of stairs and down another hall. Her footsteps echoed off the clean, cold surroundings. It was strange, the Necanian Citadel. No art or decoration adorned the walls. Beartooth was filled with such things. Her people were a bundle of color and warmth and creativity in a shell of nature's beauty. Declan's description of the Bringers being without music struck a new chord with Wilder as she saw with her own eyes the soul missing from this place.

"You will stay here," the Necanian servant told her. She opened a black door and stepped inside.

Wilder entered. The room wasn't much different from the

rest of the Citadel. Hard lines and empty space. It was utilitarian, with just a bed, a couple of chairs with a small side table, and a tall wardrobe. All were various shades of gray or black against a white backdrop. On the wall opposite the door was a tall picture window. The cityscape offered nothing much different, but the sky was still blue. Even the Necanians couldn't steal that bit of glorious hue from the world.

"There is a bathing room just there." The servant pointed to a narrower door on the right. "You can wash...thoroughly." Her nose pointed upward at the last word with an air of disgust. "I will bring you clothes for dinner."

"I have my own clothes," Wilder replied.

"I am sure the High Ruler would prefer..."

"I understand, and mean no disrespect, but I would be much more comfortable in my own things." Wilder had no intention of putting on an ill-fitting façade.

She remembered Solomon standing at the front of the old chapel one Sunday and reading the story of a young David and looming Goliath. He had read how the king offered David his armor to fight in, but David turned it down. Sometimes such offers aren't kindness or diplomacy, but strategy and agenda.

Wilder had no desire to offend anyone, but she wanted to be sure they knew she would not be bent so easily. She would not become something other than who she was and would not succumb so quickly to their power.

"As you like," the servant replied. Her white eyebrows scrunched just a touch, and Wilder knew she was displeased. "Dinner is in one hour. You will not be late."

"Of course not." Wilder dared to offer a smile.

It was not returned.

The servant made her exit and left Wilder standing in the center of her temporary home. Small walls and tall ceilings made her feel more like a damsel locked in a tower than a guest. She was tempted to check the door to see if, in fact, she was incarcerated. It wouldn't matter if she was or wasn't. She was here for a reason and that meant staying...at least for the time being.

CHAPTER 21
WOLSTAN

Wolstan paused outside Casimir's door. It was the second time in less than a moon cycle he was bringing his brother, the High Ruler, foul news. Casimir detested failure. Wolstan spent the entire return trip home plotting his words in hopes he could convince his brother that this was the best way to proceed. The better trick would be making Casimir think it was all his idea to begin with.

Wolstan straightened his shoulders and opened the door. "Brother," he said as he brought his fist to his chest and dipped his head in a humble bow.

"I have been told your men returned with no humans for our collection." Casimir was seething already. Red flooded his eyes.

"I have returned with something better," Wolstan replied, making a mental note to find out who gave the High Ruler a report without his approval and to punish them for their insubordination and treachery. "I have brought you a gift."

Casimir sneered. "You have brought failure and weakness and that is no gift to me nor to you, brother."

"I think you will see that this change of events will serve your plans fruitfully." Wolstan needed to gain control of this exchange. He needed to steer his brother's anger elsewhere. "I was able to discover a weakness in our ranks that can be severely dealt with so that our future might be secure."

"A weakness?"

"Yes." Wolstan was about to lie to his brother but had no qualms in saving his own skin at the cost of a couple of scouts. "When the Lakota incursion did not go completely as planned, I knew there must be a crack in our armor. The scouts have been lazy with the Wayward ones. But we could use their laziness to our advantage."

Casimir didn't reply. His expression shifted ever so subtly toward intrigue, but Wolstan knew his wrath remained a breath away.

Wolstan took a slow step toward his brother, then another. "Our suspicions were proven true at Beartooth. There are dangerous details about the people in the mountains which were neglected."

"Dangerous? You can't mean these people are a threat to us?"

"Of course not," Wolstan said. "These people are no match for us. If we sought merely to end their existence, it could be done without much effort at all. But we require a little more delicacy if we want to use them in your grand plan for our future."

Casimir turned away.

"These tribes and communities in the northern regions are not as autonomous as we thought," Wolstan began, edging a bit closer to his brother.

Casimir turned back around. "Beartooth had been warned?"

"Yes," Wolstan answered, "and it gave them time to prepare and to hide." Wolstan paused. This next part would make the difference in whether or not he would leave this room in one piece. "We could have fought off their defenses and hunted down the runners, but it would have taken valuable time and cost precious cargo—perhaps at *every* settlement in the North. The High Council would have been displeased knowing we are limited in supply for the Sacrament. I would not seek to put you in a position of failure, so I did what my cunning brother would have done in the circumstance."

"And what is that?" Casimir's eyes grew darker.

Wolstan couldn't show fear. He hoped his brother couldn't smell it. He guarded his face with a grin. "I offered them a falsehood to gain their trust so we could use them to our advantage. They will become our ally against themselves and not even realize it."

The red began to retreat leaving only crystal irises as Casimir calmed.

"And it will allow us to complete a purging of the Wayward in less time than estimated."

Casimir raised an eyebrow. "You have accomplished all of this?"

"No, brother," Wolstan responded, putting his hand to the High Ruler's shoulder. "You will accomplish it. It will be your victory." Wolstan sealed his favor. "That is why I brought you a gift in the form of one of their leaders."

Casimir stiffened under Wolstan's hand. "You brought one of those vile creatures here, to our Citadel?"

"Yes, one who can give you information on every settlement in the North. Unlike the beast you've kept in the dungeons, this one will hand them all to you because she thinks she is protecting them, bartering for their peace." Wolstan kept his concerns about the girl's intentions to himself. He was putting Wilder in his brother's hands, and if she was at all treacherous, it would be at Casimir's expense and not his own.

"She will exchange information for a treaty of peace," Casimir said. "And she has no concerns that we will not keep our word?"

"If she does, I am certain you can convince her otherwise," Wolstan replied with a last squeeze of his brother's shoulder before removing his hand and adjusting his own coat. "She is just a naive young woman who thinks we want to protect her people from the intolerance that killed one of their own in the spring."

"Good," Casimir said and smirked. "Then you have done well, brother."

CHAPTER 22
WILDER

The same servant from earlier returned exactly one hour later. Walking behind her down the halls, Wilder wiped sweaty palms on her skirt and hoped her apprehension would wipe away too. The servant offered no comfort, giving Wilder a wide berth, her nose turned up with prim distaste.

The heels of Wilder's boots clicked along the marble floors and echoed their rhythm off the hard walls invading the peace. It was alarming, the way this place was so quiet. Even in the serenity of the night in Beartooth, owls and crickets sang. Here there was nothing.

Wilder wouldn't have thought it so disturbing had someone merely described it to her—the cold silence—but in reality, it was beyond chilling. No wonder Declan fell so madly in love with their music and reverie.

Declan. He should be the one here. He should be the one leading their people and negotiating with the Necanians. Negotiating probably wouldn't be his preferred approach though. Wilder hoped she was making the right decision.

"You will sit at the end opposite our High Ruler," the servant told her as she turned the handle and pushed the tall doors open. Wilder's mouth was cotton. She licked her cracked lips and pasted on a soft smile as she was ushered into the dining room.

Surrounding a long black table were several Necanians. Wolstan stood, staring at her as she approached. He smiled, but it was a shallow courtesy that didn't reach his luminous eyes. Beside him sat a female Necanian. She offered only a crisp glance in Wilder's direction, then turned up her nose and picked up her wine glass. Across the table sat another female. She smiled like the general, but there was a hint of warmth to it that Wilder might only be imagining. At the far end of the table stood another male, tall, with a stern countenance. *He must be the High Ruler.* His gaze was intimidating in its intensity. He was sizing Wilder up.

Wilder tucked a strand of her auburn hair behind her ear and fidgeted with the buttons of her denim shirt as another servant pulled out the only empty seat for her.

"Welcome," the High Ruler said and held out his hand. "Please, sit."

"Thank you." Wilder hated that she stuttered the words. She sat down, and the two males followed suit. Their polite civility unnerved her. Their etiquette was so formal, like in a Jane Austen novel. *Is this how the Necanians always behave, or have they learned these rituals and rules to better serve them here?* Wilder internally chuckled at the thought of the High Ruler reading *Pride and Prejudice* like some sort of textbook on human society. If he had, she thought he must have missed the point.

A servant placed a plate of food in front of her. It was decadent and rich. The smell of it elicited a rumble from her stomach, reminding her she hadn't eaten anything all day. While it looked delicious, she poked the suspicious contents with her fork. Would they really bring her all this way to poison her at dinner?

"Is this food not to your liking?" Casimir asked, his own fork paused in midair above his plate.

Wilder needed to pull herself together and stop acting like a skittish rabbit.

"No." She picked up her knife and began to slice into a piece of poultry. "It all looks so wonderful that I simply couldn't decide where to begin." She smiled and took a bite.

It tasted as good as it looked, but sat heavy in Wilder's gut, her stomach squeezing anxiously around each forkful.

"Good." Casimir took his own bite. With his mouth still a bit full he added, "My apologies, we neglected to introduce you to everyone. Of course, you know my brother, Wolstan."

Wilder nodded.

"His wife, Wilhelmine."

The woman beside Wolstan pursed her lips as she glared at Wilder. "Pleasure to meet you."

"And this"—Casimir gestured to the other woman who was seated across the table—"is our younger sister, Hesperia."

The younger Necanian's face lit with a bigger smile than Wilder had seen since arriving in Hope City. It looked like her eyes brightened too. Her mouth opened a bit like she was about to say something, then her expression dampened a touch with a sort of restraint, and she only nodded and muttered a sheepish, "Hello."

"Hello." Wilder caught her gaze for a brief moment, and it was not void of connection as she expected from the aliens.

Curious, Wilder thought. Hesperia bore the same pristine exterior, clean and rigid, but a softness swam under the surface.

"What do you think of the city?" Casimir asked Wilder.

Wilder thought carefully. "It seems quite...uh...majestic."

It wasn't a lie, but while the smile on the High Ruler's face seemed content with the answer, she hadn't meant it as a compliment. The city was large and gleaming, but it was not beautiful and inviting. It was no place Wilder would ever want to live. "I would love to see more of it."

The High Ruler looked over his nose at Wilder. He set his utensils down with a clank against his near empty plate. "It would not be safe for you to wander the city alone."

"No," Wolstan agreed with his brother. "Many do not look kindly upon the Wayward who retreated to the mountains. They think you are dangerous, a threat to their way of life."

"A threat? Us?" Wilder remembered Wolstan's similar insinuation back in Beartooth. How would the people in the sanctuary cities get such a view of those in the northern settlements? They had done nothing to cause such animosity.

"People fear what they do not know or understand," Casimir said, but it felt like a cheap line.

"We don't fully understand you, or those living here, but we don't fear either," Wilder responded. Casimir's jaw twitched and tightened, exposing a vein in his neck.

The High Ruler inhaled and exhaled slowly before looking back to Wilder. "That is good, quite enlightened of you, and it will serve you well in our negotiations for peace." He smiled and Wilder shivered.

"I hope so." Wilder sipped her glass of water, relishing the cool liquid against her dry throat.

"But let's not talk of business this evening. That can be saved for tomorrow." Casimir finished his last bite of food.

"Perhaps tomorrow Hesperia and Wilhelmine can take our guest on a tour of the city," Wolstan suggested. "After beginning arbitrations and talk of treaties."

Wilhelmine glared at him, and Wilder thought she heard her growl under her breath. She gritted her teeth. "Of course."

Casimir nodded. "You'll see, Wilder. We have much to offer your people."

"Yes, that sounds lovely," Wilder conceded.

*　*　*

Wilder collapsed onto the bed after supper, exhausted. Uncertain.

She tucked her knees against her chest. Tears dripped off her lashes and made the silky pillowcase damp beneath her cheek. She remembered nights in bed with Declan when he'd groan and toss and turn and twitch in his uneasy sleep. His moans and mutterings gave clues to unhappy memories playing in his mind and making him wince. Wilder would gently stroke his hair and trace his stubbly jawline. Then she'd place her hand on his chest, resting it near his heart to feel it thumping, fast and hard.

I'm here, she'd whisper so softly the words were barely audible. *You aren't alone.*

In seconds, the frantic rhythm would change, calming to a more normal pace, and his face would melt back into peace.

Every bit of safety and security in her life felt like it had abandoned her in the dark of this Citadel room. If she ever needed Declan to wrap his arms around her and whisper sweet words to her, it was now. She would give anything to feel his breath against her skin, to hear his scratchy voice in her ear.

A garbled cry echoed off the tile walls.

Wilder sat up. Was it human? She held her breath, waiting for another sound. Just when she thought it was her imagination, there came a second pained moan.

She got up and tiptoed around the room, trying to determine the origin of the noise. A vent near the far corner acted as a megaphone for the disembodied howl. On her hands and knees, Wilder inclined her ear closer. Another groan. She popped up and away, her body trembling as she stood, retreating back to the bed.

The voice bounced around her again and again. It was probably no more than a few minutes, but it felt like hours as Wilder covered her ears.

Declan?

It had to be her grief and her fear and this place playing dirty tricks on her. She needed to ignore it. Needed to push it away and not give it life or it would kill her. She needed to sleep. She knew it couldn't be him. Declan was dead.

CHAPTER 23

HESPERIA

Hesperia rose before the sun after a night of little sleep.

Wilder was a curiosity to her. She reminded Hesperia of the young servant who'd told her stories and sang her songs. Most humans in the city were too much like the Necanians now, devoid of any sort of creativity and imagination. Wilder felt warm in comparison. Hesperia wanted to know her. Her brothers would disapprove.

But her brothers need not know.

Hesperia crept into the corridor, still early enough that only the servants were scurrying about. She avoided most of them, knowing which ones were Casimir's spies. There was one, a young female, who could be trusted to be discreet. Hesperia asked her to offer to bring breakfast to the Wayward woman. Wilder's servant disliked humans and would be happy to concede the task to another.

Hesperia joined her. "I will take the food in to our guest." Hesperia took the tray from the servant girl. "You may return in an hour to retrieve it."

The servant bowed and obeyed.

Hesperia balanced the tray in one hand while knocking lightly on the door with her other.

"Come in," a voice replied from within.

Hesperia opened the door slowly. The Wayward woman stood in front of the window. The bright sun made her silhouette look like nothing more than a shadow that had lost its possessor. Her shoulders were slumped, and her head tilted just enough to give the sense that she had experienced a loss.

"I brought you breakfast." Hesperia closed the door with a gentle click.

"Thank you. Oh...I didn't expect you." Wilder shook her head and drew her mouth into a smile. "I'm sorry, I didn't mean to be rude."

"No need for apologies." Hesperia set the tray down on the table. "I'm sure my presence is a surprise. I thought we could get to know each other better."

"Of course." Wilder sat down. Hesperia heard the slight squeak in her voice and saw the tremble in her hands as she reached for the kettle of tea.

"I am not like my brothers." Hesperia reached out and touched Wilder's hand. She took the pot and poured the tea for her.

"I suppose you aren't." Wilder paused, her brow furrowing. "Why is that?"

The question caught Hesperia off guard. It tampered with something she'd tried to leave untouched. She'd thought about it many times before but could never put her finger on it. "I wish I understood it myself," she said, handing Wilder her cup of tea.

"I know what it's like, the not knowing yourself anymore, or how exactly you came to be who you are now," Wilder said as she sipped from the porcelain cup. Her eyes drifted off for a moment, like they were looking at some place, or at some time, far off.

Hesperia recognized something in her gaze...a sadness or loss. It was the same expression she saw when she looked at her own reflection in the days after Casimir's punishment. She didn't like going back to that place, but for the first time since then, she didn't feel alone in it. "I lost someone...a human servant...his name was Theo. I think it changed me."

Wilder's head jerked back toward Hesperia. Her admission had startled the human as much as it startled her.

Wilder set her cup back down on the table and folded her hands in her lap. "I could say the same." Her reply sounded rough and controlled, like it was a wave of sadness breaking on the rocks of restraint. "I lost someone very dear to me. Life hasn't been the same since."

Hesperia nodded silently. She supposed that was how loss worked but hearing the sentiment from someone else brought a confirmation she didn't know she'd needed. She was strange for a Necanian, but she wasn't alone in her peculiarity. She poured her own cup of tea. "What is your life like, in the North?" she asked, changing the subject away from painful places.

Wilder's lips curled upward the smallest degree. "It is very different from here, I presume."

"Tell me about it, please." Hesperia's curiosity pushed her onward.

The request was more dangerous than this Wayward woman could know. Hesperia shouldn't care. She shouldn't wonder about anything that didn't have to do with being Necanian. She did, though... and something inside kept nudging her to find out more.

She had become aware of a void inside her and couldn't

shake the suspicion that this Wilder, or someone like her, might be the key to filling it.

"Alright," Wilder said, then told Hesperia stories and memories of people. Light and life danced in the woman's expression as she spoke fondly of her home and her people.

Hesperia leaned in, captivated by every word. She couldn't even imagine such a place, full of color and music and laughter. Had she ever even heard laughter?

Yes...once...from Theo.

She wanted to go to Beartooth. She wanted to immerse herself in the warmth. Hope City offered nothing in comparison. Just as Hesperia felt like she would burst from Wilder's joyous recollections, the woman's tone changed. Sorrow reentered. She could see it in the drop of her head and the quiver of her lip. Hesperia heard it in the rhythm change of her heartbeat.

"There is sadness, even in Beartooth," Wilder said, seeming to feel the need to explain herself.

Had Hesperia somehow looked disappointed when the woman's mood changed?

"No place is without sadness," Hesperia said.

"No, I guess that's true," Wilder said. "Perhaps the sadness helps us remain grateful for the joy."

"Perhaps." Joy was not something she knew personally. There wasn't a Necanian word for things like joy...or love. "Is it worth it?"

"Is what worth it?"

"Love." There was no retreat now. Hesperia had already crossed a line and gotten too close. "Is love worth the sadness?"

Wilder set her teacup down. She bit her bottom lip and closed her eyes. A tear slid down her cheek, catching in the upward curve of a half smile. "Yes, it is worth it."

"You love someone?"

"Yes, I did—I do. He died a few months ago. He is the one I lost, the one I meant before."

Hesperia wasn't sure what to say. "That is unfortunate," she replied. She didn't know how humans handled such things as death. Necanians did not grieve. Not with tears and sadness. Only with silence. But silence didn't seem like the correct response. It had never felt right after her own loss, which was likely small in comparison to this human's.

"It is unfortunate," the Wayward woman said. "Declan was a good man, and he didn't deserve what happened to him."

"Can I ask what did happen to him?"

Wilder cleared her throat. "He was killed at a trading post at the edge of the city, supposedly by those who feel my people are a threat."

"I see." Hesperia took a sip of her now cold tea. A thought, an inkling, buzzed in her mind.

A knock rapped against the door.

"That will be the servant here to retrieve the tray." Hesperia pushed the buzzing thoughts away for the moment and stood up, pressing her long gray dress straight with the palms of her hands. She collected the cups and picked up the tray. "I will take care of this. It is nearly time for you to meet with the High Ruler." Hesperia turned to leave but stopped and looked back at Wilder. "It would be best not to mention to my brothers—or anyone—that we had tea together this morning."

Wilder nodded.

"And be wary of my brothers."

"Why?" Wilder tilted her head.

"I am not like them, remember?" Hesperia smiled and left.

She quickly returned the tray to the servant and made way for the dungeon. Descending the dark stairwell at a quickening pace, Hesperia let the buzzing thought take full form in her mind. What little light there was in the corridor flickered. Hesperia's eyes adjusted, and she marched directly to the last cell. The damp odor of mildew was covered by the stronger scent of despair. It was sweat and the stench of human waste mingled with vomit. Whoever this man was, he was even closer to death, or worse, than he was the last time she had seen him.

Peering through the bars of his cell, Hesperia saw the same frail body, the same stains of blood and tears. This time he made no effort to appear stronger at her presence. If it weren't for the faint sound of his breathing and the weak beat of his heart, she would have thought it too late, and that he was already lost. She needed to get his attention.

She whispered the name Wilder had said. "Declan."

Nothing happened. Maybe it was just a ridiculous notion.

"Declan."

The man stirred.

"Is that your name? Declan?"

He lifted his head and opened his eyes. They were so empty. He squinted and grunted, which she guessed was the best he could give in response.

Hesperia hesitated. If she was right, there would be no going back. Telling Wilder would mean betraying Casimir. But keeping this secret would be a betrayal to who she was becoming. The former would most certainly mean her death, but the latter would mean dying in a completely different way.

Hesperia breathed in deep. "If you *are* Declan, then you need to know she is here...Wilder is here."

The prisoner startled. His head jerked upward at the expense of every muscle in his body. Hesperia heard his heart race faster. His flesh tightened and twitched with all the effort he could muster. He growled and grunted again. His eyes filled back up with tears that mingled with fear and hope and desperation.

"Shhh," Hesperia cooed, "save your strength. Wilder is here, and for now she is safe. I will do my best to keep her that way."

CHAPTER 24

CASIMIR

C asimir studied the architectural drawings laid across the conference table. His new Insemination and Harvesting Complex was now only inked lines on gray paper, but it would soon be his magnum opus. He was finalizing the last details of the project—the renovation of a dormant hospital just outside the city's dome—before meeting with their head engineer later in the afternoon.

"Brother," Wolstan said, entering with a curt bow. "The woman, Wilder James, will be here shortly." He sat down next to Casimir.

"Good. I will be glad to get this charade over with." The High Ruler rolled the documents and placed them in a leather tube, out of sight of their guest. He didn't like having a human, much less one of the filthy mountain dwellers, in his home.

There were other ways to get the information they desired, but false diplomacy and manipulation would be easier by far. Casimir had sat across from this woman at dinner, this human, with her freckled skin and ignorance. She was small and weak and completely out of her element. Bending her to their will would not be a challenge.

"High Ruler," Felix said, opening the door. "The woman, Ms. James, is here."

"She may enter." Casimir rose to his feet, as did his brother. "Good morning, Ms. James." His polite etiquette came with a fake smile and squared shoulders. "Please, sit with us."

"Good morning," she said. "You may call me Wilder."

"As you wish." Casimir gestured for her to take the seat across from him. "Would you like some tea?"

"That would be lovely." Wilder smiled, but her fear tickled the High Ruler's senses. It was faint, just a whiff, but it was there, no matter how much she tried to hide it.

Casimir nodded to his brother who poured the woman a cup of tea and set it down in front of her before they all took a seat. "I suppose we should begin our negotiations."

"Yes." Wilder took a sip of the tea. The cup clanked against the plate when she set it back down. "I don't believe in wasting time."

"Neither do I. Tensions toward your people have gotten out of hand, and we must ensure your safety."

Wilder tilted her head. "It strikes me as odd that the people in your cities would feel threatened by those of us in the mountains. We do no harm." She reached for her cup and took another sip.

"People fear what they do not know," Wolstan responded. "Fear drives men to do atrocious things."

"Yes," Casimir said pressing his back against his chair and straightening his posture. "It only takes one incident, one mal-intended soul to disturb the peace in people's minds. When that happens, they will do anything to regain it."

That was not a lie. Casimir spent six decades watching humans writhe and squirm to keep comfortable. They equated comfort with peace. If their bodies and minds weren't comfortable, they would do anything they could to fill their emptiness, even if that meant their lives were shallow and short-lived. Casimir loathed them for it but was also grateful. Their incessant need for comfort was what made them so malleable.

Wilder returned her cup to its saucer and leaned forward, resting her clasped hands on the table. "But it's not the humans in the cities who assail us. The Lakota Camp was attacked by a group of *your* people. What fear would they have of us?"

This girl was like a twitch behind Casimir's eye. He clenched his fists, imagining his grip around her neck.

"No species is without dissidents, those who give into more carnal desires," Wolstan intervened. "There are those in our own ranks, though I assure you they are quite few, who play to the humans' fears with an aggressive hand."

"And you are willing to do something about them?" Wilder asked, barely glancing upward from her own hands.

"Of course," Casimir lied. "We want what you want —*peace*. For everyone."

"Yes," the woman whispered. Then she looked up, directly into Casimir's eyes. "And what about those who were taken by your—what did you call them...dissidents?"

Wolstan flinched. It was the slightest twitch of his jaw, but Casimir saw it.

"Are you sure prisoners were taken?" he asked.

"The Lakota camp was attacked by a group of Necanian... dissidents. When survivors reached our settlement for help and safety, they said they saw several chained and taken away."

"Wolstan, brother." Casimir laced his fingers together on the table, looking to his general. "We should have someone look into this."

"I'll do it immediately."

"Thank you," Wilder responded. "I would like to know what happened to them before we continue."

"Is that necessary?" Wolstan asked. He looked to the High Ruler.

Dark thoughts crept under Casimir's skin, and he took a deep breath to keep them from showing on the surface and in his eyes. "It's a test of faith, Wolstan." A smirk pulled at the corner of the High Ruler's mouth. "How can she trust us to keep her people safe from those on the fringes if we can't even help with this simple matter of a few captives?"

"I do not mean to appear untrusting," Wilder began.

Casimir waved off her explanation with the flit of his fingers. "My brother will get the answers you seek, and we can return to further negotiations in the morning." Casimir stood and Wolstan followed suit. "Perhaps Hesperia and Wilhelmine can escort you on that tour of the city we mentioned?"

"I would like that," Wilder said, standing.

"Felix," Wolstan called to the servant. "Please see Ms. James out and take care of a vehicle for their afternoon excursion."

Felix bowed and gestured for the woman to follow him.

The door barely clicked shut before Casimir pounded his fist against the table. The sound rattled off the glass windows.

"Brother, I know the woman is more trying than—"

"Do not patronize me, Wolstan." Casimir's eyes flooded crimson with the release of pent-up malice. "If by morning she doesn't bring the information we need, I will kill her myself, and we will take what we can from the people in the mountains. Losses be damned."

"This morning was more of a success than you give it credit for, brother." Wolstan straightened his shoulders and smiled. "You showed patience. What do the humans say? It's a virtue?

This woman feels heard; she feels as though you truly care for her. You have coiled around her, ready to constrict the very breath and life from her and her people, and she is blissfully unaware."

Casimir smoothed his coat and considered Wolstan's words. They would let her think she was in control of things, that she had the upper hand. It would only make their ultimate victory sweeter. "Yes, I was wrong to think we could bend her. We will break her instead."

"Yes," Wolstan said. "And after you break her, you will break them all."

CHAPTER 25
WILDER

Wilder fidgeted with the tattered hem of her cardigan while she waited just outside the Citadel doors for her tour guides. When she realized what she was doing, she pulled her hands to her sides, curling them into small fists. She fussed with her clothes when she was nervous, something she'd always hated. It was hard not to be nervous—hard to remind herself of her own strength and hope here among the Necanians.

"Wilder." Hesperia walked up behind her. The Necanian, with her translucent skin and gleaming white hair, shined in the sunlight.

"Hesperia, I—"

Hesperia leaned close, touching Wilder's arm. "I need to tell you something important." Her eyes flicked to Wilhelmine coming toward them. "We must speak later, in private."

Wilder nodded.

"Ladies," Wilhelmine said, walking past them.

She stood tall and regal with a long neck and a slender

form, like the other Necanians. Unlike Hesperia, Wilhelmine only had two silver circles etched on her temples.

A vehicle pulled to a stop in front of them. It was like the vessel that transported Wilder into the city, but smaller—similar to a car but with sleeker lines and hovering two feet off the ground. It was curious, that only a few pieces of Necanian technology were advanced—inventiveness seemingly reserved for transportation and weapons.

"Shall we get this over with?" Wilhelmine took the hand of a servant who helped her into the vehicle.

Wilder and Hesperia followed suit. They flew away from the Citadel, through steel gates and onto the streets of Hope City. There wasn't much by way of information given. Occasionally, Wilhelmine would point to a building and tell her what it was. Mostly they were temples used to honor the Necanians.

Amid all the sights and sounds, Wilder sensed a void. The buildings were shining and tall. The streets were clean. The people were all dressed in the same crisp clothes. Everything was black and white and gray. Bright and clean and devoid of color. Faces were devoid of emotion. It was all so very formal and detached from any real semblance of life, at least the way Wilder knew life. There were no smiles, no laughter, no connection. She wondered if they were happy like this... if they were like Declan used to be, hidden in this monochromatic world. Dormant. Waiting to be reborn through fire.

"Are you alright?" Hesperia asked.

Wilder kept to the window. "I'm fine."

Wilder could understand why the Necanians feared the Wayward. They must look like savages to them—primal and unpredictable.

Wilder grinned suddenly. Oh yes. Barbarians with fresh

baked pie and herbal tea, Monday morning reading lessons, and Sunday morning devotions.

Perception is a funny thing. The lens through which one sees the world can distort truth.

Something dark caught Wilder's eye. It was a shadow at the end of a street. Wilder sat up straighter, straining to see. Their vehicle was moving closer to the edge of the city where the dome met earth. As they got closer, Wilder spied makeshift buildings outside the clear barrier. They were short and shabby, not like the pristine structures everywhere else.

"What is that?" Wilder pointed toward the object of her inquiry.

"Nothing," Wilhelmine said. "Driver, take us home."

Hesperia barely shook her head, a signal this couldn't be discussed here. Wilder would ask her later.

Within moments, they returned to their point of origin. The vehicle halted. A servant opened the door. Wilhelmine exited as though she couldn't stand another minute in the thing with Wilder. She didn't say a word as she walked inside.

"Dinner will be served in an hour," a servant told Wilder.

Wilder wasn't looking forward to more polite pretense. "I'm not feeling well, maybe it's a bit of motion sickness from the tour," she lied.

She didn't like lying and felt guilty even for this white lie. But she was desperate for a break and didn't think she could just ask for time alone without a reason. "Would it be possible to have dinner in my room this evening? I don't wish to be rude, but..."

"It is completely acceptable," Hesperia said. "The servants will see to it, and I will let my brothers know you are resting so you'll be fit for tomorrow."

* * *

The sun set in a burst of glorious color from the window of Wilder's stark room. The Necanians controlled so much but, like the blue of a clear sky, they couldn't decide the hues the sun used as it said goodnight. Was the sunset in Beartooth as beautiful this evening? The question intensified her homesickness, but there would be no clicking her heels. She needed to make a treaty, even a precarious one, if she hoped to have a chance at seeing her home again.

A knock echoed through the door.

"Come in," Wilder called over her shoulder. She expected it to be the servant to remove her dinner tray.

"I hope you are feeling better."

"I am." Wilder recognized Hesperia's voice. "Come watch the sunset with me."

There was a moment of silence before the Necanian came to stand beside her. She angled her head, her clear eyes tracing the patterns of light.

Wilder watched her and wondered if it was the first time that she'd ever watched a sunset. "You wanted to tell me something earlier?"

Hesperia ran a finger along the windowpane. "There are things you should know. But first, you saw something at the edges of the dome, just outside the wall. You asked what it was." Hesperia paused and looked back toward the door like she was checking to see if she had closed it completely after entering, as if checking to see if someone was listening.

Wilder held her breath. *Let Hesperia talk*, she reminded herself, holding herself back from asking for more.

"We all know what it is. It's the Colony, what we have named the gathering of the outcasts."

"Like those of us in the mountains?"

"No, not like you." Hesperia's face turned grim. "My

brother—He has a talent for taking his ruin and turning it into an instrument of power. Control."

"I don't understand," Wilder said.

"You wouldn't because you don't know what we truly are, what we do. What we have done to those people."

Wilder's body hummed. "Tell me."

"Beyond the wall are those who survived the Sacrament. They are not dead but have lost themselves, and now they live between worlds. Not in control enough to rejoin society, but not whole enough to seek out the Wayward. They are broken in ways you can't imagine. Casimir does what he does best, twists the truth to suit his needs. He could just kill them, but instead he uses them to his advantage even further. He lies, says those outside the dome are lawbreakers who were driven mad by their own guilt and shame. People don't ask questions, and they stay in line so that they aren't undone in the same way. They stay away from the Colony so that they don't fall victim to those *heathens*, which is who they believe them to be, what they believe will happen, what they've been told."

"They just believe him?"

"They have no reason not to. Their lives are in his hands." Hesperia looked at Wilder finally. Her eyes were glassy but there were no tears. "He did the same with your people."

"What do you mean?"

"Several months ago, some of the Wayward were at the outskirts. There was a skirmish. Casimir told the city that yours are a ruthless people who had tried to harm an innocent man. He twisted the truth so he could proceed with his plans and the people would think him their great defender."

Wilder's head was spinning. "What are his plans?"

"There is so much to it, so much to explain. He wants to use the Wayward to fuel the Sacrament." Hesperia looked away again.

"What is the Sacrament?" Wilder stepped closer to the Necanian. She hesitated, her hand shaking as she reached out to touch Hesperia's arm. "Please tell me."

"I told you there are things about us you do not know." Hesperia removed Wilder's hand gently. "We are not what we seem, and to explain it would not be enough. But I can show you."

Wilder nodded and stepped back.

"Please don't be afraid of me," Hesperia said. Her eyes pleaded with Wilder's for a moment before they closed.

The Necanian inhaled deeply. Wilder stared, waiting for something to happen. She wasn't sure what she was looking for, what she should expect. She thought this was some odd prank until a shadow passed over Hesperia. The translucent scales covering her skin dimmed to a sickening gray that spread up her neck and over her face. Then she opened her eyes and the crystal blue faded to a deep red, like blood pooling, and her pupils lengthened and stretched into something feline. She parted her lips and perfect teeth became sharp fangs. Hesperia lifted her hands, and manicured nails grew into long, dark, claws. The beautiful, ethereal creature disappeared, leaving a monster.

Wilder gasped. She thought of Wolstan's eyes shifting in front of her and how she had dismissed it as a trick of the light. This couldn't be dismissed.

As quickly as Hesperia changed, she returned back to her brighter form. "We are not beings of light so much as darkness. We didn't come to bring peace to humanity."

"Then why did you come?"

"To sustain our own people," Hesperia said. "We're soul eaters, and the people outside the wall are those who survived the Sacrament."

"Sacrament? That's what you call it?" Wilder's stomach

turned. She tasted the bile rising in the back of her throat. "Eating the souls."

"Yes," Hesperia answered.

"The High Ruler wants to use my people for food, why? Why not the people here?" Wilder asked the question, immediately regretting the way it sounded to her own ears. What difference did it make? No one deserved this.

"There are more of us," Hesperia answered. "Many more, and this world must be made ready before they arrive. Casimir does not wish to make the mistake of our forefathers and use up a world only to require another and another. He has a plan to sustain this world's resources..."

"By resources you mean people?"

Hesperia nodded. "While those in the cities work to ready this world for more of our kind, your people...those in the mountains...those that no one will miss... they will begin the cultivation of a greater supply. When the people here are no longer useful, he will do the same to them."

Wilder swallowed down her nausea. Her people didn't trust the Necanians, didn't want their way of life. That's why they'd fled north. But they'd never imagined them to be this vile, this evil.

Wilder straightened her back and clenched her jaw. "You take part in this, this Sacrament?"

Hesperia's lip trembled as she answered, "Yes, I did before, but I haven't in quite some time, not since..."

Wilder knew what she was speaking of—the loss of the human servant—Theo. "So, you do not need this Sacrament to live?"

"We do," Hesperia corrected. "We can go a while, but without the Sacrament, we will grow weak, tired, and finally we will die."

"You'll die?"

"Yes. I will. I would rather die than be part of my brother's plan though. I was ignorant before. I thought humans were worthless, but I have seen different. It's why I'm telling you all this. To help you."

"To help me?" Wilder asked. "Why didn't you help the others? Why didn't you do something to stop this?"

"I didn't...I don't have the power to stop my brother, to stop this."

"You had the power to try."

"I'm so sorry," Hesperia said, her voice wavering. "I want to try now. I want to help you stop this."

"You think I can? Will I even get out of here alive?"

"Yes, I can get you out, and you can gather your people."

"I'm not a warrior." Wilder collapsed into a nearby chair and rested her head in her hands. "Declan was the warrior," she muttered to herself. *He should be here.*

"I need to show you something," Hesperia whispered.

CHAPTER 26
WILDER

Wilder tiptoed behind Hesperia down the Citadel corridors, battling to regain control of herself, of her fear. Trust was necessary.

"Wait here." Hesperia stopped at the end of a long hallway and peeked around the corner of the wall. "There is a guard at the door to the dungeons. I will need to distract him in order to sneak you by."

"Dungeons?" Wilder whispered. Was this the moment that it all came to an end for her? Would she follow this alien into the dark abyss, never to be seen or heard from again?

"It's okay," Hesperia said. "I promise you will be safe."

How did she...? Had she read her thoughts?

"Our senses are not like yours. I can smell your apprehension and hear your heart racing. But you needn't worry, you can trust me." She took Wilder's hand into her cold palm. "I swear it."

Wilder nodded. She pressed back against the wall while Hesperia stepped around the corner.

Hesperia muttered something to the guard there, then

footsteps marched away. She returned and beckoned Wilder to follow again. Around the corner was a large black door. Hesperia placed her hand on a sensor. *Click.* She opened the door, and they stepped inside.

A seemingly other world lay behind. All the brightness, clean lines, and smooth surfaces were replaced by darkness and old concrete. Dirt coated the steps, and crumbling cracks covered the walls. Wilder's nose wrinkled at the pungent smell of something rotting. The mold and mildew in the air made her eyes water.

"This way." Hesperia turned to the right, down a long hallway.

Chipped and faded graffiti emerged through the dust, offering some comfort, like a tinge of hope that not all had been lost inside the city's dome.

"What is this place?" Wilder asked as they walked past empty cages with rusty bars. Water dripped somewhere, and the dim lights overhead buzzed and flickered.

"I believe it used to be a metro station, but now it is where Casimir tortures his enemies."

"Why are we down here?"

"I told you. I need to show you something."

From up ahead, there came a sound—a moan like an animal in pain. Wilder tensed. Goosebumps rose on her arms, and the back of her neck tingled. Another groan. She stopped. Wilder had heard that sound before. Last night, through the vent in her room. It wasn't a hallucination. Another groan.

Hesperia kept walking until she reached the last cage in the line. She turned back to Wilder, who had stayed about twenty feet behind her, too afraid to move. "Here. You need to see."

Each step closer to that cage was a battle of Wilder's will. Hearing the truth was one thing, but seeing it with her own eyes might be more than she could take. She wouldn't be able to go back, to unknow, to unsee. But she kept stepping forward, her eyes focused on Hesperia's face. The closer she got, the more the Necanian's expression softened, the more her brow crinkled. When Wilder was just inches away, Hesperia looked into the cage and then down at the ground.

Wilder took a deep breath, regretting it when the stench hit her nostrils. She slowly turned her eyes toward the space behind the metal bars.

It was dark. The shadows so dense they swallowed the light. She could make out the line of a human body. She heard the rattle of chains when it moved. She squinted, trying to get a clear picture. The figure moaned again. It was rough and deep—a man's voice.

She gripped her hands around the bars and pressed her face as close as she could get it, straining to see. "Light, I need more light," she whispered to Hesperia, her voice a bit frantic.

"There is no more light, but you can get closer," Hesperia said. "This prison door has not needed to be locked in quite some time." She pulled and the door opened.

Wilder let go of the cage and stepped inside, inching toward the man with careful steps. Her eyes slowly adjusted. The edges of his frame came into view—the frazzled lines of his hair, his strong jaw. "Declan?" His name was a sigh, a breath escaping from a hidden place. "Declan?"

The man jerked his head up and growled.

Wilder jumped. "Declan."

He growled again, and it turned into a roar as he pulled against his chains like a beast clamoring to attack.

"Declan," she repeated his name like a mantra, stepping closer until his body was just inches from hers.

In the closeness she saw him more clearly. His eyes grew wide with fear and rage. His nostrils flared and spit dribbled from his bottom lip. Dirt plastered his face. Lines of blood stained either side of his head where it had streaked down his cheeks with tears and sweat, washing away a bit of the grime. He looked thinner. He seemed paler, but that was hard to tell in the dark. She lifted her hand to touch his face and he jolted toward her again. She jumped. Had all the softness she appreciated in him faded, leaving something primal?

Wilder's chest rose and fell with heavy breaths. Each one ached. Her heart ached. Just inches in front of her, so close she could touch her flesh to his, was the man she loved and thought she'd lost. Was he still lost? This was Declan, but it wasn't *her* Declan.

"Be careful," Hesperia said. "He is not the man you knew."

Wilder shook her head, her chest hurting. "How did you know it was him?" She didn't turn her eyes away from Declan.

"I came down to see him," Hesperia said. "Curious as to why my brother kept him here. He said your name."

Tears wet Wilder's cheeks. She trembled from the inside out—a ripple from the chambers of her heart. If he knew her name, then he remembered her. If he remembered her, then he was not lost. "Declan."

He jerked and gnashed his teeth.

Wilder reached up, this time without stopping, without pulling back, without hesitation. She touched his face, feeling his dry skin and the hair of his shabby beard against her fingertips.

The touch startled him, but he didn't move away from it. Instead, he leaned into it, closing his eyes for a moment.

Wilder pulled herself onto her toes and leaned close. Her lips grazed his, matching the quiver.

"Wild," he said, quiet and husky, like getting his voice back after a bad cold.

Wilder pressed her cheek against his so that her mouth

TABITHA CAPLINGER

was close to his ear and whispered, "I'm here, Declan. I'm here."

He pulled away. "You're...not...real." The words emitting like a cough.

"I am." She pulled his palm to her chest. Let him feel her frantic heart. "I'm real."

He melted into her, fell against her. "Thank God."

"Wilder," Hesperia warned, "we can't stay down here any longer. The guard will return soon, and it won't be safe to exit."

Declan lifted his head. "Stay safe." He said, his words broken by ragged breaths.

"I need to get you out of here," Wilder said.

Hesperia stepped inside the cell. "We will. We will find a way to get you both out of the Citadel, but it will take time. We'll need help."

Declan growled at the Necanian. Pulling at his chains again.

"She can be trusted," Wilder assured him. "She's been my friend here."

Wilder looked over her shoulder, and Hesperia's mouth curved into another small, awkward smile.

"I won't let him stay this way any longer than is necessary," Wilder said.

"I know, but we need to do this the right way. The risks if we fail are too great."

"You're right," Wilder said. "But who in the city will help us?"

"There are some in the Colony who can."

"But you said they were lost?"

"Most are," Hesperia answered, "but there are others who hide among the lost, rebels who will help you...and your cause."

The world was suddenly a much bigger place than Wilder

140

had ever imagined. Was she the right person to hold its fate in her hands? Right now, the only fates she worried about were hers and Declan's. If she could save him—get them both home —then she could figure out their next steps. They could figure them out together. "I don't want to leave you here," Wilder told him.

He kissed the top of her head. "Go. I can ...wait here a while... longer, if it means you're safer."

"Alright." She held Declan's face. "I'll be back for you, and we'll go home." She pulled him closer and kissed him again. "I love you."

"I love you more," Declan said.

Her tremble had disappeared, replaced by fierce resolve. She would not lose him again.

CHAPTER 27

DECLAN

D eclan once heard that when you're dying, your life flashes before your eyes. That cliché being true wasn't as surprising to him as the memories that made the highlight reel.

His mother humming a lullaby into his ears when he was a very little boy. Her song had always been so quiet it could barely be heard. He hadn't thought about his mother in a very long time—hadn't remembered her song—and now he understood why she had been quiet when she hummed it. It was both a secret for him and a secret from the Bringers of Peace.

His father walking him to school. He would hold his hand, but only so long as they were alone on the street. As soon as another person, especially a Necanian, came into view, his father would let go and not reach for him again.

Peeking through the keyhole of their attic door where his parents had met with friends and neighbors. Declan had tried to hear the conversation, but it was too muffled.

The smell of his mother's home-baked bread filling the whole house.

His father laughing when the curtains were drawn and the lights low as his parent's silently danced across the kitchen.

A banging at the door and his parents being taken in a fury, pulled from their home in the middle of the night while a Citadel guard had held Declan down. His father getting free just long enough to charge at the guard so that Declan was released. His father had yelled at him to run, to leave, to never come back.

His mother's tears. Understanding and crying and running. Hiding in an alley a few blocks away. Sneaking out of the city with no idea of where he would go or what he would do.

The first time he'd heard real music.

The first time he'd seen people laugh out in the open. He remembered them dancing and playing and not fearing who was watching.

His first drink, first fight, first snowfall, first kiss. Then... then he remembered her. Declan saw her as clearly as if she stood right there in front of him. Wilder, her tousled auburn hair and freckled nose and crooked coral smile.

Then she was gone again.

She always disappeared, replaced by trauma and tragedy.

Declan pulled against his bindings, testing their strength. Another memory consumed his mind taking him from his chains to a bright, white room with no windows, where he kneeled on the cold, marble floor.

* * *

One Necanian stood directly in front of Declan while two others were on either side as guards. He supposed the one staring at him was some sort of leader. The markings on his face were different, deeper, with more rings than the foot soldiers. He carried himself with confidence while the others would not even move without permission. The leader looked Declan up and down with a smirk, his tongue licking the tips of short fangs.

"I have been looking forward to this." He blinked and his shining, crystal eyes changed to a deep crimson, his pupils transforming to look less like a human's and more like the slit of a cat's. The white of his skin seemed to darken too, like a shadow was cast over his face.

"Can't say that I was, sorry," Declan said. He held his chin up as he swallowed bile that sprouted up from his stomach. It tasted bitter and burned the back of his throat.

The alien sniggered. "Your posturing is almost admirable. I would give you a chance to surrender, but I assume you won't take it, and in all honesty, that is my preference. So shall we just set aside any further banter?"

"I don't know. I like banter," Declan said.

"I do not."

If it were possible, the Necanian's eyes grew a shade darker. He lifted his hands, and the shadow dimmed his skin all the way down to his fingertips, casting him in a corpse-like gray. Then his claws, growing longer, turned the same red as the eyes. The alien placed one hand on either side of Declan's head, nails tearing through the flesh at his temples and in the back of his head, piercing into his skull.

Declan couldn't breathe. Pain seared through his head and burned behind his eyes. His entire chest and lungs squeezed tight, constricted by some force that pulled on his insides like it was drawing something out of him. Every breath took more effort than the last. It was more agony than he had ever felt before, and he was certain he was about to die. Then came a burst of sweetness like adrenaline and endorphins masking the pain with a sensation of floating. His extremities numbed.

* * *

The room around Declan dissolved into a blur returning him to his dark, dank prison.

That one scene had replayed so often that Declan could no longer tell what was really happening and what was just a figment of his imagination. Its clarity turned the rest of his precious memories into little more than singular images of a life he felt detached from. He couldn't feel them anymore.

Declan had tried—desperate to remember how it felt to be alive—how it felt to love Wilder. The Necanians had unleashed some beast that had been locked deep inside him. It was killing him and taking over his body, muddying his mind.

He needed to focus, to find something to grasp. Something to keep the beast at bay. Something to keep him alive and give him at least a chance at control. He owed that to Wilder.

Wilder.

Think of Wilder.

Her eyes.

Her smile.

Her laugh.

Her kiss.

The way she would bite her bottom lip when she was writing.

The way she moved when she walked.

The way she said his name.

Declan searched his mind for every piece of her, locking them together like a puzzle he had no choice but to solve. One by one he fit them into place until a vision of her stood in front of him. It was an illusion, a feverish hallucination, but he didn't care. She was there. Flowers in her hair, dressed in lace like on their wedding day. She smiled at him and reached her hand to his face. He almost felt it, her skin against his.

"I love you," her phantom voice echoed.

"I love you more," he replied, tears wetting his cheeks and dripping off his dry lips.

But *was* she a hallucination? Had it been an illusion? *No.* There had been a burst of light. Wilder had been here. She had just stood in front of him. He had felt her heartbeat and kissed her lips. Hadn't he?

Yes.

Wilder was here. She was close.

He shook his head. His sleeping muscles tingled. He inhaled her lilac scent and exhaled hope.

CHAPTER 28
WILDER

Every step Wilder took away from that cell was heavier than the last. Her heart screamed and begged to remain in those dungeons rather than return to the Citadel halls. The bright lights bouncing off the white walls made her eyes burn even more than the tears not yet shed.

Declan, her Declan, was just below her feet.

He was alive and had been for one hundred and seventy-six days. Had he been in pain? He looked like he was in pain. She had been in pain—so much pain.

Wilder stopped in the middle of the hallway. "Is that what the Sacrament does? Is that what made him that way?"

Shame washed over Hesperia. "Yes."

"Then it can't happen to another human soul."

"We shouldn't talk about this here, out in the open," Hesperia said. "We shouldn't talk about it anymore tonight. Spending so much time with you will be suspicious and, no matter how careful I am, there are always eyes watching."

"Tomorrow then," Wilder responded and started the walk back to her room.

"You meet with my brothers early," Hesperia whispered once they were at Wilder's door. "I will spend the morning reaching out to a... friend who might help us."

Wilder gave a stiff nod.

Hesperia grabbed her arm before Wilder could disappear into her bedroom. "My brother won't let you stall again. You will have to come to terms with him."

"And what will happen to me when I do?"

"I don't know, but whatever he has planned, if he loses his patience, it will be worse."

They were in the midst of a dangerous game, and Wilder knew that Hesperia could not stop her brother's schemes. Tomorrow morning, in that conference room, Wilder would be on her own.

She placed her hand on Hesperia's. "Whatever happens to me, get Declan out of here. Get him home with a warning of Casimir's plan to my people." She squeezed her fingers tighter. "Promise me."

"I promise."

Wilder released her and turned into her room, closing the door behind her. She leaned against the smooth wood and sobbed. She covered her mouth to stifle the noise of it, but she couldn't stop the shaking. Pain and grief and relief and fear and joy all collided, smashing around her insides like a swarm of bees. She had spent every day missing Declan and wishing he were still alive. Now her wishes proved true, but they'd lost so much time. He'd suffered.

Declan. He was alive, broken but alive. If she could get him home, he could heal, and they could go back to their simple, normal life in the mountains.

If, if, if.

It was too much to long for a future that might not come,

to long for someone else to take up this mantle. To finish what she'd started.

Focus. She took a breath and allowed joy to fill the hollow places, to quiet the hum of panic, of despair. Her husband was alive.

She breathed again. He was alive, and they had to escape. Fight. There would be no joy without escape, without warning the others. There would be no future to worry over without fighting.

Wilder needed to give Hesperia time to rally help. There would be no time, no help coming, if she didn't give Casimir what he wanted from her.

And if she gave him what he wanted, there would be no going back to her old life.

CHAPTER 29
WILDER

Wilder had barely slept the night before thinking through what she would say, what she would do —knowing Declan was just below her, chained. She'd gotten up and walked to her door a million times in the night, ready to run back to the dungeons just to see him again and reassure herself it wasn't a cruel dream.

She splashed some cold water on her face then stared at her own reflection in the bathroom mirror. She looked older. Losing Declan had aged her, but it was more than that now. It was reality blotting out ignorance, replacing it with anger. She knew things she couldn't unknow. She'd never considered herself naïve, but her eyes had been shut, at least to certain things. Now they were wide open.

A knock rattled the door.

"Coming," Wilder called out. She gave herself one last look, smoothing down her disheveled hair before meeting her escort at the door.

The path to the High Ruler felt longer than before, every inch a tortuous eternity. Wilder's heart pulsed inside her ears and muffled everything but the buzz of anxious thoughts. Her empty stomach somersaulted as they reached the looming black doors to Casimir's office. The servant knocked softly. The doors opened.

This was the point of no return.

"Ms. James," Wolstan greeted her with a cool smile.

Wilder stepped inside the large, bright room. She followed the general to the conference table.

"Good morning, Ms. James." The High Ruler's smile mimicked his brother's. He gestured toward a chair. "Would you like some tea?"

She didn't. She wanted to vomit or to run. "Yes, please," she replied sweetly.

Casimir's servant, Felix, stepped into action, pouring her tea and placing it in front of her. Staring at the steaming liquid in the dainty, porcelain cup, Wilder thought of Declan—cold, thirsty, and alone.

"Are you feeling better this morning?" Casimir asked as he took his seat. "We were worried about you at dinner."

Bile burned the back of Wilder's throat, and she swallowed it down with a sip of Darjeeling. "I am. Just not quite familiar enough with the modes of transportation here. A night of rest has done me well, though."

"Good, then we can continue with our negotiations." The High Ruler sipped from his own cup. "I hope we can come to terms quickly."

"As do I," Wilder said. "I'm eager to return home with news of peace for my people."

She didn't miss the glance between the Necanian brothers. The look they gave one another was fleeting but it sent a chill up her spine.

"Did you find out what happened to the captives taken from the Lakota Camp?" Wilder picked up where their last meeting left off. She knew the answer now, of course. She was curious as to what they would offer in response.

Wolstan sat up a bit straighter. His features softened in what might have looked like compassion to some. "I'm so sorry, but it appears that the dissidents did not leave any captives alive."

Wilder's chest constricted. How easy it was for them to lie. "I see."

"My deepest apologies, Ms. James," Casimir said. "Those responsible will be punished to the full extent of our laws."

"The full extent of your laws? May I ask what that means exactly?" There were no dissidents and there would be no real punishment, but every minute she could push this was another minute given to Hesperia to secure their rescue.

"Death," Wolstan replied without hesitation. "We do not trifle with lawbreakers. We will send soldiers to round up all those responsible for the attacks the moment our treaty is signed. They won't stop until every criminal is found."

Wilder wasn't sure if he was speaking of their so-called dissidents or of her people. His words felt equal parts answer and threat. She straightened her shoulders, steeling herself against fear and replied, "Thank you." She took a breath and looked directly at the High Ruler. "And what recompense will be made to the Lakota survivors?"

"Recompense?" Wolstan asked.

"The victims left behind family—wives and children. They depend on one another for the survival of their settlement. Should they not be given something to ease the burden made heavier by your...dissidents?"

Wolstan began to speak, but Casimir held up his hand. "I am sure we can provide restitution in the form of supplies. I would assume that would be of more value than our city's currency."

Wilder wished there were truth in it. "Supplies would be welcomed, I am sure."

"Good," Casimir said. "We will see to it then. Now perhaps we can speak more about the camps in the Northern regions. I fear our lack of knowledge has brought danger to your doorstep and if we knew more, we could better help to ensure peace and safety."

"Yes, of course," Wilder said. This was it. Hesperia's words echoed inside her mind. There was no more stalling. Casimir would lose his patience because she had no more real cards to play. "I will gladly give you what information I have, but how is that enough to repay you for this safety?"

Well, maybe she had one more card, be it a small one.

"Ms. James," Casimir said, spreading his hands. "We have need for nothing. Since the first moment we set foot in your world, we have wanted only to bring your people peace. It is our pleasure to offer it to you."

Lies. A part of Wilder wanted to believe him—to put her distrust aside and cling to a false hope for a pretend peace. Had it not been for Hesperia, she might have dropped her guard and sold her soul to the devil unaware. As it was, she was about to lay her life in his pale, white hands anyway. "What do you need to know?"

"If you could tell us how many camps there are and where they are located?" Wolstan offered.

Wilder inhaled a deep breath, internally counting her words so she didn't hand them the key to her people's demise. "I know of six, maybe seven camps. Perhaps if I had a map, I could give you an idea of locations."

Casimir signaled to Felix who left the room. "Can you tell me how the groups are in communication?"

If Wilder told them of the radios, they would find a way to jam the signals. Declan worked too hard for her to undo his efforts. "It's really rather rudimentary. We simply send couriers around two, maybe three times a year. They bring messages and information." It wasn't totally a lie. Declan had been that courier. Sarai was in the position now. Besides, the radios only worked if the other camps chose to use them.

"Couriers?" Wolstan's brow wrinkled.

Casimir looked equally dissatisfied with her answer. Was it dissatisfaction or disbelief?

"We are a simple people," Wilder added. "Until this attack, there's been no reason for anything more sophisticated. The people in the North appreciate their independence from others." She hoped they would believe her. She needed them to believe her.

Felix returned. "I have the map, High One."

They placed a tablet on the table in front of her—the screen displaying a digital map.

"Please, show us where the camps are located...as best as you can," Wolstan said.

Wilder left the device laying on the table and leaned over it to get a better look. They didn't have this kind of tech in Beartooth. Older members of the camp talked about a time when people carried similar devices around in their pockets. They still did in the domed cities, but she was used to books and paper. Thankfully a map was a map either way, and she'd had enough geography lessons as a child to read one well enough.

"Obviously, you know where our camp is located." Wilder pointed to Beartooth.

"Yes," the general agreed.

"The Lakota camp was here, to the east of us," Wilder pointed to another spot. The way Casimir tugged at his coat and Wolstan clenched his fist confirmed their growing impatience. "There's another camp farther northeast," Wilder said and pointed toward the line that used to divide Minnesota from Canada.

"Are you sure?" Wolstan asked.

"Yes," Wilder responded, looking back at the map. "I don't travel to these places myself, my husband used to do that, but I know it is in this vicinity. I'm sorry I can't be more specific."

"It's quite all right," Casimir replied. "Our transports can scout the areas to confirm and...and to deploy security, of course."

"Of course." Wilder's gut lurched.

She didn't want to give away too much, but she knew it wouldn't matter really. They already had knowledge of camp locations. She guessed they were working their way north, one camp at a time. The only thing that kept Beartooth from being first was probably the heavier forest coverage. It took their scouts longer to find them because their small vehicles couldn't decipher what was hidden under denser tree-top foliage. Perhaps they thought she could save them time and offer details to determine defense capabilities of other camps. She would do neither if she could help it.

She lifted up a silent prayer for forgiveness before telling more lies.

Wilder pointed out five more camps, close enough to not seem suspicious if they had information but not so close that it would truly accelerate their plans. She acted sheepish and apologetic in her lack of detail, promising others in her camp could be more helpful, and she could send back their reconnaissance once she was home.

"That will be acceptable." Casimir gave a side-eyed glance to his brother.

"Yes," Wolstan agreed with a smirk. "Now, what do you know of these other camps? Size? Are they like your people? Are they able to defend themselves?"

Wilder hesitated.

"Yes, we should want to know so we can offer the proper help to those who need it most," Casimir said. "Until the dissidents can be pulled up by the root, all the Wayward camps are unfortunately still in danger."

Wilder inhaled, measuring her words before responding. "Most camps are like the Lakota. They would have no need to suspect danger was lurking. They are peaceful and would not think anyone would want to harm them." She paused and looked into the High Ruler's waiting stare. His bright, crystal eyes were so full of light and beauty, she understood why people would trust him, follow him—why they had for so long. But a shadow lurked at the edges, something darker, something he was holding back. She probably wouldn't have noticed it at all. Enraptured by the false light, she wouldn't have seen the darkness had it not been for Hesperia.

Please let her have gotten help.

If the frigid chill growing in the room was any inclination, the deal was about to be sealed.

"But there are one or two camps that are of rougher stock," Wilder added. "We do not have much dealing with them, but from what I've heard, they would have no problem defending themselves."

"Which camps are these?" Wolstan inquired.

"Those furthest north, deep in the cold," Wilder answered, pointing to a spot on the map, "like Wolf Point. They are not as hospitable or civil."

"That is good to know," Wolstan replied. "If there is nothing else...?"

Wilder swallowed the sour feeling that was rising. "No, I don't think there is anything else I can offer...other than my assurance that our people are not dangerous, we want nothing more than to be left alone, to live as we have for decades—at peace."

"We know," Casimir replied. He got up from the table and smoothed his jacket and adjusted his cuffs.

"So, we can sign this treaty, and you will ensure the safety of the people in the mountains, of my people?" Wilder's question held a last bit of hope. Hope for peace—that Hesperia was wrong. Hope that Wilder might get out of this Citadel with Declan alive and be allowed to return home.

Casimir's mouth curled into a wide, wicked grin.

Hope fled.

"Ms. James, we have appreciated all your help. You have given us valuable information about the Wayward." He glared at Wolstan. "Not as valuable as my brother promised me, but enough to have made this ruse of some worth to us."

"You never meant to leave us in peace." Wilder looked down at the table, her eyes tracing a gray vein in the white marble while her heart traced the path she was about to take.

"No, but you knew that, didn't you?" Casimir almost laughed. "If I didn't find humans so vile, I might have been taken with you. You are stronger and smarter than we gave you credit for. But not smart enough." He snapped his fingers and the doors creaked open. Two guards entered.

Wilder looked to the guards then back to the High Ruler. His translucent skin was no longer a gleaming white but rather a deathly gray. Darkness flooded into his eyes like blood—crimson and frightening. He stepped closer to Wilder, reaching a hand toward her face. A single, clawed finger traced down the line of her cheek then hooked under her chin, lifting her eyes to his and forcing her to stand before the pressure punctured her skin.

"You were never trying to save us," Wilder said, her fists clenched at her sides. Angry tears threatened to blur her vision.

"It was your soldiers who attacked the Lakota, and they meant to do the same to us. But we surprised them."

"Perhaps, but we will not be surprised again...thanks to you." The High Ruler looked over her shoulder, and the guards walked toward them.

"I know what you are, what you do," Wilder whispered through gritted teeth.

"Oh, Ms. James, you have no idea." Casimir smiled revealing sharp fangs. "Take her. She will be a nice addition to our herd."

Strong hands grabbed Wilder's arms. She didn't resist. It was pointless. "My people will not be so easy to defeat." Her feet slid along the floor as they dragged her from the room. All the while Casimir never stopped smiling. As the black doors closed, Wilder grabbed onto her last sliver of hope, that whether or not she lived, her people would find safety, that Declan would still get back to them. That he would live.

CHAPTER 30
WILDER

I t was dark. Or was it? She tried to blink but nothing changed. Whispers swirled in her ears from somewhere close by, intermittently interrupted by a high-pitched beeping. Her hand stung, and the stinging sensation moved up her veins until her whole arm burned.

"Are you certain?"

"We've run the tests twice."

"The High Ruler will be disappointed."

"It's one human woman."

What was happening? Wilder needed to wake up.

She concentrated, squeezing her eyes tight then forcing them open. Slowly the noises got louder, clearer, and light broke through in a fuzzy splash. She blinked again and again. She tried to find the source of the pain in her hand, but Wilder couldn't move her arms. As her vision focused, she saw leather cuffs shackling her to a white bed. A needle stuck in her hand, attached to a tube and a bag that was dripping some sort of liquid into it, into her. A white sheet covered her clammy body. Her knees were bent, and her feet rested in metal stirrups.

"There are fertility medications and treatments that human women have used in the past. Perhaps we can give her a month and then test her again?" A Necanian stepped into Wilder's view.

"This woman is barren. Her eggs are not viable. I doubt a month will change that," another Necanian replied.

"It is worth the test. I am sure the High Ruler would agree. If we are wrong, we have lost nothing. If we are right, we have used thirty days to buy him possibly a dozen souls."

Wilder's breath quickened into short, unsatisfying bursts. They were talking about her, about her eggs, about the tiny souls that would have been her children. But she was barren. It was silly that the word, the truth of it, broke her heart when the possibility of children didn't matter in her current state. Melvina had already told her as much two years ago. She had set aside this particular grief upon Declan's death, but now squirmed in it all over again—at the word she never wanted to hear or say. *Barren.*

But Declan. *Declan.* He was here and alive and so was she, at least for the time being, and that meant there was still a sliver of a promise to be fulfilled. Escape. *Escape.*

But first she needed to get free of the binds.

"She's awake."

"I'll get another dose of the sedative and the fertility treatment to get started before we transfer her to a pod."

A pod? Wilder's eyes darted around the room. She finally saw then—the bags hanging from the ceiling in morbid rows. They were too far away to make out clear details, but she could surmise enough. She observed the human forms, curled into fetal positions between the layers of thick plastic.

Adrenaline rushed through her veins. Wilder thrashed and kicked and fought against the leather bindings.

"Now, now," one of the Necanians said, "you won't feel a thing." He held up a large needle and inserted it into the tubes.

Seconds after he pushed the syringe, numbness overtook her. The room went fuzzy again and light faded back to black.

CHAPTER 31
HESPERIA

Hesperia paced in her room.

She was too late. It had taken too long to sneak to the Colony outside the dome walls. She had taken too much time setting a plan in motion. She'd hoped Wilder could have stalled her brothers longer. Would it really have mattered? At least Wilder wasn't dead.

The harvesting ward was heavily guarded. Even if she could find a way in, getting out with Wilder would prove difficult. Should she leave her? Wilder made her promise to get Declan out. Perhaps she should focus on that task alone. It would be difficult enough on its own.

No! Hesperia stopped her pacing with a stomp. She had done enough shameful things in her life. She had taken enough from the humans and watched her brother take even more. Casimir called it survival. He called it the natural order of predator and prey. There had to be another way to live without taking the lives of others—without taking the life of her friend.

Friend.

162

She'd had a friend once, and it had cost her. He was gone now.

It was about to cost her again, but this time if she stepped in and defied her brother...

She would not survive.

She started pacing again. Hesperia couldn't let Wilder suffer the same fate as Theo. She couldn't save Declan only to tell him she hadn't kept her promise to protect his wife. There had to be a way to get into the ward and get Wilder out.

Hesperia growled under her breath. She dug her nails into the palms of her hands, piercing her skin. She smelled the droplets of blood before she felt them.

What did she know of the Citadel, the guards—the ward? There was only one way into the dungeons and tunnels, and that was nearly as far from the harvesting ward as you could get.

Wait. There was a servant's corridor. Her first friend had told her of it. Theo had taken her there once. It was what the humans used while they were still servants in the Citadel, when Casimir didn't want them seen. It was a series of secret passages running parallel to the main halls. If Hesperia could get to it, then she and Wilder would have a chance of getting into the tunnels without notice. Would the doors be locked or covered over? If not, if she could find the entrance closest to the ward, then she could map out a path of escape.

Helping Wilder would seal Hesperia's fate. Casimir would be certain of her traitorous involvement. But... perhaps helping the humans escape—it could be an escape for her as well.

She was dead either way, be it by her brother's hand or starvation when the time of the Sacrament passed. Perhaps she could have a chance to see more of the world before she died.

Hesperia stilled herself and stood straighter. She filled her lungs with air and her mind with resolve. When the sun set, and the others were tucked away for the night, she would set out to do this. Some things, Hesperia was learning, were worth the cost.

She stepped into her *en suite* bath and washed the drying blood from her pallid hands. Her reflection in the mirror looked braver and more determined than she felt.

"I am Necanian, and I know no fear." She whispered the mantra taught to their children, tainted as it now was to her, and squared her shoulders before heading out her door.

Servants bustled about their normal business. Occasionally one offered her a polite bow, and she replied with a regal raise of her chin—a subtle reminder of her status. She cared little about such things anymore, but it would keep them at bay while she searched for the hidden hallway. Her brain replayed memories as she walked the corridors. The look in Theo's eye, the sound of his whisper... both brought joy and sadness. Hesperia inhaled sharply to regain focus. A left, a right, another right and there it was, a narrow door masquerading as part of the wall. She looked over her shoulders. No one was around—no spying eyes to see her push the frame. There was a soft click before the opening revealed itself. Hesperia stepped inside, closing it back behind her.

Damp and dusty air prickled her nostrils. She remembered Theo had flipped a switch to light the path, but she didn't need it. Her irises lengthened and offered visibility even in the dark. The ward would be toward the north end and the tunnel entrance to the south. Hesperia walked toward the latter. She counted three hundred paces to the door closest to the dungeon entrance. She pressed her ear against it, listening for sounds of passersby. When she heard nothing, she nudged the door open ever so slightly. The entrance was in a forgotten corner near the servant's quarters. It was just a short distance from the dungeon, an easy walk even with Wilder. There would be one guard at the door come nightfall.

Hesperia closed the wall and headed north, counting paces again. She retraced her previous steps, then went farther. There were three turns and two sets of stairs to reach the correct level. The freight elevator would have been useful, but Casimir cut power to it when the human servants were removed. Should she switch it back on? Hesperia dismissed the idea; the noise would draw too much attention.

When she reached an exit close to the ward entrance, Hesperia stopped and leaned an ear against the wall. All was quiet. She cracked the opening and peered out. The guarded entrance was just at the opposite end of the long corridor. But the servant's hall hadn't ended with the wall. It continued another twenty or so feet into what would be the incubation room itself. She clicked the doorway closed, kept walking, listening for outside noises as she did. Casimir must have forgotten about the passageway when he set up the ward and hadn't closed it off. It was a stroke of luck, really more of a miracle. It would mean she wouldn't need to sneak past guards in two places.

Reaching the last door, Hesperia heard nothing through the wall. She pushed against the doorway, but it didn't move. Her luck may have ended. Perhaps her brother hadn't closed up the corridor but had sealed the door from the other side. This was still her best chance at getting Wilder out and reunited with Declan, so she needed to investigate further.

Hesperia backtracked, exited the secret passage, and approached the ward entrance. All the while her mind raced, searching for a reason, an excuse to step inside and spy out the area and possibly come up with a backup plan.

Just as she came within a few feet of the guards, one of the

Necanian scientists stepped out. "Practitioner Aljon," Hesperia called for the man's attention. "Just who I wanted to see."

Aljon raised an eyebrow. "Why is that?"

Hesperia held little respect among the elite, but she was still the High Ruler's sister, and that status alone would give her one maneuver. "It has occurred to me that I have fallen short in my sisterly duties and want to show my brother my full support in his current endeavor. To that end, I would like to have a tour of the Harvesting and Incubation Ward. Who better to give it to me than its head clinician?"

She wasn't asking. Aljon would know that. Respect her or not, he couldn't tell her no. She would immediately go to her brother, who would appreciate her intentions, see it as her coming back to herself, and reprimand the practitioner for his refusal. The reprimand would not be without pain and suffering.

Aljon sighed. "It would be my pleasure." He bowed then held out his hand, gesturing for her to follow him into the ward.

She had no desire to ever step foot in this place again, except to save Wilder. It had turned her stomach the first visit, and the nauseated feeling worsened this time. The sterile smell of fluids and medicines hitting her senses sickened her. But they were nothing compared to the sight of the body bags hanging from the ceiling. There were more than before. Naked forms in oversized wombs, unaware of their predicament. She wanted to close her eyes and heart to them, but it was too late for that.

Practitioner Aljon walked Hesperia around the lab pointing out instruments and explaining functions and formulas. She didn't care. She all but tuned him out, his voice just a hum on the edge of her mind. Her focus was directed to the far wall where the hidden door should be. It was beyond this room and into the next where the incubators were located.

"And what is in the next room?" Hesperia asked already knowing the answer.

"Ah, yes, the incubators where we grow the embryos until they are large enough to be transferred." He smiled and Hesperia wanted to claw out his throat.

"Show me," she commanded in a tone that was the perfect combination of soft and stern.

Aljon obeyed. She followed him through rows of imprisoned souls. One in particular caught her attention, its deep red hair standing out from the others. *Wilder.* Walking past her friend's still body, she resisted the urge to reach out or whisper, leaving her words silent in her head. *I am coming for you.*

"There are currently a dozen incubators with plans to expand to a larger facility." Aljon interrupted her thoughts and drew her back to the task at hand.

"How exciting," she replied, scanning for signs of the servant's entrance. It seemed as if it had been covered by a new layer of drywall, but the closer she walked toward that far wall, the more she realized that wasn't the case. A thin line, nearly invisible beneath a layer of paint, caught her eye. It was the doorway, and it hadn't been sealed. Rather, it was pinned shut by one of the incubators. "It does appear you could use the space," she added gesturing toward the lines of machines filing the room and pointing to the few that were pushed against the wall.

"Yes, quite," Aljon said, tapping his foot on the hard floor. It appeared he was losing patience with this tour.

She didn't want to push any further. "Well, you have provided me with excellent information. I am sure the High Ruler will be happy to know how you have helped me in my efforts to help him."

Practitioner Aljon smiled and bowed again. "It was my pleasure."

It wasn't, but Hesperia played along. "I will be sure to tell him how accommodating you have been."

"Thank you," he replied.

Hesperia nodded before striding away from him and out of the ward. She made her way back to her room as quickly as she could without drawing attention, then stepped out onto her balcony. Her hands pushed against the railing. The clean, fresh air filled her lungs, forcing out the horrid stench of her people's evil.

Hesperia had once loved this view. The bright blue sky, the warm sun, the clean lines of a perfectly constructed city. It was always perfect, always controlled—right down to the weather, thanks to the dome which protected them from unwanted elements. Perfection wasn't perfect. It could be foul and putrid underneath. There were moments when Hesperia wanted to return to ignorance and loyalty and blind faith in the schemes of her own kind. Now fully awakened to their imperfections and weakness and darkness, she wouldn't go back. She couldn't go back, only forward into what she hoped would be her redemption.

CHAPTER 32
WILDER

N oises. Muffled words. Beeps. Footsteps. Were they footsteps? They all sounded so far away. It was dark, but warm like a soak in a fresh bath. Wilder was calm. But in the back of her mind, a notion pricked—like she shouldn't be calm. She couldn't push or pull it though. It was just a thought that sat there, waiting for her to pick it up and run with it. But she couldn't.

Then there was a tear, a ripping sound, and she was suddenly wet and cold. Her body hit something hard. Pain surged through her hip and back and neck and head.

"Wilder." Cool hands gingerly touched her arms then shoulders then face. "Wilder."

Her senses floated. She blinked, and her gummy eyes opened to glaring light. She blinked again and realized it wasn't quite as bright as at first but still disorienting. Her gut did a flip and the contents of her lungs and stomach spewed out of her mouth and onto her and the floor.

"It's okay," a familiar voice cooed. "Take a moment. Breathe."

Warm, soft fabric wrapped around her. Wilder blinked again. She started to regain control of her extremities and raised a shaking hand to wipe her eyes. As she pushed the goop away, the world and her mind came back into clearer focus. Body bags hung around her, reminding her where she was and what the Necanians had done. With each realization, her heart fluttered, and her stomach churned. She thought she might vomit again.

"It's okay, you're safe," the voice assured her.

Wilder turned her aching head toward the voice, toward a face, pale with bright eyes and the pieces of a concerned smile. She knew the face. "Hesperia." She nearly choked on the name.

"Shh, don't speak. Don't do anything. I'm getting you out of here."

Wilder looked down at her naked body. Goosebumps spread over her legs and arms. She wrapped herself up tighter.

"Can you dry off?" Hesperia asked her.

Wilder nodded a yes but it was an uncertain one.

"I have clothes for you to wear. We are safe for now, but we need to hurry if I'm going to get you out of here." The Necanian took another towel and wiped Wilder's face and hair. Then she helped her dress in an oversized sweater and a pair of loose britches. "I hope these are alright. I pulled them from your belongings." Hesperia held up Wilder's satchel. "I retrieved everything before the servants could dispose of them."

"Thank you." Wilder's whisper was hoarse and burned her throat. She pulled on the shoes Hesperia handed her.

"Take my arm." Hesperia stood and helped Wilder do the same.

"How will we..." Wilder remembered the guards outside the door.

"Don't worry," Hesperia said. "I came back after dinner and told the guard that I left something in here after an earlier tour.

When they let me in to retrieve it, I was able to clear our path. And now, they don't even know I am in here. This way." She held Wilder up and helped her stagger her way through the laboratory.

Wilder's stomach tumbled again as she tripped her way past the other bodies held in wait for the Sacrament. The thought of leaving them there sickened her even more. As tempted as she was to tell Hesperia to cut them all free, she knew she couldn't. There would be no time, no way to get them all out of the Citadel, much less the city, unnoticed. Getting out was the only way she could really rescue them. *I'll come back for you.* Wilder's unspoken promise was earnest.

She would find a way to help them, to stop the High Ruler's wretched plan from moving forward.

Hesperia all but dragged her through the rows, as Wilder's legs were still mostly numb. Her shoulder bumped the doorway into the next room.

"Sorry," Hesperia whispered.

"It's okay," Wilder croaked.

She did her best to help Hesperia bear her weight as they maneuvered through the incubators. She did her best not to look under the small glass domes to see the tiny figures encased inside. Her best was not good enough. Her lungs clenched at the sight. She let her trembling fingers drift over one of the incubators as she passed. This was someone's child, someone's dream. Casimir wouldn't get away with this. Anger rose to meet pain and sadness, mingling in Wilder's lungs and heart, pumping out in adrenaline that pricked her legs back to life.

"Through here." Hesperia pushed and a section of wall popped open, revealing a dark hallway.

Wilder coughed on the musty air.

"Be still." Hesperia leaned her against the wall and then stepped back to close the entry.

What little light coming from the lab disappeared and Wilder couldn't even see the hand in front of her face. She heard a click then a buzz and bulbs overhead began to flicker.

Hesperia steadied Wilder once again and whispered, "It's quite a walk, but we can take our time. We just need to be quiet to be sure no one who might be in the halls can hear us."

Wilder walked on shaky legs beside the Necanian. With each step, she held a little more of her own weight. Her sore muscles and foggy head threatened to stop her, but at the other end of this was Declan. If she could make it to him, she didn't care what happened next.

Steps and stairs and turns. Wilder tripped once but Hesperia caught her. Her mind bounced back and forth between those left behind her and the one waiting in front of her. Declan drew closer with each step, each breath, each heartbeat. Her Declan would be back in her arms in moments.

"We're almost there." Hesperia stopped. "Can you stand?"

"Yes," Wilder replied. Her legs quivered still but her will was steel.

"We are just around the corner from the dungeon entrance. I will get the guard away and then we will have to hurry to get inside the door before he returns. Stay close to me."

Wilder followed Hesperia into the corridor, her eyes adjusting to the brighter light that gleamed off the white marble floor. They crept to the edge, and the Necanian peered around the corner. Hesperia pulled something out of her pocket, a smooth black pebble, and threw it down the hall. The click it made echoed off the walls.

"Now!" Hesperia whispered, and the two women dashed around the corner. Hesperia quickly entered the door code and tugged Wilder inside before shutting the door again.

"Your big distraction plan was throwing a rock?" Wilder almost chuckled.

"It's late. No one, including myself, would be roaming the halls. I thought a noise would be enough to draw him away and give us the time we needed."

"And if it hadn't worked?" Wilder raised an eyebrow.

"I would have rendered him unconscious." Hesperia started down the stairway into the dungeons.

"Have you always known about the secret passageways?" Wilder asked, gingerly following the Necanian past the empty cages.

"No. Theo showed them to me once, before Casimir rid the Citadel of human servants." Wilder watched the Necanian's eyes dim just a touch. "I hadn't remembered them until today."

"I'm glad that you did," Wilder replied. This Necanian woman was an enigma, a mix of warm and cool, one who had nothing to gain by helping a human she barely knew. "You know you can't go back after this."

"Yes."

"You'll come with us." Wilder needed no time to come to this conclusion. There was no hesitation in her statement. It was the right thing to do.

"Your people will allow this?"

"My people will welcome the woman who gave me my life back...twice." Wilder uttered that last word just as they reached Declan's cell.

He looked worse than before. His shackled form drooping.

Wilder wasted no time stepping into the cell. "Declan." She reached up and touched his face.

A soft groan rumbled in his throat.

Wilder pushed up on her tiptoes and whispered his name close to his ears, her cheek grazing his. "Declan."

He jolted awake and growled, pulling against his chains, and almost knocking Wilder to the ground.

"Be careful," Hesperia said.

Wilder steadied herself and stood toe-to-toe with her husband. "Are we really going to do this again?" she asked.

His heavy breath puffed against her face. His eyes were wide with fear and rage.

She placed her hands one on each of his cheeks. "It's really me, I'm getting you out of here."

"Wilder," his gruff voice echoed in the chambers of her heart.

"Yes," she said and kissed his lips. "We're going home."

"Home," he repeated.

Hesperia stepped inside to hand her a key, and Wilder unlocked the shackles around his wrists. Declan fell to his knees, and Hesperia joined Wilder at his side to help him up. He flinched away from the Necanian.

"Don't touch me," he roared.

"Declan," Wilder said as she braced his arm over her shoulder to help steady him, "she is here to help. If it wasn't for her...I...I wouldn't be here now. She is a friend."

Declan looked from Wilder to Hesperia and back again before nodding.

Hesperia stepped back to his side, ready to help him up. His muscles tensed when she did.

"She saved me," Wilder whispered into his ear. "She is saving us."

Declan relaxed a little but stayed leaning in Wilder's direction. It was a struggle to bear his weight when she could still barely hold her own, but she wouldn't let go of him, not now, not ever.

"This way." Hesperia led them to the left where the shaft narrowed. "They will be waiting for us."

CHAPTER 33
WILDER

The tunnel, devoid of decent light, seemed unending. Pain jabbed at Wilder's heels and up into her legs. Her back grew sore from Declan's weight against her. But the feel and smell of him, the real him and not mere ghostly echoes, was an elixir to her tired muscles. It was grace and strength in her weakness. She could help steady him for miles if necessary.

"It is not much farther," Hesperia said.

Wilder lifted her head up, changing her view from the two yards in front of her feet to the dim light that got closer with each step. "It's daylight?" Would they be discovered so close to freedom?

"Only just," Hesperia said, "and there are no guards watching the tunnel exit. I don't think they even know it exists or that it hasn't been covered over. Even so, they have no reason to believe those in the Colony would utilize it. They're merely wounded animals to them now and of no real concern."

"Where I come from, wounded animals can be the most dangerous," Wilder commented.

"I think your people are not as arrogant as mine," Hesperia said.

Wilder peeked around Declan to smile at the Necanian who was giving up everything for them. Did she feel it? Did Hesperia grieve the loss of her family and home and all that was comfortable for her? Was it even still comfortable? She showed such little emotion overall that Wilder was unsure if she was even capable of feeling, but then again, she had shown *some* emotions. She'd been so compassionate. Whether Hesperia realized it or not, compassion was rooted in love.

Wilder adjusted Declan's weight as they trod a few more silent yards, her eyes blinking in the growing light. A breeze swirled by. The air tasted fresh and cool. Birds chirped at the sunrise. It was the first time she'd heard birds since arriving at Hope City. Their sweet song washed over her, bringing serenity. They were one step closer to home.

As they reached the tunnel exit, leaves rustled nearby. The click of a rifle being cocked.

"It is I, Hesperia," the Necanian announced. "I bring the Wayward like we planned."

A man's voice came from the brush. "Don't move until we can take a closer look at you three." Two men stepped forward out of the autumn-tinted branches, guns aimed at the trio. Wilder didn't know what she'd expected, but their haphazard attire and mussed faces were nothing like the humans living in the city. Their sullen stares didn't quite match her people either. These men were something in between.

A third man followed them. His own rifle was angled down, but his eyes never twitched or blinked. "You understand we have to be sure this isn't a trap," he said to Hesperia.

"Of course," she replied.

The man came closer with cautious steps. "Excuse me,

ma'am," he said to Wilder before patting his hands along her back, sides, and legs.

"We don't have weapons," she told him. "We don't want to hurt anyone. We just want to go home."

The man's brown eyes met with hers. He nodded but then moved to check Declan, the first touch eliciting a growl and a flinch. Wilder almost lost her own balance trying to keep Declan from falling to the ground.

"They did a number on him," the man said, then moved to Hesperia.

After being sure none were carrying any weapons, trackers, or listening devices, the man stepped back and gestured for the others to lower their guns. "I'm Matthew," he said. "I'm sorry to have to check you, but I am sure you understand what it means to keep your people safe. I am merely doing the same for mine."

"I'm Wilder and this is my husband, Declan," she said. Without gun barrels pointed at her head and stealing her attention, she was able to really look at the man. His hair was graying, and his clothes were tattered from time and wear. There were scars on his forehead that matched the wounds on Declan's temples.

"You all were cutting it close," Matthew said, his eyes searching Declan's face. "A few more minutes, and we would have given up on you and gone home."

"Getting Wilder out safely became more complicated than I first thought," Hesperia said. "But we are here now and should probably get to the safety of the Colony before they realize she is gone."

Matthew nodded. "This way."

The two men with Matthew stepped forward to help take Declan's burden from Wilder's shoulders, but she wouldn't let them. "We've got him, thank you."

They shrugged and fell in line behind the three while Matthew took the lead.

"Will it be safe...with the Colony being so close to the city?" Wilder asked.

"Yes," Matthew replied. "I promise."

"I told you, my brother isn't concerned about the Colony or its inhabitants," Hesperia said to Wilder. "In his mind, they are no longer capable of anything that would cause him concern."

"They look capable to me." Wilder watched Matthew stomp through the overgrown weeds.

"Only a small few. The rest are shells of their former selves," Hesperia said.

Wilder looked at Declan's dull eyes. "They'll never recover?"

"Some, like Matthew, have. Others have not been as lucky. It all depends on the human."

"The restoration of a soul is tricky business," Matthew said over his shoulder.

Oxygen fled Wilder's lungs, like she had been punched. She had Declan back, and yet she didn't. He recognized her, that was something—a piece of hope to hold onto. But he may never return to the man he once was. Could she live with that? No matter. She pledged to love him for richer or poorer, in sickness and in health. She'd lived without him and, while she may not know what their future would look like, having any part of him with her was better than not having him at all. Their first concern was escape, then returning home. Home was sacred. Home was holy ground. Home would make the difference.

CHAPTER 34

WILDER

S weat beaded on Wilder's forehead and soaked through her sweater. Her loose hair stuck to the back of her neck. Even in late autumn, this southern climate was warmer than most spring days in Beartooth.

Sunlight glinted off the clear dome. It didn't appear to be metal, glass, or plastic, but it was gleaming and invisible all at the same time. The tall, steel buildings inside shined with reflected light. The bright, clean, beautiful city loomed in stark contrast to the shanty town they entered at its base—homes built of salvaged wood, metal, and cardboard. The doorways were little more than shredded tarps.

Wilder's foot slipped on the muddy path. Regaining her balance, she looked up to see a crowd of faces all watching her. Their eyes were absent of light, even the children who's cheeks were smudged with dirt. Those dull eyes clouded further with fear when they looked past her, past Declan, to the Necanian who trudged with them. Gasps and whispers flitted from person to person.

Hesperia lowered her head, looking to the ground.

"*You* are not what they are afraid of," Wilder offered. "They'll come to see that as I have."

Hesperia nodded. One corner of her mouth curved the tiniest bit upward.

"Here." Matthew stopped at one of the ramshackle buildings. "You can bring him in here. Our doctor can help tend to his wounds, and you can get some rest before we plan your journey north."

"Thank you," Wilder said, stepping inside.

It reminded her a bit of Beartooth. An oil lamp flickered on a small table with mismatched chairs. A bed with worn blankets sat to one side. Small trinkets and a few old books lined a shelf. Children's drawings were pinned to one wall. It was an amalgamation of old things brought together over years of making a life.

"Lay him on the bed," Matthew instructed.

Wilder and Hesperia did so. Her shoulders and back were relieved by the release, but her heart ached to touch him again. She stretched then sat beside him, taking his hand in hers. She stroked his rough cheek.

Declan groaned. He might have been looking at her. He might have been looking right through her. "Wilder," he mumbled.

"I'm here." She leaned closer.

A smile pricked his cheeks. His clammy hand squeezed her fingers. "Safe?" His voice was so hoarse it sounded painful for him to speak.

"Yes, we are safe."

"Home?" he asked.

She brushed her fingers through his dirty hair. "No, not yet, but soon."

Declan dipped his head a fraction of an inch in understanding before his eyes closed and his head drooped to the side.

Wilder stiffened. She bent over him, her ear close to his mouth, listening for his breath. It hit her jaw in warm puffs. It was shallow, but there. He was alive, just sleeping. She relaxed.

"His mind and body need the rest." Hesperia's hand touched Wilder's shoulder. "This is probably the first real peace he has had in months."

Wilder nodded.

"She's right," Matthew interjected. "Rest is the first step in his recovery. He needs it to heal. Let him sleep while you get something to eat."

Wilder began to protest. "I don't want to leave him..."

"I'll bring the food to you," Matthew said with an understanding smile.

* * *

The meal Matthew brought Wilder was a humble one. A flat bread and some oatmeal, at least that's what the taste and texture reminded her of. The goopy porridge was fairly devoid of flavor. It could have used a few blackberries from their garden or some honey from Ellen's hives. But Wilder didn't complain. She ate it gratefully because, flavor or not, it was a gift, a sacrifice Matthew's people had made to her growling stomach. Living at the base of the dome certainly had not afforded them any of the luxuries found inside.

"Why stay here?" Wilder asked Matthew after scraping the last bit from her bowl.

"Where would we go? Most would not survive the trek north," he replied. "Besides, with every Sacrament, there are one or two more who are cast out. We are needed here."

"Do the Necanians just bring you the survivors?" Wilder

had a hard time believing Casimir would let them just walk out of his door, whether he viewed them as a threat or not.

"Their families do," Matthew said. He picked up her empty bowl and stacked it with his and Hesperia's.

"Why? Why not keep them at home, help them heal?"

"They are afraid," Hesperia said. "If a loved one is taken, it is because they have broken Casimir's law. Most people know nothing of the Sacrament. They only know that stepping out of line leads to this, and they won't risk being next."

"The true nature of the Bringers of Peace is well-hidden." Matthew set the dirty bowls in his makeshift sink with a clank. "Some suspect there is more at play than law and order, but they wouldn't dare question it out loud. They won't risk their own comfortable lives. Those who come here know the truth but can do little about it."

"But you want to do something?" Wilder asked. Matthew reminded her of Declan. He didn't seem the type of man to just sit by and do nothing.

"There are a few, less than once upon a time..." Matthew looked to Declan. "When I still lived in the city, we would meet in secret, trying to put together a plan to revolt against the Necanian rule."

"You knew of the Sacrament then?" Wilder asked.

Without looking at the Necanian he said, "Hesperia told me when my son was killed by Casimir."

Wilder glanced from Matthew to Hesperia. The Necanian's eyes revealed the cracks of a broken heart. "Theo?"

Hesperia didn't speak, she only nodded slowly.

"Those who believed me, who were willing to join me...we collected supplies. Made a plan."

"What happened?" Wilder asked but could have guessed the answer by Matthew's downcast face.

"The Bringers found out. They captured us all. Only a few

survived the arrest, fewer the following Sacrament." Matthew hadn't looked away from Declan. "Including his parents."

Wilder gasped. She made a conscious effort to close her mouth and form words in response to such a surprising revelation. "You knew them...him?" She knew Declan grew up in one of the cities. She knew his parents had been taken and he'd barely escaped. But the world seemed too big for this type of happenstance meeting.

"When you said his name earlier, it's not one you hear that often," Matthew replied. "I would have shrugged it off as weird coincidence except he looks too much like his father...and he has his mother's eyes."

"They were your friends." It wasn't a question. Wilder recognized the answer in the way his shoulders sagged, and his jaw clenched. The air in the room chilled with sadness.

"Yes. And they would have been proud of how strong he is." Matthew's mouth curved into a half smile as he kept his eyes glued on Declan.

Wilder watched for the subtle rise and fall of Declan's chest. He looked so thin and pale compared to the man who rode out of Beartooth back in the spring. The blood that stained his head and face made her stomach lurch. His chest rattled as he inhaled. She shuddered at the sound.

"How strong is he?" *Will he make it home?*

Matthew looked away from Declan and laid his hand on Wilder's. "No one survives that long in the dungeons—the multiple feedings I am certain he had to endure... No one without a fearless heart and a powerful love."

Wilder hadn't wanted to cry anymore—she was so *tired* of crying. She wiped her tears away quickly. "No one should have to endure such things."

"No, they shouldn't."

After a moment, Wilder told him, "Declan was taken

because he was trying to protect the northern camps from attack."

Matthew's eyes widened just a hint. "The Wayward have lived in peace for fifty years. The Necanians have cared very little about the people in the mountains. Why would they attack you?"

"My brother's hunger is insatiable," Hesperia answered. Her slender white fingers brushed her long white hair off her face and over her shoulder. "And he is no longer satisfied with lawbreakers alone. He has plans. Dark ones."

"He won't stop with the northern camps," Wilder added. "We're just a testing sample to get him started. He'll come for the Colony in time and then...who knows how far he will go with this."

"Most of my people have spent years healing, waiting, and preparing. But we still aren't enough to take on the High Ruler and his general." Matthew ran his hand over the back of his neck. "I'm not sure we ever will be enough."

"I thought the same thing of my people," Wilder replied. "But I'm not sure any of us can wait any longer. Things have been set in motion."

"What things?" Matthew looked back and forth between Wilder and Hesperia.

"My brother has taken to a new sort of agriculture," Hesperia answered. She inhaled deeply and exhaled slowly. "His crop of choice is human souls."

Matthew leaned as far forward as he could get without pushing the table. "What? How?"

"The short version," Wilder offered. "Labs, insemination, embryo harvesting, incubators, and body bags. No birth. No real life. Just humans grown for food."

Matthew pounded his fist on the table, shaking it so that

Wilder's cup of water spilled over. She retrieved a towel from nearby to clean it up.

"I take it the High Ruler has already begun harvesting?" Matthew asked Hesperia.

"Yes. My brother has used those few captives from the northern raids to begin his grand experiment. Unless he can find a way to accelerate human growth, it will be years before the babies are ready. But at the next Sacrament, he will use the captives who are no longer useful."

"The barren or used up," Wilder clarified.

"The next Sacrament is in a fortnight." Matthew bowed his head and clasped his hands. Wilder wasn't sure if he was just thinking or praying or both. "We won't be able to save them."

"No, but maybe we can save the others, the children," Wilder said, trying to sound certain. Her heart was beating so hard that she thought it might break free of her chest. Sweat covered her palms at the thought of going up against Casimir and Wolstan. How would they even begin to face such an admirable foe? Her eyes drifted over to where Declan lay still and sleeping, barely alive. *He* was built for this, leading an army—even a small one.

"How do you eat an elephant?" Matthew asked.

Wilder was confused. She was not overly familiar with elephants, having only seen them in some history books others in her village had kept. "I...I don't know."

The older man smirked. "One bite at a time. We take this one step at a time. The first step is getting you and Declan back to your people. My sources tell me the northern camps have the numbers and more strength. So talk to your people; mine will monitor the city, and I'll try and reach out to any remnants from the rebellion. Maybe there are one or two willing to step back into the fray."

"You must be careful," Hesperia warned him. "If they

haven't already, it won't take long for my brother to realize what I have done. His anger will make him even more volatile. He will seek vengeance."

"Winter comes early in the mountains," Matthew responded. "It'll slow down sending soldiers after you and the others."

"But it will leave you more vulnerable," Hesperia said. "If he discovers you helped us...me..."

"I'll worry about that," Matthew reassured her. A hint of anger in Matthew surfaced through the thick layers of their shared grief—a grief that had brought them together rather than drive them both further into pain and anger. It was a testament to forgiveness. Wilder had assumed any humanity Hesperia had showed was a result of her interactions with Matthew's son, but now she was seeing that perhaps it was Matthew himself who had taught her compassion.

"I can stay here with you," Hesperia offered.

"No." Matthew shook his head. "You are strong, but there is little you can do for us if they come. If anything, your presence here will put us in more danger. Right now, they have no reason to believe we have been of any help to you. For all your brothers know, you and Wilder took off into the wilderness alone."

"Then we shouldn't stay any longer than is absolutely necessary," Hesperia said.

"Agreed." Matthew stood up. He opened the drawer of a scratched-up nightstand and retrieved a key. "We have a vehicle hidden in the brush a couple miles outside the Colony. Once the doctor treats Declan, we will get you three there and on your way. If you're careful, you can reach home in a day or so."

"Fourteen hours and fifty-seven minutes," Wilder said. Matthew a raised an eyebrow. "That's how long it takes. Every time Declan and the others would come to the city outskirts to trade, I would count every minute there and back."

"Can you drive it?"

"If you have a map, then yes."

"Good." Matthew tossed Wilder the key. "Get home. Get your people in gear, and I'll do the same with mine. Between the two of us, maybe we can figure out how to save a few, if not stop this whole thing."

"We'll need to stay in touch somehow," Wilder said. "Do you have an old radio?"

Matthew paused in thought. "Deana used to work with tech in the city. She still tinkers around with old junk we find. Maybe she has one."

"If she does, we can hopefully communicate. Declan fixed up a few back at home."

"Wolstan doesn't monitor analog frequencies," Hesperia offered as reassurance. "But if he gets even the slightest inkling—"

"We will have time," Wilder said, assuring the Necanian. "I told him the camps only communicate through couriers." A lump formed in Wilder's throat. "But I also told him locations for some of the other camps. I tried to keep it to what I knew they already knew or vague enough that it wouldn't do him much good, especially with snow coming..."

"But with you gone, they'll want to act," Matthew said, understanding.

"Yes."

He nodded his head. "Then all the more reason you need to get home soon and warn them."

CHAPTER 35
WILHELMINE

Wilhelmine stepped out of her suite and into the corridor, immediately mindful of her posture. She tilted her chin up and straightened her back, making herself appear taller, more regal. She always took care with her appearance—the luxurious clothes she wore, the perfection of every strand of her silver hair, the cold gaze she offered servants to remind them of their place.

It was her custom to stroll the halls after her morning tea, inclining her ear to whispered conversations and observing the gossip of the servants. There was a power in knowledge.

Thirty or forty feet away, Hesperia's maid (Wilhelmine could never remember her name) was knocking at her sister-in-law's door. "Mistress? Mistress?" The servant knocked again.

Wilhelmine clasped her fingers together in front of her and walked toward the servant. "Is something wrong?" She tilted her head and softened her eyes in mock concern.

"My mistress has not answered, and I am worried she is ill."

"Why would you think that?"

"After dinner last night, she said she felt worn. She told me she would dress herself for bed. Of course, I obeyed her wishes." The tray faltered a bit in the servant's hand, making the silver utensils clank together.

"And you wouldn't want to intrude on her privacy without sure cause." Wilhelmine filled in the blanks for the maid. She touched a calm hand to the servant's shaking one. "I will check on Hesperia for you."

The servant bowed her head and stepped aside.

Wilhelmine smiled then turned the cold knob, calling out in a gentle tone as she nudged the door open a crack. "Hesperia, dear sister, are you alright?"

There was no answer. Wilhelmine pushed the door fully open and stepped inside. She hadn't been in Hesperia's suite for quite some time. It was much like her own in size and layout, but it smelled sweet. The subtle scent that wafted from a dying bouquet of jasmine made Wilhelmine want to wretch. She never understood Hesperia's desire to have such a thing as flowers in her room, fragile objects that they are.

"She's not here," the servant muttered from the doorway.

"It appears not," Wilhelmine said, noting the peculiarity. What would Hesperia have to do at this early morning hour? "Don't worry, my dear, I am sure she simply took a walk for fresh air to revive her senses. I will see to her well-being."

"Yes, my lady." The maid curtsied and retreated down the hall.

Wilhelmine walked around the room. Hesperia had been quieter than normal at dinner, even excusing herself early. In and of itself, that would not raise suspicion. But pairing it with her absence now and the presence of the human woman with whom Hesperia seemed so fond, Wilhelmine was certain there was intrigue here.

She walked past Hesperia's bed, reading chair, and table, looking for signs of something. The view out the window was virtually the same from her own suite. At the vanity, she touched her slender fingers to the handle of Hesperia's silver brush. She caught her own reflection in the mirror. She stood taller than her sister-in-law. Her hair gleamed, and her eyes glimmered as clear and crystal as the other members of the royal family. The sparkling scales made her white skin seem luminescent. She touched her neck and ran her fingers along her jawline, across her pointed chin and up her cheek, pushing her hair back. Her reflection darkened like a shadow crept in front of her—the shadow of her own longing and lacking. Along the side of her face was a single, thin silver ring carved into her flesh, not three like Wolstan...like Hesperia.

It was a constant reminder that she was less than, that she'd married into the royal family but was never fully embraced by it. If she produced an heir, then she might be rewarded with another band of honor.

She abhorred the idea. Hadn't she proven herself time and time again to be worthy? She was loyal. She was powerful. Casimir must see that. She would make him see it!

Wilhelmine pounded her fist against the mahogany dresser top. The attached mirror shook, and a piece of folded paper fell to the floor from it. She bent down to retrieve the wrinkled and worn parchment, unfolding it to reveal a drawing. It was a charcoal sketch of Hesperia with fingerprints blurring some of the lines. In the bottom right corner was a scribbled name—a name she heard before, a long while ago...*the boy*. The human who somehow infected Hesperia's sensibilities, it was his name. *Theo*. This was a gift from him.

Wilhelmine crumpled the paper in her palm as if she was squeezing all the life it had once offered out of Hesperia herself. She dropped it onto the floor as she exited the suite.

Hesperia hadn't returned to herself. She hadn't regained her loyalties. She was up to something, and she wouldn't get away with it.

* * *

An hour later, Wilhelmine stood outside the harvesting ward doors on the third floor, having pieced together Hesperia's trail. Servants saw things, heard things, and never refused her when she asked questions. They feared her more than their secrets. One had observed Hesperia come to speak to a practitioner the afternoon before.

"Aljon," Wilhelmine called as she entered the ward.

Tension loomed between the clinicians, whispers and wary glances steeped in the fragrance of fear.

"I'm sorry, my lady, is there something I can do for you?" Aljon looked over his shoulder twice as he spoke to her. Behind him, some of his assistants were cleaning up a mess from the floor.

"I had thought so, but now perhaps I wonder if there is something I can do for you?" Wilhelmine used her knack for spotting and seizing opportunity. "You look quite frantic this morning. Has something happened?" She carefully covered her delight in his circumstances with a calm regard to draw him into her trust.

Aljon looked thoughtful before he spoke. "I would not want to put you in the path of the High Ruler's anger, my lady." He lowered his head, but she glimpsed the slight arching of one brow. He was baiting her. She was prepared to take his bait and use it for her own catch.

"I am sure whatever has happened, I can help soothe Casimir's temper on your behalf."

"We believe someone entered the ward last night and took

one of the humans in our charge." Aljon led Wilhelmine to the spot, still being cleaned beneath a now empty containment receptacle. "I don't know why anyone would do such a thing. Only a few Necanians have access. And what human could breach the Citadel?"

"Which human was released?" Wilhelmine knew the answer before he spoke it.

"The Wayward woman. The one Wolstan brought back from the northern camps." Aljon shrunk back when he spoke her husband's name.

"Wilder James," Wilhelmine said.

This was no human breach; this was most certainly a fellow Necanian. Hesperia did this. She wasn't quite sure how, but it didn't matter. That would be for Wolstan and his guards to determine. She would merely deliver the message.

Wilhelmine smoothed down the fabric of her silk jacket. "Don't worry Practitioner. I will speak to Casimir and make a report of this. I am certain this happened at no fault of yours. I will make sure the High Ruler points his rage in the right direction."

"Thank you, my lady," Aljon said and bowed. "Thank you."

Wilhelmine turned on her heel, heading directly to the High Ruler. Her mouth curved into a smirk as she rehearsed the conversation in her mind. The High Ruler would be angry at this betrayal, but she would be the hero of the tale, the one who discovered the mutinous plot and saved him from humiliation. Thoughts of his gratitude had her almost floating down the hallways and up the stairwells all the way to his tall, black door.

CHAPTER 36

WILDER

Wilder repeatedly glanced back at Declan sleeping in the rear seat as she drove bumpy, disintegrating roads away from Hope City, toward home. Hesperia kept her eyes toward the sky, watching for Necanian transport vehicles. They were quite the trio on the run. Wilder might have laughed at the absurdity of the situation if the reality wasn't so terrifying.

"I do not like being so out in the open," the Necanian said.

"Do you think they found out about the escape already?" Wilder clenched the steering wheel.

"I am sure they have. Perhaps not that Declan is missing, but Aljon and his technicians will know that you are gone. It will not take long to realize that I am gone as well. The real question is how much time it will take for them to build up the courage to tell my brothers."

"What will they do?" Wilder asked, not really wanting to know.

"Casimir will kill Aljon, or at least the technicians who should have been guarding the ward. He will search the

Citadel, and if they find our way of escape, they will search the Colony." Hesperia's eyes lowered.

"Will they destroy the Colony? Kill Matthew?"

Hesperia shook her head slowly. "No, I do not think he will. At least not right away. Too many in the city think of the Colony with pity and believe Casimir feels the same. It would raise suspicion for him to attack it outright if they find no proof of treachery there."

"Can't your brother fabricate proof?" Wilder found it hard to believe Casimir wouldn't blaze a trail of revenge, burning down anything and anyone standing in his way.

"My brother, the High Ruler, prides himself on his control —of others and himself. He will temper his anger with patience because it will be necessary. Especially with a Sacrament so close. There is more at play than one city and plans bigger than one Wayward woman."

Wilder snickered. "I don't know if I should be relieved or offended."

Hesperia looked at her. "Casimir is also arrogant. He does not believe your people to be a real threat. He views very little as a threat. He will proceed carefully. Losing two captives and my loyalty are not worth losing all he has plotted for the future."

"So maybe I am a little relieved." Wilder chuckled again—a nervous giggle as she squeezed the steering wheel tighter.

A weak smile tipped Hesperia's lips for a moment, then faded. "Make no mistake, he will kill us when he finds us, and he will be glad to do it."

Wilder swallowed down a deep breath of fear. "Then we need to keep him from finding us." *Or at least from getting to us before we have a chance at defending ourselves.*

Declan grunted and groaned from the back.

Wilder studied him from the rearview mirror. He pulled his

knees up toward his chest like he was in pain. She stretched her arm back and touched her hand to his leg. "We'll be home soon. Rest."

"Wilder!" Hesperia exclaimed and pointed ahead of them, just to the side of the road.

Wilder followed her gesture. Behind piles of debris and collapsing concrete walls, shadows ran. There were at least three ducking and jogging around through the remnants of this forgotten town.

Wilder resisted the urge to hit the gas and speed out of there. Declan had talked about his treks to the city in detail. He had told her every turn in the road, every safe place, and every spot which required caution. They were about three hours outside of the city, and that meant these were Ridge Runners— a lawless people with no true home. They weren't friends nor were they enemies, but they could easily become the latter if she didn't play this smart.

"Are we in danger?" Hesperia asked

"I'm not sure yet." No sooner had the words left her mouth when she saw a man with a shaved head and long beard step out into the road about a hundred feet in front of her. He held an automatic rifle. Knives were strapped to his belt, and a handgun sat in a holster on his hip. There was nowhere to turn and no room to speed around him. She considered running right over him but caught sight of his men waiting in the wings. While she couldn't be sure of their number, she imagined they were as heavily armed as he was. The man didn't flinch, well aware she would have no choice but to stop.

"Don't say a word," Wilder whispered to Hesperia as she pushed her foot against the brake and slowed the jeep to a stop about twenty feet from the man.

He didn't speak. He didn't aim the rifle he was holding. He just stared.

Wilder heard other guns cock nearby. She didn't move.

The man looked from her to Hesperia. His hand tensed as he took a step forward.

"You lost?" he finally asked. His voice was gruff and solemn.

Wilder sat up a little straighter. "No, I'm on my way home."

"Home? Her kind only have one home around these parts, and it's in the opposite direction." He pointed the rifle toward Hesperia.

The Necanian tensed, and her shimmering flesh dimmed as her eyes began to darken. Wilder touched her friend's hand.

"She's with me, and we are going to *my* home," Wilder replied, steeling her words. "We don't want any trouble."

"And you think I do?" He smirked, still taking slow steps toward them.

"I know what you are. We don't have any goods or weapons. Nothing to trade or steal. I'm just trying to get my husband back to Beartooth."

The man stopped. "Beartooth?"

Wilder nodded.

"I know a man from that camp."

Declan groaned in the backseat. He moved to sit up, and Wilder turned.

The man cocked his gun and aimed it. "Don't move."

"Noah," Declan grunted, leaning his head back against the seat. His eyes squinted in resistance to the late morning sun. He pressed a hand to his chest like he was trying to push back some pain.

"Declan?" The man, Noah, lowered his gun again, eyeing the backseat. "We heard you were dead."

"I was," Declan replied with heavy breaths.

Wilder glared at Noah. "We need to get him home."

Noah looked over Declan again. She wasn't sure if he was

considering her husband with curiosity, concern, or disdain. When he turned to Hesperia again, the disdain was definite. "Declan wouldn't be caught dead with a Necanian," Noah said then spit on the ground.

"She helped us escape. She saved us both." Wilder squeezed Hesperia's hand again. "She isn't like the others."

Noah laughed. "They are all the same, sweetheart."

"I'm not your sweetheart, and they aren't all the same. What's it to you if I bring her to Beartooth?" Heat rushed to Wilder's cheeks and down her arms. "Whether you believe it or not, she is helping us, and helping you."

"I don't need *her* help," Noah replied.

"You soon might," Wilder retorted.

"Or you might need mine." Declan finished her thought, his eyes closed, and his jaw clenched.

"You don't look like you can even help yourself," Noah said. "Besides, we do fine all on our own out here."

"That'll change." Wilder looked straight into Noah's brown eyes. "The Necanians have plans. They are coming for the northern camps, and I'm guessing they'll come for you, too."

Noah furrowed his brow then swallowed slow. "Let them come."

"Let us go." Wilder's glare never flinched from Noah's dingy face.

He held her gaze for about fifteen seconds then shifted his eyes to Declan once more. His face softened a touch. "We won't stop you." He backed away from the jeep then held up a hand. "Put your weapons away, boys."

Gravel and rocks tumbled all around them as twenty or so men revealed themselves.

"Thank you." Wilder nodded and put the jeep back in gear then hit the gas, happy to leave them behind her. Wilder didn't relax and possibly didn't even breathe until they were far enough away so that she couldn't see Noah or the other Ridge Runners in the rearview mirror any longer. She kept glancing on all sides for another three miles.

"They won't be following," Declan croaked from the backseat.

Wilder's heart leaped at the sound of his voice, though it seemed to take all the strength he had regained just to sit up and speak. She longed to touch his hand or his face, but she kept her hands on the steering wheel and her focus on getting him home.

"Who were those men?" Hesperia asked.

"Ridge Runners," Declan replied in a raspy whisper.

The Necanian seemed puzzled. "I have never heard my brother speak of humans living so close to the city."

"Maybe your brother doesn't know as much as he thinks he does," Wilder said. "But it's curious he wouldn't. Your brother doesn't seem the type to not know who his neighbors are. And why not go after the closest threat first?"

"I know my brother. Either he does not know of these Ridge Runners, or he has a reason not to cull them."

"Could he be afraid of them?" Wilder asked. "They *are* well armed."

Hesperia tilted her head, considering. "Since arriving in this world, my brother has dealt with many types of humans, including those who were well armed and quite dangerous. He never showed fear for any of them. I would not think it would be any different with these men."

"What reason could he have, then?" Wilder glanced at Declan in the mirror. He appeared to have drifted back to sleep. His chest rose and fell in shuddering breaths.

"I do not know," Hesperia answered. "But the way that man looked at me suggests they would not be on Casimir's side—at least not by their choice."

"Would they join ours?" Wilder wondered to herself out loud.

"He seems like the type of man who is only on his own side," Hesperia observed.

Wilder silently agreed. But a man like Noah, like his crew, could prove useful in the fight that she knew would be coming sooner rather than later. The Ridge Runners owned more weapons and held more fierce strength than those in her own camp.

Knowing their usefulness didn't mean that she trusted them. Declan hadn't seemed to, either. But trust might be a luxury they couldn't afford.

CHAPTER 37
WILHELMINE

T he black door creaked open. Wilhelmine took a deep breath and smoothed the fabric of her dress. She lifted her head high and pulled her shoulders back as she entered Casimir's office.

"High Ruler," she said with a curtsy.

Casimir turned from the window with a sneer. "I do not remember requesting a meeting."

"My apologies, brother." Wilhelmine looked to see if Casimir would flinch at the endearment. He didn't, and that meant his mood toward her was fair. She could proceed. "I hate to interrupt, but I come with troubling news."

Casimir's expression barely shifted to one of curiosity with the slightest tensing of his lips. "What news?"

"I happened to come upon Practitioner Aljon this morning, and there seems to have been a situation in the harvesting ward." Wilhelmine paused. The High Ruler's eyes widened a touch, and his demeanor darkened. "It seems the Wayward woman has escaped."

Casimir growled. "Who let this happen?"

"I am simply the messenger, dear brother..."

"Felix!" Casimir brushed past her to call for his servant, who bowed at the door. "Have Wolstan here immediately!"

"I am sure my husband has yet to be told of the breech or he would certainly be here himself," Wilhelmine offered. In truth she cared little for Wolstan or his reputation. He was a means to an end in the life she wanted. But the High Ruler's feelings about familial loyalty must be placated. It was why her next piece of information would certainly bring out his full wrath. "But that is not all."

Casimir turned back toward her.

"I am greatly disturbed to be the one to have to tell you more sour news but..."

"Spit it out!"

Wilhelmine clenched her fists at his impatient outburst. "Your sister is also missing this morning."

"Brother," Wolstan said as he marched into the room. "I just received word regarding Wilder James." He looked to Wilhelmine, just noticing her presence behind his brother. "Wife." He politely bowed, but she read the suspicion in his eyes.

"Our sister is *also* missing," Casimir hissed.

"Hesperia?" Wolstan stood straighter. "She couldn't have done this."

"*Of course* she did this," Wilhelmine interjected smoothly. "We are all well aware of her affinity for humans. Her servant said she even had tea with Ms. James just yesterday."

"You would accuse the sister of the High Ruler, one above your station, of such treachery against her own brothers?" Casimir's irises pooled with red.

Wilhelmine closed her eyes for just a second, long enough to subdue her own anger and remain in control of her senses in a room where she had the most to lose. "I mean no disrespect.

Hesperia is my sister as well, and I care for her." It took much effort to not choke on the words. "I only mean that it is not outside the realm of possibility that this Wayward woman somehow preyed on Hesperia's newfound empathy and used her."

Casimir stood for a moment, quiet, contemplative. He adjusted the cuff of his sleeve when he addressed Wolstan. "How is it your wife came upon such news before you, brother? How is it my general was not the first one at my doorstep this morning?"

Wilhelmine bowed her head. She wouldn't dare make eye contact with either brother in this moment. But she could not keep the smirk from twisting the corner of her lips. Had she curried favor with Casimir? Surely the High Ruler would reward her keen awareness and boldness.

"I am sorry, brother. I was attending another matter."

Casimir spoke dangerously low. "What could possibly have been more important than a security breech in the Citadel?"

Wolstan cleared his throat. Wilhelmine had rarely seen her husband appear nervous. He was always the picture of duty, loyalty, and power. It was the reason she tolerated him. Oh, she had once coveted him. Enough to marry him. Enough to settle for him though he was not High Ruler. He was the best that a Necanian female from her class could hope for—better, even. He was handsome enough, possibly more so than his brother. But she didn't care about attraction. She cared about position, and she would not let even her husband jeopardize her standing before the High Ruler.

"The ward was not the only breech," Wolstan responded, finally making eye contact with the High Ruler.

Casimir's nostrils flared, and his muscles tensed. His claws bled to crimson as he waited for Wolstan to continue.

"The man in the dungeon. He was freed as well."

Casimir looked ready to strike, but instead he walked to the large window and stared out at the city below.

"How is it that the great Necanian war general was thwarted in his own home?" Wilhelmine hissed at her husband. This was her chance to overstep even him in favor with Casimir. She would speak for her High Ruler; she would put words to the anger he must be feeling.

"Silence!" Casimir crossed back toward her in three quick steps, backhanding her with such force that she was almost knocked off her feet.

Her skin stung. Droplets of warm metallic liquid dribbled onto Wilhelmine's bottom lip. A chill flooded her body. The cold which signaled her darker features were surfacing. Rage teemed beneath her skin. She took deep breaths to tame the emotion.

"You have no place to speak such things. Where is your loyalty to your husband?" Casimir tugged his jacket back into perfect place. "Would you betray me so easily, as well?"

"Never," she responded softly. She glanced toward Wolstan, whose own scales had dimmed and saw his eyes blaze red. "It was not my intent to seem disloyal. My own frustration at these events and fears of what it could mean for your plans got the better of me, High Ruler." She bowed her head lower.

"Perhaps missing the next Sacrament will remind you of the importance of self-control."

Wilhelmine jerked up. Her heart thudded and pulsed icy blood through her veins until her translucent scales were gray. She wanted to scream. She wanted to claw their staring eyes out. She was foolish to think the High Ruler would show her favor over his brother. She would not make that mistake again; not without a more tangible foundation. "Of course," she replied.

"Good." Casimir turned back to Wolstan. "Our sister must have been behind this. The human woman could not have known about our captive. No other Necanian would dare such mutiny."

"To what end, brother? Hesperia would not seek to overthrow you."

"Our sister has grown weak. Your wife was correct in one thing: Hesperia's affinity for these humans has not faded as we thought. I hoped the situation with that boy would be enough to curb her appetite for their ways."

"What would you have me do?" Wolstan inquired.

"Send a search party to look for them. I can't imagine they have gotten far." Casimir walked back to his window. "And be sure to check the Colony. Hesperia would need assistance...but temper any violence. The next Sacrament is too close to create a controversy among the citizens. But do increase security around the dome. When they are found, bring them back to the Citadel, and I will deal with them personally."

"Yes, brother." Wolstan pressed his fist to his chest in salute, punctuating the gesture with a curt nod of his head before signaling for Wilhelmine to exit with him.

She obeyed without a word.

When they stepped out into the hall, the black door closed, and Wolstan wrapped a strong hand around her slender neck. He lifted her so that her toes barely touched the marble floor and pushed her against the hard, cold wall. She clawed at his hand, trying to break free of his grip so she could breathe again.

He leaned close, his face a mere inch from her own. "If you ever try to betray me like that again, I will kill you." His voice was full of malice but quiet and even—each word laced with a pitiless sincerity. He squeezed once more than released her and walked away.

Wilhelmine gasped. Her throat ached as she inhaled deep breaths.

Footsteps caught her attention as a servant bustled around the corner and out of her sight. Wilhelmine stood herself up and smoothed her hair until not a strand was out of place. She would not be humiliated. Not like this. They would never again remind her of her place as less than. She was not less than—not less than Wolstan and not less than Hesperia. She was more Necanian. She was more loyal, more devout, and she would prove it to them. She would be glad to kill Hesperia in the process.

Wilhelmine touched the silver ring on her temple. She ran her fingers over the smooth ridge that had been etched into her scales. She would get her revenge, and Casimir would be glad of it. He would see she was worthy and that his sister was merely a transgression to finally be erased.

CHAPTER 38
WILDER

The sun had long set when the broken asphalt and gravel roads turned to dirt trails through the tall pine trees. Though it was already colder in the mountains, Wilder cracked her window so she could inhale the scent of home. The smell of the trees and dirt comforted her, grounded her. The stars, shimmering and singing in the indigo sky, led her, calling her toward her roots. They were her stars. They were Declan's stars.

Her husband still slept in the back seat. They'd stopped twice to get him to drink some water and to stretch her sore legs. She'd kept the pitstops short because the longing for home deepened with each mile and because each glance at him had stabbed her heart with anxious pangs. But now they were so close—close to Beartooth, their bed, and hope.

She slowed the jeep around a curve which took her past their lookouts. Two more curves in the trail then up the slight hill, and Beartooth came into her view. A lump formed in her throat. Her eyes watered with joyful tears.

"We're home, Declan," she whispered to him over her shoulder.

He groaned incoherently, but she felt like he knew. In the rearview mirror, she watched a peace wash over his features and the expansion of his chest with a deep intake of the air of home.

The camp lay silent and still as Wilder pulled the jeep to a stop in front of her cabin. "They won't know what to think of you," she told Hesperia who was looking around her, eyes wide in awe.

Hesperia turned to Wilder and nodded. "I understand. I will do what I must to set them at ease."

Wilder opened the vehicle's door, and as she stepped her foot onto the dusty earth, she heard the snap of a twig nearby. She turned her head to the left to find Sam, rifle aimed.

"Wilder?" he asked, lowering his gun, blinking his eyes.

Wilder smiled. "Hi, Sam."

Her friend stepped forward and, before she could fully stand up, he wrapped her in a tight hug. She chuckled. Hugging wasn't like Sam.

Sam pulled back to look at her. "We worried we wouldn't see you again."

"Me too. But I'm not the only one you get to see again." She gestured toward the back seat. "Help me."

Sam gasped when Wilder opened the rear door. "Declan?" He looked from Wilder to her husband and back again. "How?"

"A miracle." It was the best way Wilder could explain it.

Sam stood tall and looked toward the other cabins. "We need some help here! Wilder's home!"

Suddenly the windows and doorways lit up like fireflies in summertime. Doors flew open and residents emptied into the dirt street.

"Wilder?!" A deep voice, familiar and reminiscent of rest, called above all the growing commotion.

"Solomon." Wilder turned, scanning for the old man.

He jogged toward her, tears in his eyes and arms raised, ready to embrace her. He pulled her to his chest, and she could hear and feel his weighty breaths—a mingle of relief and joy blowing against her head and face. "You're home."

She nodded her head against him. Before she could reply she was pulled to someone else. Korah.

Her best friend sobbed into her shoulder. Then she pulled back and wiped her eyes and smirked. "You are never allowed to leave again. Never. Ever."

"Never," Wilder repeated through her own happy tears.

Small arms wrapped around her waist, Neema and Finley. She kissed the tops of their heads. Then felt a hand on her shoulder. It was Melvina, who hugged her as well. They all swarmed her with welcome and gladness and it was gloriously overwhelming. She laughed and cried and then remembered.

"Declan," Wilder muttered.

"Help me get him," Sam said.

"What do you..." Solomon began but stopped himself at the sight of a familiar figure being pulled from the back. "How is this?"

"It's a miracle," Sam repeated Wilder's explanation.

"Let's get him inside," Melvina said, leading the way up Wilder's cabin steps.

Just then Hesperia stepped out of the jeep. She had gone unnoticed in the fury of emotion and shock. She shut the door and all attention drew to her white hair and opaline scales shimmering in the moonlight that filtered through the trees. She kept her eyes downcast and clasped her hands in front of her.

"This is Hesperia," Wilder said to break the tense silence. "She was our miracle."

Hesperia jerked her eyes toward Wilder at the final word. Both women shared a knowing glance, one of friendship and trust.

"Then it is good to meet you, H...Hesperia?" Korah was the one to step forward. She held her hand out to the Necanian. When Hesperia took the offering, Korah pulled her into an embrace. "Thank you," she whispered with fresh tears.

Wilder chuckled, wondering by Hesperia's tense form if she had ever been hugged before. It brought a sort of tranquility to her heart to see her people respond as such—to trust her enough to welcome one so different, one they did not know. She hoped they would feel the same after she relayed Casimir's plot.

* * *

An hour later, Wilder was exhausted. They'd asked questions and she told them the basic story of reaching the Citadel and finding Declan. Melvina looked him over where he slept on their bed.

Their bed.

It felt surreal and wonderful; Declan, her husband who had died and who she had mourned was now back in their bed. *Sleeping* in their bed. Alive.

"And the Necanians?" Solomon asked. "What did you find out about their plans?"

"Can it wait until tomorrow?" Wilder yawned.

"Of course," Solomon replied with a nod.

"I'll bring you breakfast in the morning," Korah offered. "Or if you want something now I can..."

"Breakfast is fine," Wilder replied. "Rest is more important than food right now." She sat down on the side of her bed and took Declan's hand in hers.

Melvina sighed and sat up straight. "He's lucky." She looked to Wilder. "I don't know what they did to him, but his body is closer to death than I would have thought possible." She touched her pale, wrinkled fingers to the wounds on his head. "These look like puncture marks. I've never seen anything like them before."

"They are from the Sacrament," Hesperia whispered from the corner of the room where she stood silent and still.

"Sacrament?" Melvina stared at the Necanian, then back to Wilder.

"They fed on him...on his soul," Wilder explained.

The room froze. No one spoke. No one moved. No one breathed except Declan, his raspy inhales and exhales the only sound. Wilder brushed her fingers over his cheek, along his jaw and down his chest, resting her palm against the thumping of his heart.

She surveyed the room and perceived the questions in their wide eyes and furrowed brows. "Tomorrow," Wilder said, "I can explain everything tomorrow."

Each one conceded with a nod.

"We'll let you get some sleep." Melvina stood up. "You can stay with me," she said to Hesperia.

The Necanian put a hand to her chest and opened her mouth, glancing to Wilder with a raised brow.

"Melvina will take good care of you," Wilder offered her new friend.

Hesperia smiled slightly.

Melvina took her by the arm and led her out of the cabin. "We will make sure you are quite comfortable here."

When the two women were out of ear shot, Solomon spoke. "Are we sure we can trust her?"

"She risked everything to get us out of that place. I trust her with my life," Wilder replied.

"Then that's good enough for us." Korah hugged her friend again. She and Sam offered their goodnights and reluctantly left.

"And you, will you be okay?" Solomon asked Wilder.

"I have him home. What could be more okay than that?"

Solomon's brown face crinkled with a smile. He hugged Wilder and kissed the top of her head. "See you in the morning then."

"In the morning."

CHAPTER 39
HESPERIA

Hesperia silently stretched out on the cot Melvina had offered her. The blankets scratched. It wasn't nearly as plush as her bed in the Citadel, with satin sheets and down pillows. The room was much smaller too...dirtier. Dust layered the floor and table. It smelled of a hundred different scents she could not place. The air, inside and outside, held an aroma of sweetness and musk. It filled her lungs with a sensation she hadn't felt in a very long time—not since knowing a boy who'd told her stories and sang her songs.

What had she expected of Wilder's home? Humans in the city were stoic and controlled. Humans in the Colony were hollow. These humans, Wilder's people, were full of something—perhaps joy, love of life. Things Hesperia had only heard of.

Watching them embrace their friend and cry with relief had sent pangs through her vacant heart. Had it always been empty? For over one hundred years, she hadn't known the depths of its emptiness—not until that brief, shining season of fullness. For a glimmer of time, the void had been saturated.

Then her brother squeezed its contents out onto the marble floor of the Sacrament room.

But here she lay, and her insides were filling up again—bright and warm and terrifying. Would she bring the same fate down on Wilder that she had brought on the boy? No. She would do more. She would protect this woman who regarded her with grace and kindness.

She would betray her own brothers for someone she had only known a matter of days. It was a choice of life—a real and right life over death. A choice she had already made at Declan's cell to side with these humans even if it meant her own death. Hesperia was even more certain now than she had been then: better to die than the slow demise of being emptied again.

CHAPTER 40
DECLAN

S hadows swam around Declan's thoughts and dreams. Shadows, cold with dread and emptiness. They teased and taunted the beast that had awakened in his depths. It was the monster from the prison cell. But Declan was free now. Wasn't he? No. He wasn't free from the anger and fear that flooded the space where his soul had lived before the Necanian had consumed it.

His sweaty hands clenched cotton bedsheets. A tremor started in his gut and rippled outward until his entire body shook. The tremble turned to a quake, and he wrenched his head back, straining the muscles in his neck.

"Declan?" A soft whisper poked at his mind.

He recognized the voice. He wanted to yield to its comfort, but the monster wouldn't let him. It was dark, and in the dark, he couldn't be sure what was real. Was he still chained to that cell wall? Were Wilder and their home an illusion? He smelled the musty dampness of the underground walls and his own blood dripping by his nostrils. He tasted the copper of it in his mouth.

"Declan, it's okay," Wilder's voice cooed. A small hand touched his shoulder. His mind warred with what to do. The monster won, and Declan's eyes flew open. He jerked up.

She startled from his erratic movement. He saw her and he heard her, and he felt her, but too much of him was caught up in the nightmare. He couldn't make that part believe it *was* her. He tried, oh how he tried. He was desperate to fall into her arms, but the primal creature took charge of him. Like a man possessed, he leaped from the bed and knocked over a chair. What was he doing? He swiped the vase from the kitchen table and heard it shatter on the wooden floor.

The floor creaked behind him.

He grabbed a bowl from the nearby shelf and shifted enough to throw it toward the sound.

She gasped.

Declan turned in time to discover he'd barely missed hitting her with the dish, which slammed the wall and fell to the ground in tiny bits of broken ceramic. The shock quieted him long enough to comprehend it was truly her and not a hallucination. His bare toes twitched on the smooth, wood planks of the floor. Fire cracked and popped in the wood stove. The bergamot scent of her Earl Grey tea mingled in the air. He was in their cabin. He was really home.

Declan glanced around the space, his senses fully returning. Across the room, moonlight beamed through the window and glistened off a fresh tear that traced his wife's cheek. His insides shivered once again. His own tears responded in full force, wetting his face and blurring his vision. What had he almost done? What was happening to him?

Wilder took a step toward him. He shook his head and held up a hand, desperate for her to stop. He couldn't trust himself. The monster could take over again, and he didn't have any more strength to fight it.

She kept walking.

He stepped backward, trying to retreat from himself more than from her.

"Declan, it's okay."

"I...I..." The table stopped his escape, and he nearly collapsed onto it.

"Declan." She never looked away from his blurry eyes. Once within reach, she touched his arm, and when he didn't flinch, she touched his other arm. Wilder took his hands in both of hers. "It's okay."

The sound and feel of her sent a wave of love and grace crashing into him and it washed away the residual confusion in his tormented brain. "I'm so sorry," Declan wept. He fell forward into her. She led him back to the bed, supporting the brunt of his weight.

In bed, he turned onto his side—body and heart weary again. Wilder wrapped herself around him like a blanket of security. They held hands. He closed his eyes and began to drift back to sleep while her body shuddered with silent sobs behind him. He squeezed her hand, breathing with her until they fell asleep.

CHAPTER 41
WILDER

Wilder had woken up alone for one hundred and seventy-nine days. Each morning, she'd opened her eyes to an empty bed, and it had cracked her heart all over again. This morning, as she opened her eyes to bright, warm sunlight shining on Declan's sleeping face, the cracks in her heart began to seal. The sound of his breathing was like an offering of new life to her own fragile lungs. She wanted to reach out and touch him but stayed her hand instead. She wanted to whisper his name but remained silent. Last night's episode replayed in her mind; she didn't want to repeat it—didn't want to shock his frail mind.

Wilder sighed. She yawned. She stretched carefully so she wouldn't disturb him.

Declan grumbled. He slid his hand under his pillow before nestling into it. His eyes blinked open then circled around the room until they landed on Wilder's face. His lip twitched. "I'm sorry." His voice was hoarse.

Wilder took his hand in hers, brought it to her lips and

kissed it. His skin was cool and dry. She smiled at him, and a giggle started to form in her chest and rise up her throat. "I'm fine. It's my vase and bowl who really need the apology."

He chuckled softly. The mirth of it didn't reach his eyes, but she didn't know whether it was because it was a bad joke at a bad time, or because he'd been hollowed out—vital pieces stolen from his soul. Wilder prayed he would not be a living ghost like the other Sacrament survivors.

"Korah will be here soon with breakfast." Wilder moved to get out of bed but Declan didn't release the grip on her fingers.

"I love you." He leaned forward, mimicking her kiss by bringing chapped lips to rest on her hand.

"I love you more." Wilder bent forward and kissed his forehead, then his mouth. It was barely a touch, but it sent a spark jolting through her veins. He was here, and she could touch him and smell him and taste him and feel him and that was enough for today. More than enough. She hoped it would be enough for him—at least for the day.

* * *

Declan was quiet and reserved while they ate the bacon, hard-boiled eggs, and scones that Korah had brought. He'd flinched when Korah hugged him. It was momentary, and he settled into her friendly embrace, but it was there. He dove into the food with ferocity, but it seemed to sour for him after a few bites. He said his stomach needed to readjust. It made sense. He was weak—his movements slower and more calculated from pain and infirmity. She fought the fear whispering in her ear that she could lose him still. She could lose everyone still.

Wilder sipped the last bit of tea from her cup and stood up. "We should get to the council meeting. They'll be waiting for us."

"You should go without me." Declan stared at the glass of water in his hands.

"You are leader of this camp. You should be there," Wilder replied. "I want you there."

His hands trembled. He pushed the cup away and it tipped over. Water spilled over the table. Wilder grabbed a towel hanging near the sink to wipe it up.

Declan stood up, supporting his weight with a hand on the table. "I can't, Wild. I'm no use to anyone like this. I'm weak. I can't think straight. I can't control myself..."

"Declan..."

"I almost hurt you." The volume of his voice didn't raise so much as the tone changed, getting deeper, heavier.

She stopped her cleaning. "You didn't hurt me. And you don't have to lead, but they will want you there. They will want to know what you think. You can help even as you heal. It will take time."

"I can't help anyone. Don't you see that?" He pounded his fist against the table. "I'm broken..."

"Look around you!" Wilder raised her own voice, not in anger, but because she needed him to stop, to really hear her. "My favorite teacup, the chair on the porch, our clothes, the bum table leg. Our whole life is nothing but broken things once cast aside, but we made use of them, and we have cherished them. Just because something is broken doesn't mean it can't be fixed—be useful. You may feel fractured right now; I get that and it's okay to feel it, but you aren't finished yet. Far from it." Her chest tightened with each quick breath, and her legs wobbled beneath her at the ferocity of her own words.

A slow tear slid down Declan's face. His jaw clenched as he turned his eyes to stare straight into hers. "They took my soul, Wild."

Wilder's heart quaked at the brokenness in his voice. She

closed the gap between them, took his damp cheeks in her hands, and stared into his green eyes. With all the truth and strength she could muster, she replied, "Then you can have part of mine."

CHAPTER 42
DECLAN

The breeze carried an invigorating chill, and the bright sun warmed Declan's face. He squinted as they walked through the camp to the chapel where the elder council met. Aching muscles loosened with each step. He realized that threads of his frayed mind were tethered to the scents and sounds of home—the associations grounding him in the reality of his safety and freedom.

A squeal echoed across the way. Declan jerked his head.

"It's okay," Wilder whispered and squeezed his arm. She smiled and nodded to the left.

Declan turned in that direction. Neema and Finley were racing toward him. The two children crashed into him with full force, wrapping their small arms so tight around his waist he coughed. "Who are these kids?" Declan winked. "The ones I knew were three inches shorter, so these must be impostors."

Neema looked up at him and stuck out her tongue. "You know it's us!"

"You were gone a long time. We grew!" Little Finley exclaimed with hands on his hips.

"I *was* gone a long time," Declan replied with a lump forming in his throat. "And I missed you both."

"Of course, you did. We're too adorable not to miss," Neema said and giggled.

Declan tousled Finley's hair. "This is true."

"We need to get to our meeting," Wilder said with a laugh, extricating Declan from the children's grip. "You can come see Declan when we're done."

The children pouted but hugged Wilder, then let the couple go on their way.

"Griffin will want to see you, too," Wilder said to Declan, taking his hand.

It had been Griffin's first run. Declan remembered the young man trying to hide his fear when the jeep was blocked. Remembered him screaming when Declan was pulled away. Remembered him looking through the rear window before everything went black.

"You okay?"

"Yeah." He squeezed her hand, and she rested her head on his shoulder as they walked to the chapel. He *wanted* to be okay. Holding her hand, walking through this camp, it gave him hope that he could be, eventually. His mind and memories felt like muddled darkness, but there was a spark in the distance, calling him.

Stepping into the chapel, Declan tried to hide his trepidation and hold onto that spark instead. The night before, he had barely been conscious, but now, seeing his family, brought about a joy mixed with fearful sorrow. With every embrace, he teetered on the edge of screaming or shattering. He knew them and trusted them, but did he know or trust himself anymore? He sucked in deep breaths and tensed his muscles in an exhausting effort to maintain his composure.

"Let's sit." Wilder took his hand and the light and peace

rushed back in.

Declan inhaled another breath so long and deep it filled his lungs to capacity, stretching his rib cage to the point of pain. He released it and attempted to exhale his fears with the air as he sat down at the rectangular wooden table.

"It hasn't been the same without you," Solomon said to Declan.

Declan swallowed and nodded.

"Should we jump right in?" Melvina asked. "Small talk just seems like a luxury when there are so many important questions."

"I agree," Sam replied. He looked a different kind of worried—one Declan hadn't seen in his best friend before. He looked toward the Necanian at the table, and his jaw clenched. "What's going on?"

Wilder sighed and squeezed Declan's hand. He rubbed a thumb over her skin to offer some support.

Wilder glanced at Hesperia then spoke. "The Necanians are not what we thought...not exactly...not completely."

"The Sacrament you mentioned last night?" Melvina asked leaning forward and propping her elbows on the table.

Wilder nodded. "The Necanians feed on human souls. It is how they stay alive."

Declan tensed at the words, at the collective gasp of the council. He glanced at the Necanian who kept her head down. Was she ashamed or just anxious?

"The marks?" Melvina turned to Declan.

He touched the puncture wounds on the sides of his head but said nothing. What could he say? Forming the thoughts of the torture poked the beast residing in his hollow place. The act of uttering the words would surely release it or push his emotions off the ledge.

Solomon jumped in though, sparing Declan from having to

respond. "How could no one know this? How could they be doing this, and no one questions it, no one stops them?" Solomon's voice cracked in a mix of shock, anger, and grief.

"I don't know," Wilder said. "Hesperia?"

Barely lifting her gaze to anyone but Wilder, the Necanian opened her mouth to speak. Declan's wife called her a friend; she'd risked everything to save them. But he'd spent his entire life hating these beings and could barely stomach being at the same table with one, much less hearing what she would have to say on the matter of their murder of millions.

"Our species is very old," she began, "and we learned long ago that while some beings can be taken over with brute force, manipulation is easier and less costly to us. We wasted many other worlds far too quickly to reach that end, and my brother is determined to not make the same mistake on your world."

"Brother?" Korah asked.

"Hesperia is the sister to the High Ruler Casimir," Wilder explained.

The tension thickened. A heaviness settled in the silence.

"Please continue." Melvina looked at Hesperia with a wide, waiting, somehow still warm, stare.

The Necanian nodded sheepishly. "We became choice architects. When we first arrived on this world, every image of us, every interaction, was plotted and planned to create a perception which served our purposes. Subliminal nudges and small gestures of persuasion brought tiny moments of control which grew into the power we...they...now have."

"So you're con artists?" Declan grunted.

"It couldn't be that simple," Solomon argued. "You can't control an entire planet of free-thinking people with just manipulation."

"You assume all people are free-thinking and that we started with the whole planet in mind," Hesperia replied gently. "We started by showing ourselves heroes with the intent only to help you. We built relationships with those in power. We promised *them* more power while offering the world only more peace. More primitive groups who could not be controlled in this way were culled. Those who were forgotten or hated, followed. Any voices that rebelled were secretly silenced until no more voices rebelled. The offer of peace and comfort is so very seductive, most rarely recognize it as the form of fear it truly is."

"But we rebelled," Wilder said. "The people in the mountains didn't relent to Necanian control."

"No." Hesperia's mouth curved into the most subtle hint of a smile. "No, you didn't relent. You didn't relinquish your love or truth or faith, but you also didn't truly rebel. Your numbers were small enough and your voices quiet enough that no one even bothered to listen or watch you."

"Then why attack us now?" Sam asked, brows furrowed.

"The Necanians need food," Wilder said. "And until they are fully self-sufficient on this planet, they can't afford to keep feeding on people in their cities now that they have expended other sources like prisons."

Questions rose from every seat at the table. How long can they feed on us? How many Necanians are there? What do you mean by fully self-sufficient?

Wilder lifted her hand, and everyone fell silent. Declan's chest puffed with pride at the leader she had become. Truth be told, she was always a leader here, she'd always just led from the background.

"Long story short, the Necanians plan to grow people like food. An agriculture of incubators and stasis containers that steal any real life completely away." A tear peeked from the corner of Wilder's eye but never fell.

Everyone stared in shock. In little more than a half century, the entire planet had succumbed to the hunger of a species they'd thought came to save them from war, famine, and disease. Memories of his parents in hushed attic gatherings flashed again through Declan's brittle mind. They had known. If not everything, they knew enough and had endangered themselves, sacrificed themselves to stop it. If they had told him, would he have been able to do something? In the years since their death, could he have saved more people, done more, said more?

Wilder must have sensed the apprehension tightening his muscles because she placed a gentle hand on his arm. When he turned to look at her, she offered him a soft, reassuring smile.

"We need to run," Korah said. She looked down at her hand resting on her rounded stomach. Was she pregnant? Part of Declan wanted to jump up and hug his friends and congratulate them, but congratulations felt ill-timed after all that had just been revealed. A sudden ache in his stomach kept him seated.

"We pack everyone up and we move north," Sam said. "Forget the caves. We go farther. Shoot, we make our way to Alaska if we have to."

Hesperia was the one to respond. "It will buy you time. But it will not save you. My brother will not stop until—"

"Someone else will fight," Sam interrupted. "Someone else can fight it. Someone stronger."

"Who?" Wilder asked. "Who exactly will fight? Does anyone else even know what we know?"

"Then we tell them." Declan's throat felt sore and dry as he spoke. "We get on the radio, and we send messages. We tell everyone we can think of. If people know the truth, they will fight."

"If they believe it," Hesperia said. When everyone turned to her waiting for more, she explained, "The High Ruler and the

Lieutenants leading the other domed cities have done well in creating a people who do not question them. They have made themselves look to be the light... people may not be able to fathom that they might actually be the darkness."

"Then we show people the darkness," Solomon said. "We show people the truth."

"How?" Melvina asked.

"We set the captives free," Wilder suggested. "We can send messages to whoever will listen. We can't control what they'll do, we can only hope they'll believe us and be willing to help. And then we go into that Citadel, and we get every man, woman, and child out of there. We can't allow them to spend any more time than necessary in those prisons."

Declan shuddered at the memory of being in his cell.

"What good will that do if the Necanians will only come for them—for us—again?" Korah asked.

"Can we broadcast this Sacrament?" Solomon asked. "Perhaps others will see and believe. You can lead them out of the dome."

"There might be a way." Hesperia sat up straighter and clasped her hands together. "Casimir will retaliate. He will fight because his pride won't let him relent or retreat, but the Necanians are outnumbered. If he can't control humanity, he can't overpower it."

"Wouldn't it be better to just kill him?" Declan asked quietly. He couldn't be the only one thinking it.

"Violence will only beget more violence. Innocent people will get hurt," Melvina offered.

Declan twisted his wedding band around his finger. "Innocent people are already getting hurt, and I'm not sure we can avoid raising weapons."

"We have to be better," Solomon said. "If a fight comes for us, then we will certainly defend ourselves. But we can't draw first blood. The Necanians rule by fear. Stirring more won't bring anyone freedom. We have to trust that the truth can do the work. I am sure I can quote a scripture or two on the matter." The old man raised an eyebrow and grinned.

"That won't be necessary." Declan shook his head. "I'm certainly not looking for a fight. I don't think I'd even have the strength." His insides tumbled at the admission. Wilder touched his leg under the table. He rested a hand on hers. "But some others might not agree."

"Wolf Point and the Ridge Runners?" Wilder asked. Declan nodded, and she continued. "I tried to tell Noah. He didn't believe me then, and I doubt he would believe me now."

That sounded like Noah. He mostly only worried about himself and likely wouldn't help them anyway. "We'll just have to be clear. This is a rescue, not a revolt."

Was it all too optimistic? To think they could breech the city and the Citadel without a fight? To think they could put the Necanian plans into such upheaval without battle?

"It'll be a different kind of battle," Wilder said, reading his expression. "But we will have to be ready for anything. We'll have to be smart and time everything right."

"Two weeks," Hesperia muttered, looking at her hands.

"What?" Korah asked.

"The next Sacrament is in two weeks. The Necanian High Council and all of the servants will be in the ceremonial chambers. There will be very few guards keeping watch."

Even after everything she'd done, all the information she was giving them, Declan didn't trust her. He wondered if all her help was really some ploy. Was she just a spy sent by her brother?

Wilder trusted her though. And Declan trusted Wilder.

Wilder nodded her head once, then said, "Then that's when we'll go."

CHAPTER 43
WILDER

Wilder warmed her hands near the wood stove. In the two days they'd been home, the cool air had turned frigid. Gray clouds now hid the golden autumn sun, and snow drifted down in fluffy white specks. It wasn't abnormal for snow to come this time of year in the mountains.

Wilder considered it a blessing—a cleansing of sorts. Hopefully the snow continued to fall until it blanketed the whole of her world and covered her soul, just as serene and fresh as the winter tide.

"Korah sent me home with fresh bread," Declan said, closing the cabin door and brushing white flakes off his coat.

"Dinner is just about done," Wilder said, stirring the mixture in the cast-iron pot. "The bread will go perfectly with this vegetable soup."

Declan sniffed the pot's contents, then kissed her cheek. "It smells delicious." He set the warm loaf of bread, still wrapped in a checkered towel, on the table then grabbed two plates and two bowls from the kitchen shelf.

It was all so normal—like every evening supper since their wedding—quiet and peaceful.

But now it was somehow alarming.

The world wasn't normal anymore. The world wasn't quiet or peaceful, and Wilder felt out of sorts with the dichotomy. Should she relish this gift of homespun ordinary while they had it—a gift she'd begged God for night after night when she thought Declan was dead? Or should she turn their mealtime conversation to the Necanians, prisoners, Citadel, and Sacraments?

"Korah said she's starting to feel the baby kick," Declan said as he handed her a bowl.

Wilder ladled soup into it. They hadn't yet spoken of Korah and Sam's baby, or set-aside dreams for a baby of their own. Talk of alien overlords might be an easier one.

"That's nice," she replied, filling her own bowl with steaming stew before sitting at the table across from her husband. She picked up her spoon, but then just stared at it.

"It's okay to be happy for them." Declan reached across the table and took her hand in his.

"I know." Wilder turned her gaze to their intertwined fingers. She inhaled her anguish and fought to keep her words from erupting with the exhale.

Declan's brow wrinkled a bit just before his lip curled into a half smile. "It's a good thing."

Wilder nodded. "It is. But..."

"But we hadn't..."

"We can't." Her correction was sharper than she meant it to be.

Declan's eyes widened. His fingers trembled against hers.

"The Necanians. They ran tests on me...when they thought they could use me for their breeding program..."

Declan squeezed her hand, and her trembling grew stronger.

Wilder's chest burned and heaved. She closed her eyes in an effort to shut out the reeling of the room and her emotions. "They ran tests, and I can't. I'm...I'm barren." Saying the word out loud was more than her cracking heart could bear. The guilt and sadness spilled out with a sob.

Declan rushed out of his chair and knelt in front of her. He pulled her against him as she cried. The released confession broke yet another chamber of emotion in her still crippled heart. Though the deluge only lasted a minute, the exhaustion in her body and ache in her head made it seem like she'd cried for hours.

She nestled her damp face against Declan's chest. "It seems a silly thing to worry over now when we may not even survive the winter. When we just got one miracle, it feels selfish to still want another."

"It's not selfish." Declan pushed her back enough to look in her face. "If anything, we know now that miracles happen. Big miracles can happen." Tears gleamed in his eyes.

"It's not even something we should think about right now." She wiped her face.

"Why? Because the Necanians want us dead?" He tucked a curl behind her ear and held her chin between his thumb and finger. "Dreams for the life we want are the only thing that will keep us going."

"Even if the dream is a foolish one?"

"It's not foolish to keep hoping for a miracle. I mean, you're looking at a very handsome one right now." His mouth quirked upward.

Wilder laughed. "It's true. You are a handsome miracle." She leaned forward and kissed his cheek.

"A handsome miracle. I like it." He chuckled.

"It's not a nickname that's going to become a thing. You know that right?"

"Oh, we'll see about that." He winked, then pulled her back into his chest. He kissed her head and whispered, "I love you."

When he was seated again, Wilder dipped her spoon in her bowl and watched him tear a chunk of bread from Korah's perfect loaf. This was their normal—the warm safety of the life they'd made together—a mixing of love, pain, joy, grief, and peace—all meshing haphazardly together into a home. She took a bite and smiled as Declan wiped a dribble from his stubbly chin. *Her handsome miracle.* If God gave her one miracle, perhaps He would be generous enough to give her a second? Even if He didn't, was her hope in the miracle, or in *Him*?

* * *

Wilder mulled over miracle thoughts as she lay in bed, unable to sleep. The moonlight sparkled off the fresh snow outside her window. Declan breathed in a calm cadence beside her. Occasionally a mumble or groan broke his rhythm. He would flinch or twitch, and pain would flash across his face.

"I'm here. You're safe," she cooed in his ear, careful not to get too close or touch him.

The past two nights were devoid of outbursts. His trauma twitched below the surface of his skin and in the mumbling of his mind, but it didn't get him out of bed. The possibility, though, was just a breath away. While sleeping, he was least in control and the most unaware of the differences between reality and the frightful memories still plaguing him.

Wilder turned over to watch him, her handsome miracle. He'd survived and come back to her. He was still coming back to her, and as painful as this imperfect reunion was, she was grateful for it. She hated to see him broken, but she would remain with him in that brokenness. *In sickness and in health.* She had meant those words. She meant them still. And she knew he offered her the same promise in her own barrenness.

Was that a miracle too? To have and to hold someone who would take you in your broken and barren imperfections, who would find joy in a life void of certain desires because it was a life with you? Rarely noticed miracles—small or wrapped in a very ordinary packaging—filled her life. They were ever-present. They knit her to something—someone—stronger than herself.

"Knit him back together," she prayed into the moonlight, then closed her eyes, offering the rest of her prayers in silence.

CHAPTER 44
CASIMIR

C asimir studied a diagram on his desk. It was plans for a new harvesting ward. A renovation of an old hospital that could house fifty times the capacity of their small third-floor experiment. He told Wolstan, "I want you to go to the Colony."

"I thought you wanted to wait until after the Sacrament?"

"I've decided these treasonous actions must be dealt with swiftly. Waiting only gives them more time to sow discord. With snow in the north halting troops from retaliation against the people in the mountains, the Colony is our one recourse." Casimir walked to the picture window and stared down at the tiny humans who bustled about, oblivious to reality, warped and twisted into the truth he'd offered. "I can handle the people, should they even question. Their disdain and dehumanization of the others—the societal lepers in that Colony—will most likely keep them from even looking."

"And if they look?" Wolstan asked cautiously, flinching when Casimir turned toward him.

"Then, as always, we will make sure they see what we want them to—a danger to their way of life and security."

Wolstan smirked. "Yes, High One."

Casimir nodded curtly in response. A smirk of his own was playing at his lips, but he let it fade. "However, handle this with care and quiet. We cannot be made to seem like brutes. We are the Bringers of Peace, the Saviors of Mankind, after all." He scoffed at the nicknames given to his people. It brought fond memories of their arrival on this world and how quickly the humans had fallen into his grip.

He'd built such a brilliant charade, so bright a glamour that even those who questioned could never pinprick its surface enough to disrupt the illusion. Some spent too much time fighting the wrong enemy—the seen one versus the unseen. Perhaps others felt the truth—dark and foreboding beneath the veneer—but they couldn't grip it and bring it into the light until it was too late. Except...

Cold ran down Casimir's arm, and his skin darkened a shade. Except for this Wayward woman, this Wilder James. She was a problem. She knew and had seen too much, and she had gotten away. Others had gotten away. These people in the mountains were proving to be a problem. He shouldn't have let them exist this long. He should have hunted them decades ago like the pitiful prey they had always been.

"And, brother," Casimir said, "when can we do something about the rest of the Wayward?" He felt the tension in his muscles, the disgust and frustration building at the thought of letting those vermin live even one day longer than required.

"Soon," Wolstan replied. "The snow in the north is likely to only last another few days, and once it is gone, we will be able to reach the deeper camps with more ease. If we go now, we likely won't be able to hit every camp with the force desired to take them out all at once."

His brother had a point. "Which means they can inform the others and retreat to shelter, prolonging their capture and my annoyance?" Casimir loathed the weakness of his people in the colder temperatures and denser forests. Necanian bodies weren't built for freezing temperatures. They became too sluggish, reflexes slowed, and metabolisms increased, making their hunger insatiable as their systems labored to regulate. It would be little more than discomfort outside of battle. But they had learned early on that discomfort turned disastrous in a fight. Casimir had weighed the cost of ignoring this weakness now and, while he was willing to lose Necanian foot soldiers, he wasn't willing to just all out lose. Too much was at stake. In this instance, patience would prove virtuous.

"Yes, High One. But I am mobilizing our best soldiers, and the moment we have an open window we will be ready." Wolstan appeared confident, nevertheless Casimir noted the twitch of his jaw.

"See to it that you are. I'd like to have this whole sordid business wrapped up sooner rather than later." The darkening cold coursed through Casimir's entire body, and the room tinted red.

"I live only to serve and please you. We will not fail you again." Wolstan placed a fist on his chest and bowed his head.

"No... you won't."

CHAPTER 45
HESPERIA

Hesperia had spent most of her past few days at Beartooth in Melvina's cabin. Her body did not agree with the sharp cold. It made her muscles lethargic and her mind foggy. Melvina had given her a sweater and blanket. The warmth coating her skin was worth the itchiness of the fabric as she contented herself with sitting by the fire. Wilder visited her each day, checking in to make sure she was comfortable.

Hesperia was discombobulated in this very different place. It wasn't just the terrain or foliage. It was a life that contrasted with everything she was. Wilder's people were a people out of time and step with what the world had become. It was glorious and frightening. Could she ever really make a place for herself here—in a world like this? She'd lost her place among her own people. Now she was out of time and step with herself.

"Would you like some tea?" Melvina asked, holding a whistling kettle in her hands.

"Yes, that would be lovely," Hesperia replied, holding her pallid fingers closer to the warm flames.

Melvina brought two cups over. "May I join you?"

Hesperia nodded. "Of course."

She and Melvina had shared several conversations by the fire during her stay. They'd shared histories. She'd answered questions about Necanian culture, and Melvina had taught her about herbal remedies. They'd discussed faith and shared heartbreak. This older human woman was half her age in years, but so full of wisdom. Hesperia felt safe in her gracious kindness.

"Are you warm enough? I know the cold doesn't suit you." Melvina sipped her tea.

"I am fine, thank you."

Melvina cocked her head and pursed her lips. Her eyes stared into Hesperia's. "Are you sure?"

The question startled Hesperia. It wasn't the word choice but the tone—that look. It was the haunting notion that this woman across from her could see something beneath the surface. Something she was afraid to share, afraid to admit.

Hesperia thought for a moment. "I do not know."

"The Sacrament is coming," Melvina said, watching Hesperia.

Hesperia nodded and sipped her own cup of warm tea. The steaming liquid chased away the cold inside her.

"It is a source of ..."

"Sustenance for my people? Yes." The admittance was grotesque. It sounded vile in Hesperia's own ears.

Melvina nodded in understanding. "And you need this sustenance to live."

"Yes." Hesperia said, shame creeping into her core. She looked down at her chipped and faded mug. Such an imperfect thing would never be allowed in the Citadel.

Melvina asked gently, "How long can you survive without a Sacrament? Without a human soul to feed on?"

"We usually host a feeding once each Necanian moon cycle. It would be every three months by your calendar," Hesperia explained. "This is usually enough to satiate and keep us strong. One could go six or nine months and feel weak—feel the hunger take hold, but they'd survive."

"And longer than nine months?" Melvina leaned a little forward in her chair.

"No one has gone longer." Hesperia realized where this conversation was headed before Melvina spoke her next question.

"And you? When was the last time you participated in a Sacrament?"

How long had it been? When had Theo died? That was certainly longer than nine months. It had been years. She'd wanted to stop feeding after being forced to watch her brother drain the life from someone so precious to her—valuable in a way so different from the way her family and her people placed value on things. That awful moment changed the way she viewed humans and Necanians.

But she'd needed to feed, hadn't she? The two Sacraments following his death she'd refrained, but her brother saw weakness growing in her and would not allow her to continue her protest. He'd forced her to participate in the Sacrament. He'd told her it was their way. It was survival of the fittest. Necessary, even. The way he had said it left no room for argument. She had been afraid—afraid of Casimir and afraid of death.

The fear became its own kind of death and had morphed into a self-loathing that fed on her insides. Something had happened to her. Knowing Theo, connecting with his humanity, it had changed her in a way more profound than she first realized. It wasn't something that would fade with time or distance. It was like a seed had been planted, taking root. Those roots gripped her—grew deeper into the fibers of her being. She had known then that she couldn't keep feeding. She wouldn't keep taking.

She wondered now why she hadn't just stopped then—with thoughts of the boy and his dying gift to her. Why hadn't she just let Casimir kill her? Wilder would say there was purpose in it, that her choices led her here, and they had. She chose to leave the humans more intact. She chose to take less and less until she was really taking nothing at all. It hadn't been enough. Another Necanian would always finish them. Casimir didn't believe in waste, and he certainly wouldn't give her the satisfaction of pardoning their deaths.

So, she didn't save anyone. Not really. Perhaps she had saved herself, and that is why she saved Wilder.

"I guess it has been twelve months," Hesperia said.

Melvina tilted her head slightly to one side. "And you are not dead." The old woman scrunched her nose and wrinkled her brow. "Are you hungry?"

"No." Realization sprang up. Hesperia always waited for her body to weaken and her appetite to flare. She knew it would mean succumbing to her own hunger or death. But no. She hadn't been hungry. "Why?"

"You're asking me?" Melvina sat up straight, eyebrows raised and a hand to her chest.

"No, not really," Hesperia said and smiled. "I'm sorry I just never thought about it. I have seen others punished and forced to miss a feeding and how it makes them wretched and empty and ravenous—"

Melvina leaned forward and interrupted. "But you've never felt that?"

"I have not." It was a wondrous realization. Freeing and frightening.

"Curious," Melvina said. "Why do the Necanians feed?"

"Nourishment," Hesperia answered plainly. Hadn't they already discussed this?

"Yes, but what kind?" Melvin asked. "Because you also eat food. What nourishment do you gain from human souls that your bodies cannot gain from food?"

Hesperia considered the question, taking a long moment to ruminate. "Food does fill our stomachs. The Sacrament fills something else...something deeper in us. Something like a well always being dug."

Hesperia couldn't quite explain the look on Melvina's face. It wavered between inquiry and revelation with every crinkle of her eyes. "Your own souls perhaps," she finally offered. "Maybe you feed on human souls because your own soul is depleted...decrepit." She paused and then shook her head and reached to touch Hesperia's hand. "I'm sorry I did not mean that to be as offensive as it sounded."

Hesperia had not been offended and so ignored the apology. The theory presented had commanded her attention. "What do you mean?" she asked.

Melvina inhaled a deep breath before replying. "Well, we have talked about your culture and history. Your people have no art or music or love or sense of community. No joy. You don't even have words for things like joy and love. These are things that nourish the soul. They make life worth living. They provide a strength that is deeper than our physical bodies." She paused, stood up and paced the room with her hands on her hips. Twice she started to say something but stopped and paced again. Finally, she jerked back toward Hesperia with wide eyes. "You spoke once of a boy who was music and love to you. Could it be that he taught you how to feed your own soul, and so you no longer need to steal from another's?"

It was so simple and yet so profound. "I never thought..."

She let her own words drift into shocked silence. To Necanians, the need to feed on other creatures was natural and necessary. There was no disputing it. When you added in the arrogance that teaches Necanian superiority, there is no questioning it. They were taught that humans and the like were lesser—food. "We are symbiotes. We are but parasites." Could the food they needed be given instead of taken? "Can we change?"

Hesperia hadn't really meant the question for Melvina, but the woman answered, nonetheless. "I don't know. Time will tell that. You are the experiment, my dear."

"If I can change, perhaps others can as well." Hesperia looked up at Melvina.

The old woman crouched down to stoke the fire. "But will they?"

"Wilder believes that truth can bring freedom for the other humans. Can truth bring freedom for my kind as well?" Hope began to swim inside Hesperia's limbs and lungs. What she assumed was hope.

"It's worth trying. Because you're not like the others. You've proven it is within your kind to have compassion and kindness and to be selfless. If others would do the same, risk themselves." Melvina paused to add another log to the fire. "Maybe the truth will set them free to live something better too."

"We would not have to be enemies," Hesperia said.

"No, we wouldn't." Melvina smiled and returned to her seat.

Both returned to sipping their tea.

CHAPTER 46

WILDER

I t snowed overnight, a clean canvas to cover the muddy world beneath. Declan was stoking the fire while Wilder was putting on the tea. She'd just started warming scones on the wood stove when a knock sounded.

Declan opened the door. "Solomon...and Sarai, is that you?" He smiled wide and embraced the woman.

"You're back," Wilder said, moving in to hug this new friend herself. "Come in. Have tea with us."

"Thank you," Sarai replied, and she and Solomon entered, stomping the snow off their boots.

Wilder grabbed two more cups and filled them with dried herbs. Her tin was nearly empty. She made a mental note to ask Melvina to make her more. The kettle whistled. She pulled it from the stove and poured the steaming water into the cups.

They handed coats and hats to Declan who hung them on hooks by the door before they were all seated at the table. "They told me about what happened to your camp," Declan said to Sarai. "I'm sorry. But I'm glad you made it here."

"As am I, friend." Sarai reached to touch his hand. "And I

243

must say, getting back and hearing of your resurrection was a wonderful gift." She smiled at Wilder. "Perhaps wishes do come true," she said, winking.

Wilder remembered their conversation and weeping on this stranger's shoulder—now a new friend. She returned the knowing smile. "Do you take honey in your tea?"

"Yes, please," Sarai said.

Wilder retrieved the honey and set it on the table as she took a seat with the others. "I take it you have news?"

"It's why I brought her here first thing." Solomon reached for a scone. He slathered it with fresh-churned butter and Korah's blackberry jam and took a large bite.

"I was able to make it to three camps…" Sarai began.

Declan blinked. "Just three?"

Sarai looked down and briefly closed her eyes. "Three was all that was left."

Wilder reached to take Declan's hand. She imagined how this must feel to him. He would blame himself for not pushing them harder. He would want to bear the burden of responsibility, but she would not let him bear it alone.

"The three remaining took the radios and antennae. They're keeping them on and awaiting word." She took a sip of her tea. "Solomon filled me in on your plan…on the Necanians' plans…" The teacup rattled as she set it back on the saucer. "I'm sure the other three camps will help. All understood we must work together if we are to survive. If you tell them the news you brought back to Beartooth, they will certainly join you in infiltrating Hope City and the Citadel."

"Even Wolf Point?" Declan raised an eyebrow.

"Even Wolf Point," Sarai replied. "But keeping them from acting with wanton aggression will prove difficult. They tend to view violence as the first response."

"Yeah." Declan wrapped a hand around his mug. "I'm not sure they'll take orders from anyone either."

"If they provoke the Necanians, it will put all of us—the captives and the infants—at risk." Wilder knew they needed all the help they could get. She knew if a fight couldn't be avoided, Wolf Point would prove helpful. But was it worth the risk?

"I can talk to them," Declan said. "If I can make them see that those in the harvesting ward are our priority, they might listen."

"And if they don't?" Solomon asked before taking another bite of his scone.

"Then we don't take the risk." He placed a hand on Wilder's arm. "We won't let the ends justify the means. We won't put others in more danger unless it becomes absolutely necessary."

"And we can pray they put their own vengeful tastes aside long enough to help us." Solomon leaned back in his chair. "What they do beyond that, we can't control. Perhaps in seeing our way, they will change theirs?"

Sarai reached for a scone, still steaming slightly as she nibbled on it. "We can contact the others. Take turns monitoring the radios, maybe set up a schedule..."

"Good idea," Declan said. "We can ask them to start preparing, sending those who can join us to Beartooth. The sooner the better."

"Hesperia says the snow will keep the Necanians away," Wilder interjected. "But this time of year, it won't last long, so the other camps will need to hurry before they're found out."

"If we're lucky, the snow will last long enough to get us to the next Sacrament," Declan said.

"Well," Solomon responded, "we've already had a record

snow fall for this time of year. Signs point to it hanging around a while longer. Thank God."

"If it doesn't?" Sarai asked.

"Then we need to be ready to move," Declan said.

The table fell into a heavy silence at Declan's words. The next Sacrament was ten days away. Ten days that felt too soon and like an eternity all at once.

* * *

There was a small shed behind their cabin. Wilder had rarely ever bothered with entering, given it had always seemed to be in a state of chaos. Declan insisted that it was organized chaos, but the clutter made her twitchy. Declan and Sarai had left breakfast and immediately had made a beeline for the mossy structure. After a visit to Hesperia, Wilder joined them and brought lunch with her.

"Any luck?" Wilder asked, setting a plate of tomato sandwiches on the dusty table. They were one of Declan's favorites—Korah's sour dough bread with sliced tomatoes, a slather of mayonnaise, and a hearty sprinkle of salt and pepper.

Declan grabbed a sandwich and took a large bite. Through his full mouth, he replied, "Yeah..." Tomato juice dripped from his chin.

"We've been successful at reaching the other camps," Sarai continued for him while he wiped his mouth and finished his bite. "They are distressed, of course, but they are with us."

"And Wolf Point?" Wilder asked.

Declan swallowed his food. "I think we will be able to count on them. When I told them about the incubators...I think they got it."

"Good." Wilder breathed a sigh of relief.

"I was actually just about to bring the radio inside in case anyone tries to make contact..."

He'd barely finished the thought before the radio crackled.

Declan grabbed for the speaker microphone. "Hello?"

Static.

"Hello? Is someone there?" Declan asked again.

Static. Another sputter through the speaker. "Is this Beartooth? Come in?"

Even through the broken connection, there was something familiar about the voice. "Matthew?" Wilder inquired. She took the mic from Declan. "Matthew? Is that you?"

"Matthew?" Declan asked with a wrinkled brow and squared shoulders.

"He helped us get you out of Hope City," Wilder replied. "He lives in the Colony outside the dome with the others who have survived the Sacrament."

"I bet they all wish they hadn't," Declan muttered.

Wilder's heart lurched at the way he said those words. Did Declan wish he hadn't survived or was he merely referencing an understanding of their pain? He took her hand, squeezing it and offered a smile in answer to her unspoken question.

"Something's happened," Matthew's voice crackled over the airwaves again. "They sent a squadron to cull the Colony. It was dark. Most were asleep when they snuck in. It was a surgical strike." The static of the radio broke up the man's sorrowful tone. "Most were taken before we even realized the Necanians were there."

Declan took the microphone. "How many survived?"

"Declan, I assume? Good to know you are doing better. I told you he was strong, Wilder." There was a pause. "There are only about a dozen of us left. I was able to sneak them out into the brush and hide them away until the Necanians left."

"Will they come looking for you?" Declan asked.

"I doubt it. To my knowledge, they don't know how many of us even lived in the Colony. They wouldn't know that they didn't get all of us. We didn't confront them for that reason...among others."

"Others?" Declan asked.

"The people here aren't in fighting condition."

Wilder remembered the state of the Colony residents—shallow stares, dying eyes, and weak shells. Some barely seemed alive. Others seemed in too much pain to do much of anything.

Declan wiped a hand over his face. "Where are you now?"

"After you two left, we hid some supplies, another radio, and an antenna that could boost our signal far enough north, all about two miles away. Just in case." The radio cracked and popped again after Matthew's answer. "We've got shelter in the town ruins, but we can't stay here long."

Wilder grabbed the mic. "Can you make it nine days?"

"Yes, if we ration carefully. Why nine?"

"In nine days, the next Sacrament happens. We have a plan," Declan said.

"Don't share it over the radio," Matthew ordered. "I know you said the Necanians wouldn't monitor these channels, but..."

"Yeah, emergency use only. We got it." Declan set the speaker down and looked to Sarai.

Wilder caught the worried glance. "We can't worry about it. If his camp was just attacked, they wouldn't have had time to search and monitor yet, assuming they even do." It was possibly foolish optimism on her part, but they couldn't do anything about it if she was wrong.

"Any messages you need to send, I'd do it now before they have time to put it together." Matthew's response bolstered her assurance.

"Will do. Can you come here or send someone?" Declan asked.

"I can make it," Matthew answered. "We have another old truck and a road map. I can be there within twenty-four hours."

"See you then," Declan said before shutting the radio off. He looked to Wilder. "Can we trust this guy? Really?"

"He knew your parents," Wilder offered as a reply.

Declan's face paled a bit. He swallowed, and his eyes widened.

"He was their friend. They were part of a group trying to take down the Necanians. I don't know much. I know the Necanians fed on him. I know they killed his son. I know he helped save us."

Decan nodded. "That's enough for me."

CHAPTER 47
WILDER

Representatives from other camps arrived in Beartooth to flesh out their plans.

The camp buzzed with a mix of excitement and anxiety. Wilder echoed it in the pounding of her heart and tremble in her lungs. Everything seemed to be coming together so fast that her mind and emotions swirled and spun to keep up. Anxiety knocked at the door of her thoughts, and she worked to focus on the tasks at hand, desperate to keep it from entering.

"You okay?" Korah asked as they walked from the greenhouse.

"I should be asking you that question," Wilder replied.

Korah rubbed a hand over her baby bump. "I'm not. I'm terrified. But if all this is what we need to do to give my daughter a safer and brighter future, then we have to do it. I keep reminding myself of that."

"Daughter?" Wilder couldn't help but smile wide through her worry, remembering not so long ago, before so much had changed, that her friend had guessed she would be having a boy.

"Just a hunch." Korah shrugged, her eyes brightened a touch and her mouth curved upward.

Wilder stopped walking and took her friend's hand, looking into her face. "We will do what we have to do to make things right, to protect you and your baby and..."

"I know you will," Korah interrupted her. "I know." She squeezed Wilder's fingers.

"Wilder," Sam called from near the chapel. "Declan is looking for you. Matthew's here."

She and Korah picked up their pace to the chapel. Sam held the door open for them. Inside, voices chattered from all corners.

She identified Declan's deep rough tone. "Glad you made it safe."

"Glad to see you doing better," Matthew said, shaking his hand.

Wilder stepped toward them. "Matthew."

He turned and smiled. "I'm glad you made it home," he said as he hugged her. "Both of you."

"I'm sorry about what happened to your home," Wilder said.

Matthew nodded. "That place was never our home, though. It was a stopgap, a waiting room until we could find something real again."

"Hopefully you will." Declan inched closer to Wilder and took her hand.

Matthew looked Declan up and down then stared into his face with a tilted head. "It's amazing how much you look like them," he said. "Your parents would be proud of you, of what you're trying to do." Matthew patted Declan's shoulder.

Declan tightened his grip on Wilder's hand for a moment. He cleared his throat. "I hope so."

Declan, Wilder, and the whole council of Beartooth took seats at the front of the chapel while everyone else filed into the wooden pews. There were about twenty in all, between representatives from the other camps and a few residents of Beartooth joining to help. It was nerve-racking—sitting in front of them all, watching their reactions to Declan's plan and more so to Hesperia. She'd reluctantly arrived with Melvina. Wilder had wanted her there. She was an ally, and when questions arose about her allegiance, Declan surprised even Wilder when he vouched for her.

"She saved my wife," he told them. "She saved me. She gave up everything." He nodded at the Bringer. Hesperia returned the gesture in kind but said nothing.

Their guests' crossed their arms and their stern glares didn't relent, but they seemed willing to take Declan's word on the matter. He always used to tell Wilder that if you serve others, you respect them and care about them. Don't do it for gain but because it's right, and it will be like keeping coins in your pocket. He'd earned some coins with them. It looked as though he was spending them all to defend her friend and to sell their strategy.

"So why not just go in and blow them all to hell?" Jacob, one of the leaders from Wolf Point, asked.

"Because Hope City isn't the only Necanian Citadel," Declan replied. "Because faith in the Bringers is so deeply entrenched, it might turn even the humans against us."

Solomon sat forward in his chair. "We are too small in number to take down the Necanians as a whole on our own. We need people to see what they truly are, what they are really doing. The hope is that as word spreads, more and more will abandon Necanian rule."

"And if they don't?" Jacob retorted.

"They will," Sarai said. "It may take some time, but they will, and the Necanians will lose power."

"Then what?" another man asked.

"That isn't up to us," Wilder blurted out. She looked up from her lap to see them all waiting for further explanation. She swallowed. "Each Citadel, each corner of the world, will have to decide together. That's the point, to give them a choice. They can bring the Necanians consequences or force them to leave. The Bringers have plagued the whole world, and it will be up to the world to choose their fate. Not us, not today. Today is about Hope City."

Declan squeezed her bobbing knee. She turned to him. He smiled, and his face was the embodiment of hope to her. Her dead-but-not-dead-husband had returned to her. Hope kept him alive, and hope would keep them going. They would be hope dealers and truth speakers and it would make a difference, even if just one heart at a time.

"We will have some help from within the city," Matthew said into the silence. "There are a few left in the city who have been waiting for another chance to take down the Necanians. They will be ready when the time comes."

"Good," Declan said. "Then we gather in three days at the rendezvous point outside the dome. Jacob, you and your men will help Matthew's people with the trucks and monitor the exit. Matthew and Sarai will lead the team into the communications room, and the rest of us will surround the Citadel, incapacitate the guards, and rescue the captives."

"Three days," they agreed and then dispersed.

CHAPTER 48
WILDER

Wilder grabbed her journal, wrapped in her favorite blanket, and curled up in her favorite porch chair.

In twelve hours they would start their journey to Hope City, and there would be no turning back. She should probably be doing something useful—packing her bag, prepping supplies, finalizing plans. The last few days had swept by without breathing or pausing, a hurricane of activity.

Now, all was quiet.

Sitting on her porch, Wilder heard soft music wafting from a cabin a few doors down. She longed to hear the choir of the summer insects once more, but they had already been silenced by the cold. She sipped her tea and imagined the chirping of the crickets and croaking of frogs echoing through the trees. She hoped she would have the chance to hear them again.

Declan came around the corner of the porch. "Aren't you cold out here?"

"Nah." She smiled and patted the seat next to her, inviting him to come sit like they used to.

Declan obliged, moving the seat close enough to intertwine their fingers.

There were so many things to be said, but Wilder couldn't find words. Declan remained silent as well. The electric tension of unspoken fears and hopes charged the air between them.

Declan inhaled through his nose, and a puff of air blew from his mouth. He didn't look at her when he said, "This isn't what I wanted."

She tilted her head.

"Tomorrow," he said, and took another deep breath. "I wanted to raise children with you, to walk through a simple life loving you until we were old and gray. Then I wanted to sit on this porch and watch the sunset with you. I didn't want any of this...this rebellion..."

Wilder turned in her chair so that her knees were touching his. She took both of his hands in hers, their warmth chasing away the chill on her skin. "Neither did I. But you know the truth, and you couldn't have lived any kind of life that was good while knowing others were suffering—knowing the suffering would come for our children or grandchildren one day. That's one of the things I love most about you. I cherish your heart that fights for those who can't fight for themselves, and I'd rather walk into the fire with that man than live a hundred years with one who did nothing when he could have."

Declan leaned forward. He touched her cheek then ran his hand through her hair before kissing her lips gently. "If this is the last moment of any kind of normal we have, I need you to know it has been enough. And, at the same time, it hasn't been *nearly* enough."

Wilder stood up from her chair and crawled into Declan's lap, snuggling against his chest, settling her head in the crux of his shoulder and neck. He wrapped his arms around her and kissed the top of her head.

"I love you," she whispered.

"I love you more."

"I love you most."

"We will have to agree to disagree." He kissed her head again.

They returned to silence, but it was softer, full of peace and not anxious. Wilder closed her eyes and imagined a chorus of crickets and frogs as the stars glittered into view across the darkening sky.

CHAPTER 49

WILHELMINE

Wolstan's deep voice boomed through the black door.

He had not spoken to Wilhelmine and had taken to sleeping elsewhere since her infraction with Casimir. But she was still a member of the High Ruler's Council, and therefore invited to the Pre-Sacrament convocation, though not allowed to participate in the Sacrament itself. Wolstan, she knew, might find himself in the same predicament if he weren't careful and more proactive in his dealings with the Wayward.

"The snow has held on longer than we anticipated for this time of year, brother." The quiver in Wolstan's voice echoed through the wood where Wilhelmine was listening. "The Sacrament is in two days, and once it is over, we will be ready to strike."

"My patience is waning, Wolstan." This voice was Casimir's, just as deep but more ominous. "I have tolerated enough weakness."

"I mean only to ensure our victory," Wolstan said.

"You think it is not ensured? You think these humans can defeat us?" Casimir spoke louder, his tone more fearsome. Wilhelmine found herself wishing, almost hoping for her husband to face the High Ruler's wrath. Why should she be the only one questioned and doubted and punished?

"I think..." Wolstan hesitated a second and Wilhelmine imagined the anxious look he must be wearing. "I think we want more than victory, we want a decisive one. We want to put an end to this faction once and for all. No loose ends. No sweeping up afterward. I want to remove any obstacles which might give them reason for hope."

All Wilhelmine could now discern were footsteps moving across the marble floor. She wondered at Casimir's response, but voices traveled down the hall behind her, alerting her to the arrival of the rest of the council. She stepped back from the door and straightened her jacket. She ran slender fingers down her silky hair and stood up tall to greet them.

* * *

Seated next to Wolstan at the long council table, a lesser being might feel awkward and tense. Wilhelmine relished it.

His glare had not gone unnoticed when she'd entered the room, but he could not remove her. He could not change places. He was forced to acknowledge her—they all were, in some small way. Gossip about her had circulated through the Citadel and city. She would have no voice at this meeting, but she had presence, and she would not let it be one of regret and deficiency.

It didn't escape Wilhelmine's notice that all talk of the Wayward was conveniently neglected. Even if that business had been whispered about, the other Necanians were too smart to bring it up to the High Ruler so close to the Sacrament. They listened to his plans with flattering smiles painted across insecure faces.

"By the start of the next lunar cycle, building will begin on an insemination and incubation facility capable of expediting our final phase of rule over this world." Casimir smiled over the hologram modeling the architectural scheme. It was a renovation of a vacant hospital that would become the home to Hope City's food supply. "Schematics and logistic details have been sent to the other twelve domed cities that they may soon follow suit."

Murmurs of excitement and adulation floated around the table. Wilhelmine kept silent. She did not doubt Casimir, but she wanted a piece of it all—the glory and gratitude.

"This Sacrament," Casimir continued as they all quieted, "it will be a celebration of the glorious future to come, where we are no longer shackled to these humans and the facade they require of us. A future where we can live as we were meant to —one abundant in power and freedom."

Wilhelmine's chest heaved, and her heart pounded with pride and possibility. She resolved to stay vigilant, watching and waiting for an opportunity to prove her value. She *would* have her place in this new future.

CHAPTER 50
WILDER

No one spoke. Wilder didn't mind. She'd left all her words back in Beartooth—tearful goodbyes and uncertain promises of return. She offered silent prayers as she helped set up camp for the night.

She and Declan, with their team, had arrived a few miles outside Hope City. Korah, Sam, Solomon, Melvina...her family... had been left behind, ready to move farther north on a moment's notice, which was all they would get. Her gut toppled at the thought. She settled her anxious heart with a ragged breath.

"Do you fear?" Hesperia asked from beside her.

"I wish I didn't," Wilder said.

Hesperia fastened the tent to its pole. She appeared so serene to Wilder—almost detached from the reality they would be facing with the next sunset.

"Do *you* fear?" Wilder asked in return.

"I do not," Hesperia said matter-of-factly. "But I am not sure that it is better to be unafraid, necessarily."

"What do you mean?" Wilder asked. "Fighting anxiety is exhausting. I can't see anything better about fear."

"You fear because you have something to lose." Hesperia looked to her with softer eyes, their brightness dimming. "I do not, because I have nothing to lose."

Wilder closed the gap between them and put her hand on Hesperia's arm. "You are part of us now," she whispered. "Whatever happens, you are one of us."

The Necanian's eyes brightened again, and her skin shimmered with a muted glow of belief. "But I still will not fear. My friend has taught me what it is to have faith." Hesperia lowered her head so that her forehead touched Wilder's.

"We have a visitor!" one of the men called from across their temporary base.

Declan came from around a next-door tent where he had been helping Matthew. He joined Wilder, and together they watched a familiar figure saunter into their site.

"Declan, it's good to see you looking less dead," Noah mused as he approached, reaching out a hand.

"Noah." Declan's muscles tensed as he accepted the gesture. "What brings you here?"

"I came to ask you the same thing," Noah replied. "I live out here, after all."

"We aren't trying to intrude. We'll be here one night then out of your way." Declan kept his eyes locked on the leader of the Ridge Runners.

Noah sent a disgusted glance toward Hesperia. He looked back to Declan, his lip curling in a halfhearted smile. "I don't suppose you'll enlighten me on the purpose of your visit?"

"We have business in Hope City," Wilder said.

Noah nodded.

Wilder followed his gaze around their makeshift campsite.

He looked at every face, every tent, and paused upon seeing the four trucks parked in a line at the opposite end.

"I'm not a stupid man, Declan." Noah touched the rifle clipped to his tactical vest. "This isn't about trade or tourism..." He paused and stared at Wilder. "I'm thinking this is about that help you mentioned I might be needing. But the thing is, I still don't see where I need any help. It does look like you are about to stir up some trouble though, and I can't abide that so close to my home without knowing why."

Declan growled softly.

Hesperia stepped forward. "The High Ruler is planning to enslave humanity using their bodies as a continual food source for the Necanians."

Noah inclined his gaze toward Hesperia. Wilder couldn't read his expression. Anger mingled with confusion and what looked like a tinge of amusement all played across his dirty features.

"It speaks," Noah finally chuckled. "But that's a hell of a tale to believe."

Hesperia tilted her head. "It is true. Seeing as my brother is the High Ruler, I presumed it would be most believable coming directly from me. But you can believe what you wish."

Noah's jaw tensed, and his brow crinkled. He kept his eyes fixed on Hesperia but spoke to Declan. "You trust her?"

Declan didn't hesitate. "I do."

"And you mean to stop them?" Noah asked.

"We mean to rescue the test subjects they've already taken from the northern camps," Declan replied.

"And the babies already in incubators," Wilder added. She couldn't forget the tiny faces seen through small glass domes.

Noah kicked the dirt at his feet then stepped back and turned around, staring somewhere into the distance.

"I know it's a lot to take in..." Declan began.

"I believe you." Noah turned back around. "But I don't see nearly enough fire power to take on the Citadel."

"That's not the plan," Declan said.

"Then what is?"

"Sneak in, get the captives out, let the people in the dome know what the Necanians really are."

"And what are they?" Noah raised an eyebrow.

"Soul eaters." The answer came from Hesperia—full of disdain and remorse.

Noah cursed under his breath. "You're damn fools if you think this will work."

"Then help us," Wilder pleaded.

"I'm not one for taking sides," Noah said.

"They're going to build a facility. How long do you think you have before you won't have a choice?" Wilder didn't trust Noah, but she'd rather have him with them than against them.

"I'm not exactly the quiet rescue type of guy." Noah patted his gun. "I'd have a different strategy."

"You and your guys watch the perimeter," Declan offered as an option. "If things go sideways, you'll be our cover, and we'll probably be thankful for your guns."

"But," Wilder cut in, "violence isn't the answer here, not yet. We have to try it our way first or we are no better than the Necanians, putting value in power over life." Heat rose in her cheeks.

Noah sighed. "I still think you should go in guns blazing. It's what I would do, but for your sakes, I hope you're right."

"If we're wrong, you'll be free to do it your way," Declan said.

Noah looked between them and at Hesperia again. Wilder was proud her friend didn't diminish under his gaze like she had before. She kept her posture tall and her eyes focused.

"We'll have your six," Noah finally said. "But if things go sideways..."

"Blazing guns, we know." Declan nodded in agreement. "We move at sunset."

"Why not fully after dark?" Noah inquired.

"The Sacrament," Wilder said. "The Necanians will be gathered together and distracted."

"They will not suspect any humans to even know of it happening," Hesperia added.

Declan smiled. "They won't see us coming."

CHAPTER 51
DECLAN

They left the trucks parked behind a ridge a mile away from Hope City's dome. Declan would send a signal to the drivers when they were leaving the tunnel, but they couldn't risk the noise giving them away before their rescue attempt even started. He looked back toward them, squinting at the light from the lowering sun.

"You okay?" Wilder tugged at his jacket sleeve.

"Just running it all through my head one more time," Declan said.

"We all know the plan," she assured him.

She was right. They'd gone over it three times that morning. Everyone knew their roles. Everyone had memorized Hesperia's map of the secret passageways. Everyone was as ready as they were ever going to be.

Declan had to stay focused—had to keep himself centered on their mission because with every step closer to Hope City, his body only wanted to remember the torture.

The city glistened beneath the clear dome with the bright colors of the retiring sun. Outwardly it was breathtaking.

Declan briefly admired the spectacular beauty of its steel drenched in sunset. There was no real life or beauty in that place, but God could still find a way to show off. Perhaps it was the Maker's way of reminding them He was present, even in this darkness—that He would be with them.

"The tunnel entrance is up ahead," Matthew said. "There may be guards posted, so be ready.

Declan pulled his taser from his belt. Part of him would be more comfortable with a gun in hand. The rage bubbling up inside him whispered its hunger for vengeance. The beast that haunted his dreams growled to be set free. He swallowed down the pain and glanced at Wilder.

Her ivory cheeks were flush with freckles and what he guessed was fear. Her red hair blew in the breeze, and her bright eyes were fixed ahead. The still broken pieces of him cried for more time with her, lamenting what the Necanians had stolen from them. His own fear threatened to release that beast of his affliction. Just when he thought it would win, Wilder looked at him. The determination in her gaze softened, and she smiled. His heart rate slowed, and his breathing calmed. The tormented parts of his insides shrank back.

"We can do this," she told him.

He only nodded.

Carved out of the concrete ahead, the tunnel mouth came into view. Declan reached out and took Wilder's arm. As they stepped out of the fading daylight and into the darkness, he pulled her close and kissed her. "I love you," he whispered against her lips.

Her mouth curved into a smile against his. "I love you more."

* * *

As they walked farther into the bowels of the city's past, the haunting scent of mildew and death tickled his nostrils. His muscles tensed at the memories. Walking past his cell, Wilder brushed her fingers against his. That primal anger wanted to pulse through his veins, but he walled it in with sheer force of will. He couldn't lose control now. He wouldn't. He thought about the next step. They would exit the dungeons and have to navigate a left and two rights in open hallways before reaching access to the passages.

Hesperia led the way through the dark and up the stairs to the doorway. She paused before entering the code. Matthew stood beside the door as it clicked open.

The single guard on the other side turned with a look of shock. Before he could raise a weapon, Matthew tased him and Hesperia dragged him through the door. They bound and gagged him, tossing him into a nearby cell. Hesperia peaked through the open doorway, then nodded that it was safe to follow.

Declan's body was on the alert—muscles taut and blood thumping through heated veins—waiting for a Necanian to turn the corner. None did. They turned left, and it was clear. They turned right, and it was clear. As they made the last right toward the access point, a young Necanian servant girl stepped from a doorway on the left. Hesperia moved to action, quickly clasping a hand over the girl's mouth.

"I am sorry, friend," Hesperia whispered to her as she rendered the girl unconscious and pulled her into a storage closet.

They restrained her, then continued their course.

Declan's chest burned. Was this too easy? The Sacrament would be a diversion, but something in his gut told him the other shoe was going to drop. If getting in was this easy, he became more and more certain that getting out would not be.

CHAPTER 52
WILHELMINE

Wilhelmine stood at the back of the white room. The rest of the Necanians formed concentric circles in front of her, the higher classes before the lower. All were dressed in lush black robes that glided against the contrasting marble floor. They stood tall and lithe and hungry, staring at the center point—waiting.

The door on the opposite side of the room clicked, and the sound reverberated off the walls. Wilhelmine watched her brethren split, creating a pathway from the entrance to the room's center. Casimir walked through them, and they bowed in a wave that made Wilhelmine shiver with delight and jealousy. Behind Casimir walked Wolstan, and the chill in her spine became nothing but contempt. She should be beside him —her husband—and behind her High Ruler. She should be standing in a place of honor and respect, not cowering in the shadows, wishing for a morsel of mercy to be cast from her master's table.

"For power and for sovereignty we feed," Casimir uttered the ritual words.

The congregation repeated the phrase.

A gong peeled.

Through the door, two guards carried a young man. He blinked rapidly and sweat glistened off his forehead. Wilhelmine smelled his fear even from her position in the distant corner.

The gag in the man's mouth muffled his pleading. He tried to wrestle himself free but failed. When he was placed in front of the High Ruler, his fear all but paralyzed him. Color drained from the man's face as he watched Casimir's skin and eyes darken.

The High Ruler stepped forward, and the guards forced the man to his knees. Casimir lifted crimson claws and dug them into the man's temples.

There was another muffled scream. Then silence.

Casimir leaned his head back, and his eyes closed. He opened his mouth and exposed his long fangs. A sigh of satisfaction escaped his lips, then he released his fingers. The man collapsed onto the ground, his head bleeding, and his body lifeless.

Wilhelmine's own hunger surged inside her. The emptiness formed into envy. The High Ruler's punishment was this hunger—a hunger he would never know. He could feed whenever he chose. It was his preferred method of torture after all. He never had to feel the weakness and cravings—the longing for strength. Wilhelmine hated longing for anything. But she was always longing, always craving, always wanting more.

"For power and for sovereignty we feed," the assembly resounded again.

Another human was brought in. There was more muffled begging and more fear. Wolstan stepped forward and Wilhelmine snarled. He should be the one suffering punishment. He was the weak one. She wished him dead.

"For power and for sovereignty we feed."

The cycle went round and round. One Necanian at a time stepped forward to satisfy themselves on the souls of these subordinate and ignorant humans. If one was left alive, Casimir would finish them off. Slowly the room filled with the aroma of sweet fear and coppery blood and fresh death. Wilhelmine stifled her own screams of frustration.

A soft clacking echoed through the wall behind her. She stepped backward and leaned her ear against the cool tiles. Footsteps? Who would be moving about the Citadel during the Sacrament? The few guards and servants not participating should have been in dutiful positions or their private quarters. It was curious, potentially suspicious.

Wilhelmine discreetly stepped to the back exit. She turned the door handle slowly and pushed the door open only enough to squeeze herself through. Once in the corridor, she closed the door with barely a click.

There was no one to be seen. But she had heard something. She would rather chase a phantom than remain only a spectator to the Sacrament a moment longer. She looked left, then decided to walk right, taking cautious steps around the corner.

She heard a whisper. "This way...quickly."

Wilhelmine turned another bend. A doorway had been opened in a wall. Several humans, dirty and ragged, were stepping into a dark passage. She hadn't even known such a walkway existed. More important to her than the humans crawling like rats into the walls was the Necanian guiding them. Stationed at the entrance to the hidden corridor was none other than Hesperia.

"Sister," Wilhelmine said. She touched a hand to her chest. "What are you doing?" She feigned shock.

Hesperia turned toward her with a calm face. Wilhelmine

would have wanted her to have seemed at least a bit surprised or anxious, but she didn't offer the pleasure.

"What I do is no business of yours," Hesperia replied.

The couple of humans at her side paused and looked between the two Necanian women. They, however, did show the fear and concern that Wilhelmine so desired.

"Go without me," Hesperia whispered to them. "I will find you."

The woman nodded and Wilhelmine recognized her ginger hair and pale skin. *The Wayward woman.*

"I see you and your *friend* have returned," Wilhelmine said.

Hesperia closed the disguised door. It clicked back into place, leaving only smooth wall like it never even existed. "I don't wish to hurt you."

"Ha!" Wilhelmine couldn't hold in her contempt. "You are not capable of hurting me." She stepped closer to her sister-in-law—slow, calculated steps that gave her time to consider her next move. "I could scream. I could call for help and expose you."

"Yet, you haven't."

"No, not yet." A cool burst rushed through Wilhelmine's veins. Her skin dimmed from shimmering white to a deathly gray. She stretched her fingers as her nails lengthened and sharpened into blood-red talons. "See," she explained, "if I call for help now, your friends will be killed, and you will be arrested. Which would be lovely to behold, but I cannot be sure how your brother will punish this transgression. I fear his loyalty to family will leave you alive. And I want you dead."

"So, you mean to kill me first," Hesperia said. "You are so certain that you can?" She tilted her head. The almost naive expression on her face made Wilhelmine want to snap her neck.

"Let's find out," Wilhelmine said, then lunged at Hesperia.

Hesperia deflected the punch. Wilhelmine jabbed with her other hand, and Hesperia deflected it again then spun out of the way. Wilhelmine kicked, her foot landing hard against Hesperia's abdomen. Hesperia doubled over and stumbled back. Wilhelmine grabbed her by the hair and pulled her head up before shoving it hard into the marble wall. The sickening crack it made echoed around the empty space.

Pressing Hesperia's head into the tiles, Wilhelmine leaned in close. "After I kill you, should I tell them of your treachery? How it was all in self-defense to keep you and the Wayward from enacting whatever evil scheme you have concocted against the High Ruler?" She pressed her claws into Hesperia's luminous skin. Blood dribbled. "Or should I tell them that the Wayward woman did this to you. That they used you, forced you to help them infiltrate the Citadel, then left you for dead when they were done with you?"

Hesperia struggled against Wilhelmine's hold.

"Either way, you and your friends die, but one version might mean their deaths are slower and more agonizing..."

"I'm not dead yet." Hesperia writhed again.

"No but choosing not to feed has made you weak. There is no hope for you." Wilhelmine pressed her harder into the wall.

Hesperia's body relaxed a bit. Her breath drew in and out in heavy heaves. "My body is weaker," she gasped. "But my hope is not." Hesperia's arm reached out and a prick stung Wilhelmine's abdomen. A shock coursed through her skin. She jerked backward, collapsing to the cold floor. Hesperia steadied herself against the wall until she stood straight again. She limped toward Wilhelmine holding a black object in her hand.

"I suppose you will kill me," Wilhelmine choked, pain still pulsing through her body.

"No. I won't kill you." Hesperia leaned down, and the

object in her hand buzzed and crackled before she held it to Wilhelmine's chest.

Electricity surged in excruciating pangs. Hesperia's face blurred. The brightness of the hallway burned Wilhelmine's eyes, then everything turned black.

CHAPTER 53
WILDER

Wilder hesitated in the dim corridor. "I don't like leaving her behind."

She could barely make out muffled voices through the walls. She didn't dare imagine what Wilhelmine would do.

"We risk more in trying to help her than going ahead." Declan took Wilder by the arm and tugged her forward.

He was right. Hesperia could handle herself or she wouldn't have risked it. Hesperia wouldn't risk them or this mission. And if things were going to go sideways, they needed to keep pushing forward in hopes that they'd at least save some. There was no waiting nor turning back now.

Their crew inched forward through the dusty hidden hallway and up secret stairways toward their destination. Wilder listened to Declan breathing—a break from the otherwise tense silence. At the second floor, Matthew and Sarai diverted their team toward the control room.

"Be careful," Wilder whispered to them.

Matthew only gave her a glance and a stiff nod before stepping through the egress and into the light of the open. Sarai followed suit, but not before adding a reassuring smile.

The doorway closed again. Wilder's eyes readjusted to the dark as she listened through the wall. She heard no shouts, no real commotion. She muttered a fervent prayer and followed Declan onward.

They went up another flight of stairs and walked twenty or so paces beyond the first left turn. This was it. It had been her way of escape when Hesperia pulled her out and would be a path to freedom for the souls in the harvesting ward on the other side.

Declan looked to each of the men and women with them— ten in total. Each gestured their readiness. Then he turned to Wilder. The silent question he held for her was deeper. It was more than asking if she was ready; it was asking if she still wanted to do this. It pleaded with her to be careful. It masked his own fear and assured her they would be fine. It promised a happily-ever-after. Even though they both knew it was a promise they might not be able to keep, they made it anyway, mouthing, *I love you.*

"Once we open this door, we won't have time to hesitate," Declan said to the group. "We take care of any Necanians first, then we get to work getting the humans out. Quick and quiet." He pushed the wall.

White light inched through the widening expanse of the doorway, brightening the dim hallway. Wilder blinked several times before stepping into the ward. She saw the incubators first, then motioned to her left. Before she could react, Declan was already grabbing the Necanian, who jerked and fell to the ground. Two other Wayward rushed past her, into the other room. She followed, entering the space just as they took down two more Necanian guards at the doorway.

One of the men, Jeremy from the Lakota camp, glanced out

into the corridor. "All clear," he said. Then pulled chains from his backpack. He wrapped them around the door handles and secured them with a hefty lock.

Kate and Seth, members of Beartooth, pulled the unconscious Necanians together, binding their feet, hands, and mouths.

"Let's get to it then," Declan said.

It was only then that any of the Wayward really looked and saw the horror surrounding them. As they stared at the body bags suspended from the ceiling, Wilder watched them. Mouths open, tears glistening in wide eyes. Knowing it was happening and seeing it in real life were two very different things. Wilder presumed they all felt the same twisting in their guts and aches in their hearts that she had before—which she felt again now.

Declan snapped back to reality and into action. "We have to hurry."

He and Jeremy began to cut the bags down, opening them to release their human residents. Wilder and Kate pulled blankets and towels from their packs. They went to work wiping the clear goo from the shivering bodies.

Confused eyes blinked up at them.

"It's okay," Wilder cooed. "We're here to help you."

More than one vomited up the contents of their stomach and coughed out the fluid from their lungs. All of them struggled to stand on weak legs.

A noise came from the incubator room.

Wilder and Declan looked to one another. Declan furrowed his brow then walked to investigate the noise.

Wilder held her breath. She watched and waited—a few seconds feeling like hours to see if they had been found out.

"Hesperia!" She gasped as Declan returned with her friend.

"We need to hurry." Blood dripped from Hesperia's head and stained her teeth.

Wilder rushed to her side. "Are you okay? What happened? Did Wilhelmine...?"

"I am fine," Hesperia assured her. She took Wilder's hand and squeezed it. "I will be fine. Wilhelmine is taken care of...for now." Hesperia turned to Declan. "But they will find her. And when they do, we will be out of time."

"We need to get everyone out now." Declan moved to help one of the rescued stand.

There were only about five men and two women in the ward. "I swear there were more," Wilder whispered to the others.

"There were," Hesperia confirmed. "They were probably used in the Sacrament."

A sob stuck in Wilder's throat. It made sense, yet she hadn't thought about those who would be lost because they waited for the Sacrament. Maybe she wouldn't let herself think it. She'd wanted to save them all, and yet they couldn't. They would save these few. They would stop this and save countless others.

Declan was suddenly right next to her. "There was no other way." He put his hands on her shoulders and gazed into her face. "There was no other way."

Wilder bit her lip and nodded. "We need to keep going."

They began to lead the men and women back toward the passageway, unsteady legs and adrenaline carrying them all forward. Once they were safe, leaning against cobwebbed walls, they returned for the incubators.

There were twelve. A dozen little lives growing under individual glass rotundas.

"The incubators have a fail-safe. Once you unplug them, they will generate their own power to keep the children alive for sixty minutes," Hesperia told them. "If they aren't in the trucks and attached to the generators by then, they won't survive."

"There are more than a dozen of us, and, thank God these things are on wheels," Declan said. "We all take one."

They unplugged the machines which beeped frantically, and the lights under the domes shut off. The lights powered back on after a few seconds and each incubator whirled back to life. The first six they brought to the corridor. Each one of the rescued Wayward used the rolling machines for support as they followed Jeremy down the hallways. The second six were rolled on by their crew. Declan, Hesperia, and Wilder took the rear.

Declan closed the wall behind them. The corridor wasn't as dark this time, lit by the lamps of a dozen children getting a chance at new life. Seeing the glowing orbs push back the darkness around them gave Wilder a new, strengthened faith. They were so close to freedom.

Instead of moving back toward the stairs, they went the opposite direction. Hesperia told them of a service elevator about fifty feet beyond the ward. Matthew's first job in the control room was to turn it back on, and they hoped he had been successful, because carrying those incubators down the stairs would take more time than they had left. On the other hand, the elevator would make noise, so once they summoned it, they would likely be heard and that meant only minutes to get to the tunnels. Either way, their time was running out. Wilder wished for the minutes to slow down while they sped up. *We are so very close.*

CHAPTER 54
MATTHEW

Matthew nodded to Wilder before stepping out of the dark of secrecy and into the bright open hallway.

There were no guards there, but he was certain one or two would be stationed outside the control room. They had no way of knowing how many would be inside. The Sacrament meant a skeleton crew of Necanians but was that one...two...five? He and his crew had to be ready. He reminded himself they were ready.

Slinking stealthily down the corridor, they halted at an opening in the path. The control room was to the left. Matthew peered around the edge of the marble wall. The entry to the room was thirty feet away and, sure enough, a single guard stood sentry—a tall Necanian, stoic and staring straight ahead.

Matthew looked to James, a member of Wolf Point, and held up one finger.

James nodded then rushed around the corner.

Matthew counted to ten in his head, an ear inclined to the shuffle of feet and smothering of voices around the corner, before leading the others in the same direction. He saw James lowering the Necanian guard to the ground.

Matthew's crew of four split into two pairs—one on either side of the control room doors. There was a lock with a hand-print scanner. James lifted the unconscious Necanian to his feet and Sarai held its limp hand to the scanner. The red light flashed green, and the door clicked. James dropped the body quietly before Matthew gave the signal, and they burst through the door.

Two more Necanians sat in front of screens. They looked up with wide eyes. One jumped to its feet but got no farther before Sarai sunk a taser into its chest. It convulsed to the ground. The second Necanian reached for something on the display in front of it, but Matthew grabbed its arm and pulled it behind the being's back.

"Not today, fella," Matthew said as he pressed his taser into its side and pushed the trigger. The Necanian jerked and fell sideways out of his seat.

James and Sarai dragged all three Necanians into a corner and restrained them. She stood with eyes alert for any stirring, tasers at the ready.

"You're up," Matthew said to Harper, turning his attention to the screens.

Harper was only eighteen years old but was a wiz with technology. She had come into the Colony with her mother, who'd survived Casimir's torture...but barely. The woman died within a few weeks—her body never able to fully recover from the feeding. Harper had spent all her time distracting herself with old computer parts. The kid had a knack for this stuff, and Matthew hoped she would be able to do what they needed. Fiddling with old hardware was a far cry from hacking this kind of system. But before the Colony, Harper had studied on a programming education track. She definitely had a better chance than any of the other Wayward.

"Let's see what we've got." Harper tightened her ponytail and started typing on the station keyboard.

There were eight or nine screens lined in front of them. Most showed security footage of Hope City—street cameras and feeds from local businesses. A single screen zoomed in on the main entrance to the Citadel.

"Hesperia was right," Harper said. "There are no cameras monitoring the interior of the Citadel. Nothing on the halls, corridors, or rooms. They've all been powered off." She clicked away on the keys and a schematic of the building popped onto the center display. "But there are sensors being monitored at locked and guarded doorways."

"They really are that arrogant," Matthew chuckled. Years ago, Hesperia had told him of Casimir removing any humans from service within the Citadel—after murdering his son. The High Ruler had closed up the servant hallways and said there wasn't a need for constant surveillance. He would regret his pride now. "Do you see the service elevator?"

"Yeah." She pointed to a spot on a digital map. "Hopefully they only disconnected it remotely or this is gonna get more complicated."

"We've been lucky so far," Sarai said.

"Don't jinx it," replied James. And the Lakota woman rolled her eyes at him.

Harper punched more buttons. Her fingers moving faster than Matthew could comprehend. Once upon a time, he'd considered himself good with computers, but it had been a long time since he touched any tech more advanced than a car engine. He barely understood what their little genius was doing.

"It looks like today is our lucky day," Harper said, glancing at Sarai with a smirk. "The elevator is back online."

"Good." Matthew tapped the talk button of his two-way radio in a series of dots and dashes—a quiet signal to Declan that they would be good to go. He turned his attention back to Harper, leaning over her shoulder to look at a camera view of the city. "Now on to other matters. Once that elevator starts moving, we won't have time to waste."

"Already working on tapping into the citywide feed," Harper said. "I just need a couple minutes to get around their security, and we'll be in business."

Matthew recounted what he would say in his head. His skin grew clammy. He wondered why he, a guy who hated public speaking, had volunteered to put his face on camera for all of Hope City, and really all of the domed cities. He prayed for the right words.

"Okay, I'm ready when you are," Harper said. "Here's the camera." She pointed to a small lens resting above one of the monitors. "You tell me when, and we start broadcasting."

"Are we sure this should be me?" he asked, looking around at his team.

Sarai stepped to stand next to him. She placed a hand on his shoulder. "You are a face the people of this city will recognize. They will believe you before any of us. Besides, you understand even better than we do what is at stake here."

She meant the loss of his son. Matthew sat down in front of the device—staring—unable to move or speak. *God give me the right words.*

Sarai touched his arm. Her big brown eyes looking at him with confidence. "Just tell them the truth."

Matthew nodded and swallowed the lump in his throat. "Yeah. Okay. Ready."

Harper pushed a button, and a red light came on. "You're

live," she whispered.

Matthew took a long, deep breath. He'd been leading people in the shadow of the dome for decades. Now was the time to step into view and lead anyone else who would listen. *Dear God, let them listen.*

"Citizens of Hope City," he began. His voice and heart were shaky. "You don't know me. But I was one of you once. I lived in a row house on Fifth Street with my wife and my son. We believed, just like you, that the Necanians were the Bringers of Peace and the Saviors of Mankind. But it was a lie.

"These... creatures..." Matthew cleared his dry throat and swallowed. "These creatures who came and made us feel safe and comfortable—who made themselves look beautiful and heroic—they are soul eaters feeding on all that makes us good and bold and wonderful. They gave us peace and safety, but in receiving it, we sacrificed ourselves to them. We gave up music and art and the beautiful diversity of humanity. We gave up our lives."

An image of his son—young and bright and lovely—flashed in his mind. His heart pounded, and his chin quivered. He swallowed again, willing himself strength. "These Bringers of Peace who say they are protecting you are feeding on your very souls. One at a time, they are destroying us for their plea-sure in secret rooms. Even this minute, they are using humans for food."

Matthew nodded to Harper who hit another few buttons on the keyboard, patching into a forgotten security camera.

The video feed on the monitor shifted to a grainy image in a bright room. Necanians stood in circles, but they weren't bright with life, they looked gray and frightening. At the center, a Necanian was gripping a human's head with long claws. Dark blood dribbled down the woman's face. The Necanian smiled then released her, and she fell to the ground.

Matthew's voice played over the live footage of the Sacrament. "This is who the Necanians are. Not Bringers of Peace, but of death. They stifled our souls long before killing our bodies. Slowly, they have fed on us.

"First, those we would call enemies. And maybe you could be okay with that—with the vile and the evil dying by their hands if it meant you did not have to worry. But their hunger only grew. And now they look to turn us all into nothing more than a crop they grow to sustain themselves."

Harper clicked more buttons and an image appeared on the screen.

"Found these," she said clicking through the file showing architectural plans for a building renovation. A laboratory. Schematics of body bags and incubators.

Matthew's limbs went suddenly weak. He knew and yet he had no idea. They truly had let the devil into their lives. For what? Whatever Casimir sold to them was a hoax. It wasn't peace. It wasn't life. It wasn't comfort. It was fear and manipulation, and they'd bought it. *Dear God, don't let it be too late.*

Matthew nodded to Harper, and she returned the feed to the video of his face. He looked at his image in the monitor. He wasn't a young man anymore. But somewhere under his speckled gray hair and the dark circles around his old, tired eyes, he saw pieces of his son. His boy wouldn't have a future, but others still could.

"We have believed lies," he said into the camera, "but it is time for the truth. And the truth is, I know you are scared. I know this won't be easy. We lived outside the dome once before. We lived in homes and communities, and we served each other and loved and laughed. We can do it again. Together we can do this. You won't be alone. We will help you."

CHAPTER 55
CASIMIR

Casimir stood in the center of the Ritual Hall. One by one, watching his brethren take their fill from the souls of their chattel. His blood coursed with strength, invigorating his flesh, at the visceral sensation of Necanian power.

The Sacrament always reminded him of his place—of his people's place. They were built to rule. They were built to have dominion over lesser beings.

The feeding Necanian hissed through elongated fangs, then withdrew its claws from the human head. The female fell to the ground with a soft thud. Two Necanian guards dragged the corpse away, droplets of blood smearing on the white marble floor, while two others brought in the next soul.

"For power and for sovereignty, we feed," the chorus rang out with confidence.

Casimir never tired of the refrain. He closed his eyes and let the deep tone of a unified, Necanian voice, splash against his psyche like a strong wave against a stone.

Exhaling, he opened his eyes to watch the human struggle

against her bindings. Her eyes widened with fear as fingers gripped her head, claws dug into her flesh, and blood dribbled. Casimir drank in the metallic sweetness of it. These wretched humans were vermin. They were fools if they thought themselves a formidable match against his people. Especially the Wayward, who were nothing more than a pest to be exterminated.

"For power and for sovereignty, we feed."

Casimir pulled himself out of his thoughts and back to the ceremony. He glanced proudly about the room. Something flashed. In the black and white room there was a spot of red—a blinking light in the upper corner. A camera.

Casimir leaned to Wolstan, whispering in his brother's ear, "I thought all security cameras inside the Citadel were powered off?" He gestured his head toward the small half-globe attached to the wall near the ceiling.

"They were," Wolstan murmured. "I will investigate."

"Go."

Wolstan exited. A few Necanians watched him with curiosity, but when they turned to Casimir, brows raised in question, the High Ruler smiled and lifted his chin. A sign that all was well.

It was then that Casimir noticed Wilhelmine's absence.

CHAPTER 56

WILDER

Wilder waited by the service elevator door, her palms sweaty and muscles twitching.

They were still hidden in the secret passage-ways behind the false wall, but the delay heightened her anxiety about all the things that could still go wrong.

Had Matthew reached the control room? Had he sent his message to the city? Were they able to get power to the elevator? The newly woken Wayward still struggled to find strength for waking limbs. The incubators hummed softly, but she knew they were on a limited power supply. The little lives inside depended on them to get out of this building.

Wilder glanced down at one of the glass pods. Inside was an infant that looked to be about thirty weeks—fully formed but still too tiny to be born in a dusty hallway. A couple of the others seemed a little bigger, a couple smaller. Hesperia had told her this was a test crop for the Necanians. They fertilized and incubated the embryos at roughly the same time while they perfected the process and waited for larger labs to be built. She'd started to tell Wilder of the previous test crops, the ones that failed, but Wilder couldn't stand the thought. She still couldn't.

She shivered, and Declan placed a hand on the small of her back.

"It's okay," he whispered. "Matthew sent the signal a few minutes ago. We will get out of here. It's all about timing..."

A soft rumble echoed below them, getting louder as it rose.

"See," Declan said and smirked. "Everyone get ready to move. We need to get on and off the elevator fast."

Relief and tension mingled through Wilder's muscles. They'd managed to get this far with little interference, but would getting out be this easy?

The elevator reached their floor, and the rusty door squealed open.

"Going down?" Sarai said from the doorway.

"Where are the others?" Declan asked.

"Waiting," Sarai said. "We may not all fit so..."

"Got it." They started wheeling incubators inside.

The freight elevator was large but not big enough for everyone at once. They squeezed in as many as they could, then helped Sarai pull the door down.

When the elevator rumbled back into motion, Declan took Wilder's hand.

His green eyes were so full of hope and doubt and love and fear. Their whole future depended on the speed of a ninety-year-old elevator.

No. It was dependent on something greater, something far more trustworthy and stable. All day, Wilder had wrestled with anxious thoughts, with the fear of what could go wrong. At this most vulnerable moment, she was overcome with thoughts of what could go right.

They had come this far—from the brink of death and the

blackhole of grief—into something bigger than their life and their love.

The floor shook under Wilder's feet as the elevator moved toward them again. Her heart sped up, and her arms tingled with adrenaline. Just like before, the elevator rose, and the door screeched open.

Sarai didn't smile though. "Some Necanians are on the move, we need to hurry."

Without a word, they pushed the remaining four incubators into the large metal box. Declan pulled the door down, and Sarai hit a red button. The elevator jolted as it started its descent.

"Has Matthew made it back to the tunnels?" Declan asked.

Sarai shook her head. "No, he said to get you all out and come back for him."

"My brother will come to the tunnels," Hesperia said. "When he sees that we have used these passages, he will know that is our way of escape."

"There's no changing it now," Declan said.

All along, they knew their plan was a risky one. They realized it was unlikely they would get in and out without notice and without confrontation. They had hoped. They had prayed. But they were aware of the probabilities.

The High Ruler was arrogant. The Sacrament was a distraction. Those facts were enough to get them inside. As the elevator came to a slow stop, Wilder's gut twisted with the notion that she would not be getting out. They would save the lives they came to rescue—even if it meant sacrificing her own.

Sarai opened the door. Jeremy was there, ready to help. They hastily exited, incubators first. Declan was the last one off the elevator, and as soon as his foot crossed the threshold, Sarai was pulling the door closed, ready to retrieve Matthew, Harper, and James.

"Jeremy," Declan said, "you lead the others out, I'll wait for Matthew and his crew."

"I'm waiting with you." Wilder planted her feet and gripped his hand in a way that let him know she wouldn't be persuaded otherwise.

Declan's jaw clenched, but he nodded.

"I will remain as well," Hesperia said.

The blood on her head and mouth had dried, leaving a crusty residue on her shimmery scales. Droplets had stained her white attire. Wilder looked down and noticed dirt smudges along the hem—dirt from the muddy streets of Beartooth no doubt.

Hesperia, who had never been less than a pristine picture of perfection, was marred. Her appearance was flawed, but her expression reflected more life than Wilder had seen in the time they had known each other. This Necanian looked more human, more like one of her people—dirty and imperfect and beautiful.

Wilder touched Hesperia's shoulder. "Thank you."

Hesperia stood beside her now, unflinching in the face of fighting her own family.

Did Necanians have souls of their own? The human soul connected people as image-bearers of God. They were the seat of depth and beauty—real, true, meaningful life—the expression of the Maker. If that was a soul—creation longing for connection with its Creator—Wilder couldn't imagine *this* Necanian to not have one now.

Heavy footsteps pounded overhead.

"Guards," Hesperia muttered.

Wilder met Declan's gaze. Another silent conversation ensued behind his worried eyes and furrowed brow, asking her to go, to run, and she refused with a sigh and a shake of her head. He placed a rough hand on her cheek and tugged her close for a kiss. His lips crushed against hers with longing and a lifetime's worth of love and devotion. A goodbye kiss.

A quake. The screech of breaks, the squealing of the elevator door flinging open. Wilder pulled away from Declan.

"They've sounded the alarm," Matthew said as he charged out of the elevator. "I say we run."

"Agreed." Declan grinned and patted a hand on Matthew's back.

"Please do," a slithering voice echoed down the corridor. "It will make the hunt so much more fun."

Wilder couldn't move except to turn her head toward the dungeon stairwell. Standing under a stream of light from the dim overhead lamps was Casimir. A triumphant smirk curled his lips, but his eyes were red with anger. Wolstan stood beside him with two Necanian guards.

"Matthew, get out of here," Declan muttered. "Make sure they are safe...and ready."

Matthew nodded. He gestured for Sarai, James, and Harper to go first then jogged down the corridor behind them.

"Would you like me to stay or go?" Hesperia whispered to Wilder.

Hesperia's skin dimmed to gray and fangs protruded from her gums. Hesperia was ready to fight, to defend them. But there was turmoil written in her darting eyes. Was it hesitation in standing against her brothers? Hesperia glanced toward Matthew and Wilder knew. This wasn't doubt, there was no questioning of loyalties. Hesperia had loved Matthew's son and wanted to protect the father in a way she couldn't protect Theo.

"Go with Matthew," Wilder replied. "Keep him safe...and the children."

Hesperia turned to exit, but paused, looking back to her

brothers. She opened her mouth to speak but closed it again quickly.

Casimir sneered at her. "No goodbye? No apology?"

"I owe you nothing," Hesperia said and chased after Matthew.

Casimir moved forward, slowly down two steps. "I could pretend I don't know how you turned Hesperia against me, but she has always had a weakness for your kind. She has always been weak."

"She's not the weak one," Wilder said. She squeezed her fingers into fists, her nails digging into her own palms, an attempt to keep herself calm. "You think you're better, higher, but you are the lesser being. You need us."

"In the same way you need turnips and milk." Casimir sneered. He took two more steps, Wolstan and the guards following.

"If that were true, you wouldn't hate us so much," Declan said with a smirk of his own.

"I remember you," Casimir said. "I still don't like the banter."

"Yet you keep talking," Declan chided.

Wilder linked her arm around her husband's, worried he would provoke a response they wouldn't be prepared to fend off. Declan only tugged her close. He pulled a radio from his pocket and held the button. "Get clear and blow the charges," he ordered.

A crackle of static. "The whole Citadel could come down."

Declan looked into her eyes, his own glassy. Wilder smiled at him with quivering lips, and he smiled back. "We know. Do it."

"So that's your plan?" Casimir laughed. "To save a few worthless humans then blow yourselves up? You would die for this?"

"To stop you?" Declan asked. "You bet we would."

Casimir laughed again. "Of course. And you think you are doing good for your fellow humans. But the freedom you offer is messy and sacrificial, and most humans aren't interested in sacrifice—even in view of our darker faces. They will lie to themselves about our motives, justify our feasting on souls by saying it won't happen to them. They will make you the villains to protect their comfort. Do you really think they will just give up the easy life we offer?"

"Enough will," Wilder responded. "Enough will feel the chains break in their hearts and minds, and once they taste the freedom the truth offers, you will lose control. Your lies may have made life easy, but they also made it cheap. The truth may be painful, but it offers so much more than the false peace your fear brought." Her heart pounded fast, and her stomach flipped.

Standing face-to-face with Casimir—a powerful evil—felt so beyond her feeble courage. She was just a girl from the mountains who wrote stories and picked berries and was ignorant of the happenings outside her small circle in Beartooth.

Her own ignorance had once given her a sense of security in her place in the world. She hadn't seen the oppression and bondage others faced. She had lived as though life at Beartooth was life everywhere.

Until she couldn't.

Seeing the reality of Necanian rule pulled and stretched her heart. She didn't even realize it had needed to grow. Her people were people of big hearts, and yet, even as she feared she wasn't enough, her heart had grown to fit the whole uncomfortable, painful, messy world.

Wilder inhaled a long, deep breath through her nose, filling her lungs. She thought of smelling the pine trees again. Of sitting on her porch and hearing the birds sing. She didn't want to die in this musky tunnel. But while darkness might be all around her, light was bright inside her. Love was pushing back her fear.

Seconds seemed to slow to minutes. She looked at Declan's steeled face. Once upon a time, they'd shared so many dreams of what their future would look like. Dreams for children and grandchildren and so much joy. One only ever dreams of joy. Not pain. Not death.

She pulled his hand to her lips and kissed it, knowing their dreams might never come true. Not the way they thought. She wouldn't birth a legacy, but there were children who would have a chance in this world. Humanity was being given a choice at real freedom—soul-deep freedom—the kind that wasn't about getting what you wanted, but of serving others. The story told of her and Declan—that would be their legacy. There would be joy in the world again. Wilder hadn't stopped dreaming after all. Now she just dreamt her ballad of sacrifice —her song of being lost and found—would point others to the path of liberty.

"You shouldn't underestimate us," Declan said. "That has been your biggest weakness."

"It won't matter," Casimir said. He glanced at his brother.

Wolstan nodded. "Guards are already on their way to the tunnel entrance. They will find your comrades. They will end this and take back what belongs to us."

"It is a pity the two of you will not live to see your friends fail." Casimir gestured to the two guards.

They began to step forward when a sound like thunder, loud and booming, echoed from somewhere above.

"No, you won't live to see our friends succeed," Wilder said.

The ground shook and debris began to tumble from the walls and ceiling.

"This won't be worth it," Casimir hissed. "My plans have been sent to other cities."

"So has our message."

There was another boom. The wall cracked and the stairs crumbled. Casimir, Wolstan, and the guards fumbled to find new footing.

Declan pulled Wilder close. His eyes darted around them. "This way!" He tugged her, stumbling into a cell at the corner of the structure.

They huddled together on the floor. Declan wrapped himself around Wilder.

Another low and deep clap echoed from down the corridor, sending a shockwave through the space, followed by smoke and dust and heat. The ceiling and walls around them quaked, shaking off large chunks of concrete. Wilder and Declan pressed themselves into the corner. Wilder squeezed her eyes shut tight and muttered prayers.

"I love you," Declan whispered into her hair, then kissed her head.

"I love you more."

A high-pitched ringing filled her ears, drowning out all other noise until only silence remained.

CHAPTER 57
HESPERIA

The bitter wind carried the last remnants of winter away even while the sun worked to offer fresh warmth. Robins pulled worms from the moist ground as bits of green poked through the earth.

Hesperia soaked in every detail of spring—of new life vanquishing death. In the dome, she'd never noticed the change of seasons. In the dome, she'd missed out on so very much. Melancholy melodies. Abstract art. Soul-touching stories. Faith—not in oneself, but in something far greater. *Someone* far greater. The Necanians didn't comprehend such beauty...such love.

"Hesperia, can you go grab the potatoes from my kitchen and bring them to the table?" Melvina rushed past with a basket of bread, still steaming with freshness.

"Of course," Hesperia said, and headed toward Melvina's cabin.

"Hesperia," Matthew called as he jogged toward her.

She smiled. "Hello. I am glad you made it in time."

"James and Deanna have things under control in the

Colony...at least for a few days." Matthew fell into step with her as they walked the dirt street.

"Have there been many more citizens of Hope City to leave the dome?" she asked. Matthew had sent updates, keeping them informed since they'd returned to Beartooth in the weeks after the rescue, but it had been a while since she'd heard any news.

"There are a few more every week." Matthew tucked his hands into the pockets of his jeans. "They all have questions. Some have stayed and made a home in the Colony. Some returned to the city, but we've started several support groups within the dome to help them relearn how to live together and rebuild a sense of community."

"And the Necanians?" Hesperia's brothers were entombed under the fallen Citadel—she had seen their corpses herself when the Colony's rescue teams had dug through the rubble. There were others who had died in the explosions. Some escaped, survived, and were put into holding until it could be decided what should be done.

"We're still sorting out what to do with them," Matthew replied. "Without their High Ruler, most are compliant, not causing any trouble. Some people want them freed, while others want them killed. Neither seems like the right response in view of their crimes."

They paused outside Melvina's cabin. Hesperia didn't say anything. What could she say? These were her people. She understood them. She even had compassion for many who, like her, were only living as they had been taught. They didn't know any better—didn't know they had a choice. If Hesperia had been asked a few months ago, she would have said that skipping the Sacraments would mean her death. Yet here she was, completely alive, possibly *more* alive than she'd ever been —stronger, more at peace.

She reached for the door, and Matthew touched her arm. "Some have heard your story. They want to change, to learn to live among us as you have, as part of us."

"Can they?" Hesperia wondered. "Those who wish to change, could they be shown mercy? Forgiveness? Would humans welcome them?"

"They've welcomed you," he answered. "Perhaps you could return to the Colony with me, help me show everyone that there's a way to move forward for all of us. If anyone is a picture of what the future of this brave new world can look like, of what redemption can look like, it's you."

Could she go with him? Did she want to? Hesperia was making a home for herself in Beartooth. This was where she was learning what it meant to live and love like a human

"Think about it," Matthew said and patted her arm. "We can talk more after the meal." He smiled, then walked away.

Hesperia watched him for a moment before ducking into Melvina's home. She grabbed the large ceramic bowl of mashed potatoes from the table and headed back outside.

Stepping back into the sunlight, Hesperia changed her focus from the changing season to the people bustling about the camp. The street was full of chatter and laughter. An upbeat tune strummed from a guitar somewhere close by. Everyone carried trays and bowls of food toward the far edge of the little village. Hesperia mingled among them, and no one flinched at the sight of her. No one wrinkled their eyebrows in concern or widened their gazes in fear. They smiled at her like she was one of them. Did she want to go back to a place where she would have to face expressions of loathing and terror?

"Put the potatoes over here," Melvina called to her. She stood beside one of two long tables placed in the clearing near the woods. It was covered in platters of food from one end to the other; fried chicken, ham, potatoes in various forms, vegetables of every kind, and fresh baked breads and pies—a banquet of favorite dishes all made with joy and love.

The second table was really several tables lined together to form one long piece. It was surrounded by mismatched chairs and set with mismatched plates and cups. Everyone from camp gathered around, finding their places.

"Hesperia," Korah shouted. "I made the pie you like. But I have an extra one back in our cabin if you don't snag a piece." She winked.

Hesperia mouthed a thank you as Korah adjusted the nursing infant in her arms. Sam walked up behind his wife, kissed her cheek, and kissed his baby girl's head before sitting in the chair next to Korah.

Neema and Finley chased each other around the table.

"You two need to find a seat." Griffin reached to stop them but was unsuccessful. "With the kids," he corrected when they went for two empty seats just down from him.

"How come you get to sit at the big table," Neema protested.

"Yeah, you're just a kid too!" Finley added.

"Griffin is eighteen as of last week." Solomon came up and put one hand on the young man's shoulder while his other was full of blueberries. "So, he gets a seat at the big table now."

The two children pouted as they shuffled to sit with the other kids on picnic blankets.

"I'm not sure if I'll live to see those two turn eighteen." Solomon chuckled. "They might actually be the death of me." He popped a berry in his mouth then walked to the head of the table.

"I thought I told you not to touch any of that food until we were all ready to eat," Melvina grumbled.

"They're from my greenhouse," Solomon defended. "Plus,

I'm old and need to keep my blood sugar up." He tossed another blueberry into his mouth and grinned.

Hesperia smiled at the antics.

"Isn't everyone here anyway?" Solomon added.

They were. Almost every seat at the table was filled with warm souls full of light and life. Hesperia looked for where she might sit.

"Hesperia," a friendly voice sang out over the crowd. "We saved you a seat by us."

Wilder James sat near the head of table, waving for Hesperia's attention. The smile spread across her face made the corners of her eyes crinkle. The breeze tousled her red hair, and she pulled wispy strands from her face. The scar on her forehead was barely noticeable now—just a thin pink line served as a memento of the day the world had changed. Wilder and the red-haired baby that bounced on Wilder's lap were both miracles of that day.

The baby cooed and gurgled as Hesperia approached. It reached out it's chubby little arms to the Necanian. Hesperia took tiny hands in hers and kissed its fingers before taking her seat by Wilder.

"She loves you so much." Wilder kissed the baby's rosy cheeks.

One would never know that the little miracle wasn't Wilder's own flesh and blood. The same cinnamon hair and rosy skin. The same soul-warming smile. The baby even had Declan's green eyes. Wilder may not have birthed this child, but Hesperia suspected it was always meant for her.

"And I adore her," Hesperia tickled the baby's belly. "My sweet little Lottie."

"Did you see all the pie?" Declan took his seat and leaned to kiss little Lottie's cheek, then Wilder's.

"I did," Wilder said and giggled. "Just save some for the rest of us."

"I make no promises." Declan feigned a serious look.

Metal clinked against a glass.

"Welcome!" Solomon stood behind his chair. Everyone quieted. "We have gathered around this table to celebrate the goodness God has bestowed on us. And not just us, but the greater community beyond this camp. Fear plagued this world for too long...even long before the Necanians came. It isolated us and imprisoned hearts and minds. But not anymore."

Declan took Wilder's hand in his and scooched closer to his wife.

"We give thanks to God for walking us to freedom—even if it meant going through darkness." Solomon looked to Declan and Wilder. A tear glistened in the corner of his eye. "May we remember that our freedom comes with the responsibility to lead others—to take them by the hand and guide them to the Truth and Love that casts out fear. That's what community is. That's what we are. That is what we want this world to be."

"Amen!" Shouts echoed around the table.

Hesperia's heart echoed their joy.

This is what life was meant to be. Not power, but community. Not control or selfish comfort, but a love that served others.

If she could get her Necanian brethren to understand...

But she feared that she couldn't. They had no category for this, no frame of reference. This couldn't simply be told. It had to be shown.

Hesperia leaned toward Matthew who had taken the seat on her right. "I will go with you back to the Colony. I will help show my people that there is a better way."

"Are you sure?" Matthew asked. "You would leave all this?"

"Yes. Wilder introduced me to something that has

breathed life into my soul—real, joy-filled life. Now it is my turn to introduce that same life to my people."

"Not only them," Matthew said.

Hesperia touched his hand. She noticed the differences in their flesh and was reminded of the differences in their histories. Yet they were not so different. Not anymore. Perhaps they never had been as different as they were led to believe. She was thankful for his son, who had opened her eyes to something outside her knowing. She was thankful for Wilder, who had seen past her outer shell and into her true being. Hesperia had lived over one hundred years, and if she lived another hundred, they would be spent sharing the good news of this kind of freedom with the world.

She leaned a touch closer to Matthew and smiled. "I will tell everyone who will listen."

ACKNOWLEDGMENTS

This is my fifth book, and with each new project I only grow more and more grateful for those in my life who encourage and support this passion for telling stories.

Brian, thank you for believing in this dream and fighting for it with your constant encouragement when I feel too tired and discouraged to fight myself. You hold my arms up. I am daily reminded of the blessing you are to me in every way. I cannot imagine a better partner in life. You are my Declan, my Rohan, my forever love.

Lila and Lorelai, your energy, spirit, and grace show up in every woman I write. I am thankful to be your mom, and hope that you grow in strength and beauty. You both make me fierce and brave.

To my parents—Gary and Etta—your love, wisdom, and support has been a strong foundation for every area of my life. You have taught me what it is to love Jesus and love others. You have loved me unconditionally and been my greatest cheer-leaders. I am who I am, in large part, because of who you are.

Emerald, thank you for being a sounding board for this and every story. For reading and talking me through plots and scenes. For being a source of support. I am so glad God connected us.

Victoria, thank you for always loving my characters as much as I do. Talking through my stories with you has become such a valuable part of my process. Your friendship is even more valuable.

Katie, thank you for fangirling, Triscuits, and making me laugh when writing is hard. Your encouragement is lollipops and pie.

To the tribe of women who keep me grounded and centered, not just in writing, but in life—Lauren, Fawn, Misty, Mandi, Ashley, Sylvia, and the ever growing group of coffee table women—your love, grace, and prayers mean the world to me.

To the Blue Ink Press team—Sherry, Amanda, Stephanie, Christa, Morgan, and Liz—the investment you pour into me and my stories is beyond what I could ask for. You take a rough and ragged thing and make it gleam. Thank you for believing in me.

To the authors who I call friend. There are too many to name, but you inspire me, encourage me, and motivate me more than you can possibly know. I am thankful for a writer community who makes me feel like I can do this too. (And I need reminding with each new book.)

To my dear readers—you rock all the socks. It is my honor to connect with you over a story; over the laughs and tears, over the characters to love and the ones we love to hate. I pray that something in these pages sticks with you, gives you hope, and reminds you of your purpose and value in this world.

Finally, but most importantly, to my Maker—You are Light in the darkness. You are Truth amidst lies. You are my saving grace and the hope I run to. Your love sustains me. I pray that this meager offering brings You glory.

ABOUT THE AUTHOR

Tabitha Caplinger gets way too emotionally invested in the lives of fictional characters, whether it's obsessing over a book or tv show, or getting lost creating her own worlds. Tabitha is the author of Christian fantasy such as The Wolf Queen and The Chronicle of the Three Trilogy, and a lover of good stories and helping others live chosen. When she's not writing book words, she's reheating her coffee, binging a new show or teaching God's Word to young adults. Tabitha, her husband and two beautifully sassy daughters desire to be Jesus with skin on for those around them. They live to love others...and for Marvel movies.

CPSIA information can be obtained
at www.ICGtesting.com
Printed in the USA
BVHW070932310123
657510BV00001B/34